DEVIL'S LAIR

ALSO BY MICHAEL A. BLACK

DEVIL'S LAIR

TRACKDOWN SERIES: BOOK 8

MICHAEL A. BLACK

ROUGH
EDGES
PRESS

Devil's Lair
Paperback Edition
Copyright © 2023 Michael A. Black

Rough Edges Press
An Imprint of Wolfpack Publishing
9850 S. Maryland Parkway, Suite A-5 #323
Las Vegas, Nevada 89183

roughedgespress.com

Paperback ISBN 978-1-68549-410-0
eBook ISBN 978-1-68549-348-6
LCCN 2023944622

For Officer Andres Vasquez-Lasso
Chicago Police Department
R.I.P.
03-01-23
And for all my brothers and sisters in uniform, both military
and civilian who stand or have stood on the line.
Stay safe and God bless.

Yield not thy neck
To fortune's yoke, but let thy dauntless mind
Still ride in triumph over all mischance.

King Henry the Sixth, Part III
Act III, Scene 3
William Shakespeare

CHAPTER 1

**THE HIGHWAY NEAR THE MCNAMARA RANCH
PHOENIX, ARIZONA**

A quick look over his right shoulder confirmed once again that no one was following him as he pushed on through the near darkness. A hint of a yellowish-orange nascent glow to the east was just starting to tincture the velvet sky over the mountains. Not much traffic, but it was the Sabbath. And it was early.

Very early.

Steve Wolf wondered how many times he'd run this same course over the past year or so when he was training for a fight.

A fight...

The one with the Russian was supposed to have been his last bout.

Supposed to be...that was the operative term.

Nothing ever turns out the way it should.

He contemplated this, and the other recent developments in his life as he ran along the highway carrying a five-pound weight in each hand. And also wondered how many times he'd worn the Glock 19 in the shoulder rig under his left arm.

More so in the last several months than in the ones before.

Insurance.

Pulling his left arm closer to his body, he felt the reassurance of the solid metal. It was Mac's gun—the same one he'd worn on so many of his early morning runs. He was going to have to remember to wipe it down with some oil so all the sweat he'd deposited on it during the trek wouldn't corrode the smooth elegance of the dull gray finish.

He owed Mac that much. That and a helluva lot more.

His eyes swept back again, first glancing over his left shoulder and then over his right.

Nothing. No one followed him.

I'm turning into a paranoid idiot, he thought.

However, as they say, it's not paranoia if it's true.

His feet skipped over the gravel on the side of the road.

Paranoia.

But damn it, he had his reasons. How many times had they tried to kill him since he'd gotten out of prison?

Even now, a few months after the big fight, the biggest one of his career, and the climactic shootout that had followed it, he still couldn't shake the constant urge to keep looking back ever so often to make sure that nothing or no one was creeping up on him.

Having to deal with numerous attempts on your life every couple of months will do that to you, he reflected. But now all the danger was supposedly over with.

Wasn't it?

That's what Pike had assured him, and Wolf had gone through a lot to see that it was.

Or was it as they say, the more things change, the more they stay the same?

He seemed permanently stuck in Alpha Blue status— possible threat of hostile activity.

Maybe Pike was right. Wolf had to admit that after the fiasco in Las Vegas during the big fight with Dimitri Rakhimanov, and the gruesome gunfight that followed, Wolf's constant fear of assassination had lessened substantially. The Mexican drug lord who'd marked Wolf for murder, Esteban Cortez, and his main body- guard had both been killed in the melee of the hotel shootout, as had a bunch of others.

"It's all over but the cryin,'" Special Agent Lucian Pike had said. He'd given Wolf his utmost assurance that his problems were finally over with.

And then the cryptic text message yesterday from Pike had popped up on Wolf's phone like a yellow warning light flashing alongside the road.

HEY, WE GOTTA TALK. IMPORTANT. BE IN TOUCH SOON.

Important.

Good old Pike, always good for throwing out a message with a bit of mystery to keep things interesting.

And anxiety-laden.

That SOB had been more or less responsible for getting Wolf into one tight predicament after another for the past several months.

A brownish jackrabbit dashed across the highway about fifty feet ahead of Wolf, its faint shadow dancing along in a distorted mirror image on the pavement.

That makes two of us, Wolf thought. *Me and Mr. Jack Rabbit. Both easy pickings for some unseen predator.*

The solid comfort of the Glock bouncing against his side reassured him once more.

Yeah, Cortez and his bodyguard were dead. So was the big Australian ex-French Foreign Legion son of a bitch who'd been hired to orchestrate Wolf's demise, courtesy of that rich bastard in the Caribbean whose name Wolf didn't even want to repeat. The asshole's nefarious femme fatale was also in government custody. She'd tried to stab Pike, and would have if Wolf hadn't saved the big fed's ass.

Again.

You'd think the man would be grateful, Wolf thought.

But he hadn't heard from him in weeks. At least he could give me an update on the case against Von-what's-his-name.

After a few more steps, Wolf corrected himself: Von Tillberg. There was no sense in avoiding saying the name. According to Pike. This one was the nephew of that other infamous Von-something who'd ruined Wolf's life when he'd been in the army over in Iraq.

Framed him and sent him to prison.

Von Dien. No sense tiptoeing around that bastard's name either, even sub-vocally.

Jesus, the story was so complicated, but so was life.

Wrongfully convicted for a war crime he didn't commit, sent to prison and doing hard time, getting out and being stalked by a series of ruthless killers…Wolf had his doubts it was ever going to end. Or that he'd clear his name.

And then it was, and he did.

Not only had he survived, but he'd triumphed.

Or so he'd thought.

Clearing his name, conviction reversed, reinstatement of all back pay and privileges…it had all seemed like he'd come out of a bad dream and with quite a windfall. And he'd even won the World Heavyweight Mixed Martial Arts Championship and gotten a huge payday.

Sort of.

It turned out he'd won the battle and then lost the war, so to speak.

Wolf came to the dirt road cut off that led up the face of the mountain. This was the most grueling part, but the air was still cool, and the heat of the day was yet to come. He took a deep breath and started up the incremental incline.

A mile to go to the top, he thought. *To the first plateau.*

His legs were starting to feel the strain now, but that was a good thing and it felt good to be off the pavement and running on the less-impactful dirt. His knees would thank him later.

His knees...the big Russian had done a good job working them over in their fight back in mid-July. He recalled the pain of each leg kick that the big guy had slammed into him. Wolf had given as good as he'd got, though. It had been an epic battle. And afterward, Wolf had secretly vowed it would be his last, too.

But that wasn't meant to be either.

Had he somehow known this?

Was that the reason that even after winning the title, Wolf had kept up with these early morning runs?

Reno, his friend and trainer, had been all for that.

"Now that we've won the big one, for all the marbles," Reno'd said. "We'll be in line for some real decent big-money matches."

Wolf hadn't told him that he was going to retire...that fighting the Russian, winning the title, was going to be his last fight. He'd decided it, and it was...

Until it wasn't.

Wolf's feet stirred up little cyclones of dust on the trail as he continued up the slope, each step hitting the ground with a scraping precision. It was a fitting accompaniment to his recollection of Reno's anger.

"What the hell do you mean, you're withholding our damn purse?" Reno had shouted into the phone about a month after the fight. "And that title is *ours*. We won it fair and square."

Wolf recalled the cords in Reno's neck bulging out in bas relief as he argued with the commission. The title meant more to him than it did to Wolf. "That's some goddammed bullshit, and you know it."

Bullshit or not, that's what happened.

Citing an obscure clause in the contract regarding one of the principals failing to notify the commission, the hotel, and the other camp of any possible contingency developments that might pose a security issue, the commission had subsequently advised, was in violation of the good faith clause in the document.

The attempt on Wolf's life in the triage center of the hotel after the fight, and Dimitri and his trainer getting shot at sort of fit that aforementioned definitive clause, even though Wolf had advised the commission and the hotel prior to the fight of the possibility of danger. At that time, all the tickets had been sold, the closed-circuit TV rights were locked in, and everyone concerned brushed off the vague possibility of Cortez posing any real threat.

Or so they said.

"Oh yeah?" Reno shouted into the phone. "Well, lemme tell ya, we're gonna sue your asses. When this is over, we'll own you and that damn hotel too."

He'd punctuated the sentence with a colorful bit of profanity, which Wolf was sure would cement the possibility of a long and protracted court battle. But what the hell, he'd just come through a bigger, longer one of those, and his high-priced attorney, Maxwell H. Ozmand, was always spoiling for another court fight. He'd just won a real huge one against the US Army through the Military Court of Appeals.

Hell, what were a few thousand bucks more in billable hours?

The Great Oz had expressed the perfect mixture of outrage and confidence when Wolf and Reno had approached him about initiating a lawsuit.

"Don't you worry, Stevorino," the lawyer had said, his slicked-back gray hair artfully arranged in a pompadour that Elvis Presley would have loved. "When I get through with those bastards we'll not only get your title and paycheck back in full, but we'll go for a million or so in damages. Just leave it to the Great Oz."

And so they did. But in the meantime, Wolf had to start paying off the mountain of legal bills from the Military Court of Appeals fight and all the other debts he'd accrued. The wrongful conviction settlement from the army was another pending court battle, and had put the skids on a reinstatement of rank and privileges and any back pay. The Great Oz had assured him that it would be forthcoming too, but so far, all Wolf had gotten was the satisfaction of knowing that his name was finally officially cleared. As far as the money that was coming, Wolf was certain that between Uncle Sam and the Great Oz, whatever was left would be substantially reduced. To make matters worse, an unexpected and expensive medical procedure that had suddenly popped up back in North Carolina had eaten up most of the other money he'd saved from his previous MMA matches. His uncle, who had no insurance, had to have emergency bypass surgery. At least that seemed to have turned out okay, but it was shaping up to be what Dolly Parton would call a hard-candy Christmas in about a month. He'd even had to scrap the long-anticipated Caribbean get-away vacation that he'd promised his lady-love, Yolanda.

So Wolf, even though now a vindicated man, had a voluminous collection of bills to pay off and no prospects for a good-paying job. Being able to pick up a few bucks going to college on his reinstated GI benefits was something, but certainly not enough. Those gaps in the job application he'd filled out, even the ones for something like a security guard position at a Chuck E. Cheese restaurant, came with too many suspicious-looking blanks staring back at him.

List your employment history for the past five years.

Four years at Leavenworth.

Have you ever been convicted of a felony?

Well, yeah, but you see my record is clear now. The conviction was reversed...

Thanks for your application, Mr. Wolf. We'll be calling you.

But they never did.

So he was back where he started when he'd gotten out of prison: living in the apartment above Mac's garage and eking out his existence in the dwindling field of bail bond enforcement.

Bounty hunting.

And the promise of those big money fights that Reno had talked about had somehow gotten shuffled to the bottom of the deck. Nobody in the big leagues wanted to touch him with the pending litigation. He'd taken a few club fights, all of which had ended in one-round knock-outs, and then his luck seemed to take a turn for the better. Reno had gotten contacted about a televised, non-title bout on an undercard from one of the smaller, lesser-known MMA leagues against an up-and-coming Brazilian fighter named Juan Dos Pastos. While the money wasn't that good, and was far beneath Wolf's status as a world champ, he grabbed it, short notice or not. And now it is coming up in seven days.

A week.

Wolf's jeweled heavyweight championship belt, the one he'd gotten in the ring after the Rakhimanov fight, still hung in the glass case in Reno's gym. And the sign out in front said:

STEVE WOLF, WORLD HEAVYWEIGHT MMA CHAMPION TRAINS HERE.

Wasn't it pretty to think so?

Wolf remembered that line, or something close to it, from a Hemingway novel he'd read for one of his lit classes. Now it really rang true.

His breath coming in sharp gasps now, he saw that he'd reached the initial mountain plateau with the one-mile marker and reached out and grabbed it as he made his circle and started back down.

It felt good to touch something solid and fixed, like the marker, in this uncertain world, and this ceremonial grasping filled the bill. He thought about how many times he'd done this same thing before circling his way back down the mountain.

The more things change, he thought, *the more they stay the same.*

* * *

On the way back, everything looked quiet and pretty much unremarkable. Mac's Escalade was in the long driveway alongside the specially modified, reinforced black Hummer that had once belonged to Reno when he'd been a bounty hunter. There was no sign of Kasey's tan Honda, which suited Wolf fine. He'd always had a rather contentious relationship with Mac's daughter, even though she still ran the office for the family bounty-hunting business. Thankfully, he'd seen even less of her since she had remarried and moved out with her young son, Chad. Wolf did miss inter-acting with the boy, but it was just as good the kid was gone. Now it was only Mac in the main house and Wolf in the apartment over the garage—right where he'd started a year and a half ago after getting out of prison.

Two steps forward, he told himself, three steps back.

Scanning the roadway in both directions as he ran alongside the asphalt, he saw a few cars whiz by. None appeared threatening, but he couldn't help but wonder who or what would be coming at him next. That seemed to be the natural state of things.

Wolf sprinted the last hundred yards down the long access road branching out from the highway before turning onto the driveway at Mac's place.

The soles of Wolf's shoes made slapping sounds on the asphalt as he came to a stop. Bending over, he continued his subdued, cool-down march, going around in circles until he recovered his wind.

"Jesus H. Christ," Jim McNamara said, stepping out from the shadows next to the garage where Wolf had his upstairs one-room apartment. "You make more noise than a herd of zebras. You're lucky I'm not some bad guy staking this place out."

Wolf grinned. Mac, his best friend and mentor, was ex-special forces and never let anyone forget it.

"Zebras?" Wolf said.

McNamara shrugged. "I was watching an old Tarzan movie on TV. I guess, given the season coming up in another month or so, I coulda said reindeer, huh?"

"I'm just wondering where the hell you're getting all these distinctive metaphors."

"Metaphors? Is that what they're called?" McNamara clicked his tongue. "Sounds like all them college courses you've been taking are making you into one helluva smart ass." He smirked and shook his head. "Just count your lucky stars I wasn't some ne'er-do-well sneaking around here to do you in."

"No self-respecting bad guy's gonna come sneaking around here with you on patrol," Wolf said. "How come you're up so early?"

"Got some business. Plus, I figured you'd be going to see the mountain, and I wanted to make sure you got back okay."

"Appreciate it," Wolf said.

He took it as a good thing that he wasn't really all that winded despite the ending sprint. Maybe he wasn't that far out of fighting shape. He'd find out shortly.

"You heading over to the gym this morning?" McNamara asked.

"After I shower and eat. Why?"

"Skip the shower and let me buy you breakfast at McDonald's. How about coming with me for a quick pick-up?"

Wolf knew a quick pick-up could easily stretch into a prolonged surveillance, but he owed Mac more than he could ever repay. McNamara had been the one who'd picked Wolf up when he'd been released from prison and helped him get his life back on track. Wolf still lived in the upstairs portion of McNamara's huge garage, and it had been Mac who'd let Wolf work for him as a bail enforcement agent. The work had been interesting, too. And then there was the little matter of McNamara saving Wolf's life a time or two, but Wolf had also saved Mac's, so that account was pretty much even, but with some things you didn't keep score.

"Sure," Wolf said. "Just let me change clothes."

He was dressed in dark sweatpants and a loose-fitting sweatshirt with the sleeves cut off. Both were drenched.

"Damn straight," McNamara said. "Don't want you to stink up the seats on the Hummer in case I have to give it back to Reno someday."

Wolf chuckled.

"And don't forget to bring your bail enforcement agent's badge, but you'd better leave the Glock at home," McNamara said. "Your concealed carry still ain't come through yet, ya know."

Wolf knew that. And with his record, he doubted it ever would. Even a reversed conviction and a now-clean record couldn't erase the fact that he'd still spent four years inside. If that wasn't a red enough flag for some pencil-pusher in the state police to flag his application, he didn't know what was. Some things never changed.

Once an ex-con, always an ex-con.

"We don't want to lose that baby if some overzealous cop rousts us and finds you packing," McNamara said. "Besides, I always got Jammin' Jenny in the backend if we get in any firefights."

Jammin' Jenny was Mac's nickname for an M-16 he'd smuggled out of Vietnam back in the day. He'd described how he'd disassembled the "combat loss" weapon and had the parts wrapped in metal and layers of plastic and then secreted in several Plaster of Paris Buddha statues that he had made in Saigon. When it was time to DEROS, it was easy to have the statues shipped home in his hold-baggage. Once he'd rotated back to the world, both McNamara and Buddha got smashed, and Jammin' Jenny got liberated. And subsequently reassembled. Mac had advised Wolf to do the same back when he first got sent over to Afghanistan and Iraq at the start of Wolf's military career.

"I could use one of them new M-fours," Mac had told him. "And they're smaller than a sixteen."

The thought of trying to smuggle out contraband, much less a military combat rifle, had weighed heavily on Wolf's conscience, but Mac had been his mentor when Wolf's own father had abdicated that role. He wanted more than anything to please McNamara.

But that wasn't to be, either.

Wolf texted him back that there was no plaster and no friendly villages in Afghanistan or Iraq, along with a couple of smiley face emojis.

McNamara texted back a two word response, and it wasn't "Let's dance," but he'd included a humorous emoji of his own to show that he wasn't pissed.

Different wars, Wolf thought. *Different rules.*

Which brought him back to the present.

"I got about as much chance of getting my concealed carry permit as I have of winning the lottery," Wolf said.

"Quit being so damn negative," McNamara said. "You just got your damn name cleared, for Christ's sake. But we can't afford not to be careful. So…"

Wolf knew what he meant.

"I know, I know," Wolf said, heading for the garage and his apartment. "Leave the gun and the cannoli."

* * *

They were rolling down the access road toward the highway ten minutes later, the Hummer sounding like a diesel truck, even though it wasn't. What it was, however, was fourteen years old, and showing its age. Reno, during his bounty hunting days, had the vehicle's doors reinforced so it was damn near bulletproof. After a round through the leg down in Mexico had ended both his bounty hunting and MMA fighting days, Reno had given the Hummer to McNamara, despite them once having been competitors and enemies. Now Reno was Wolf's manager and trainer.

How things change, Wolf silently reflected.

"What time you got to be over at the gym?" McNamara asked.

Wolf shrugged. "Nine or so, I guess."

The dashboard clock said 0650.

"I'll get you over there in plenty of time," McNamara said. "This boy's been stayin' at his sister's place, and she's got to go to work."

"It'd be nice if you told me who we're looking for."

"File's in there." McNamara patted the leather console between the seats. "His name's Willie Jones."

Wolf popped the lid open and took out the manila file. He opened it and studied the picture paper-clipped to the first page. The face of a young Black man seemed to stare back at him from the color photo replica of the mug shot.

Willie Jones, male Black, six-two, one hundred ninety pounds, black hair, brown eyes.

"What's he wanted for?" Wolf asked.

"DWI, burglary, auto theft, and fleeing and eluding. Seems he was drunk when he broke into somebody's house and then stole their car out of the garage. He wrecked it while the cops were chasing him and they caught him."

"Sounds like he should have skipped the booze and taken his job more seriously. He's got quite a sheet here. Assault and battery, a couple more burglaries, strong-armed robbery, and a whole bunch of resisting arrests." No listed weapons charges, but that didn't mean anything. "Why the hell did Manny post bond for this piece of shit, anyway?"

"He's desperate for business," McNamara said. "The way the courts are, they're letting everybody out on their own recognizance. He's worried they're gonna end cash bail in this state just like they're trying to do in Illinois and already did New York. Make things even worse. Put all the bondsmen out of business."

A revolving door, Wolf thought. *Or better yet, a merry-go-round.*

Regardless of the metaphor, Mac was right. It most likely spelled the eventual end for bondsmen and hence, the bounty-hunting business.

"So now the son of a bitch has missed two court dates, and Manny's set to pay out ten grand if we don't pick him up before the fifteenth."

Wolf chuckled. "Mac, that's tomorrow."

"Damn right, it is. You don't think I woulda bugged you unless I really needed the help, do ya?"

Same old Mac, Wolf thought.

"His mama put up her house as collateral," McNa-mara said, "but you know what a pain in the ass it is to try and foreclose on something like that. Besides, turns out she don't own it anyway, like she claimed. Mama's not any more honest than her son is."

"So where we headed?"

"Penway Gardens."

Wolf cast a quick look at him. Penway Gardens was a low-income housing project and also a pretty rough area.

"You sure he's there?"

"Yep. He listed his mama's address when he got arrested, and I been staking the place out. Ain't seen hide nor hair of the asshole. Then Kasey's got a friend working for the phone service he uses. Secretly pinged it for me and I'm pretty sure he's staying with his sister now. She's working at a gas station and has to be there at eight. When we get in position, I'll have Kasey call there and ask for him."

That was one thing about Mac's daughter. She was a wizard with the computer and getting into various databases.

"What if he answers?" Wolf asked.

"Well, then we'll know he's in there. This time of the morning, most of the other shitheads will be just getting in bed to go to sleep, so we shouldn't have to worry about them interfering. We'll just tell his sister to either open the door up, or we'll take it down."

Wolf was familiar with those solid, often reinforced metal doors of the projects.

"You bring a sledgehammer?" he asked.

Mac grinned. "Does a bear shit in the woods?"

Wolf grinned as well. "We'll probably need a pry bar as well."

"I got one of those, too."

Suddenly Wolf was wishing he had brought along the Glock.

"Here we go," McNamara said, swinging over to the curb and stopping. Before them on the right side of the street were two massive cement pillars which had a decorative sign in white and green suspended between them announcing YOU ARE NOW ENTERING PENWAY GARDENS. The base of each pillar was decorated with crude graffiti ranging from gang symbols to misspelled profanity.

"Better put on our Kevlar, just in case," McNamara said. "And take some of that pepper spray. You want the Taser?"

Wolf would have rather had the Glock, but chances were good that they'd be encountering the police sooner rather than later, and the last thing Wolf needed was to get arrested with a firearm. After slipping on the Kevlar vest and fastening the Velcro flaps, he stuffed a can of pepper spray into one of the pockets and the Taser in the other. It was shaped like a TV remote and had a purported effective range of ten to fifteen feet.

McNamara was dialing his daughter's number now, and she answered on the first ring. He put her on speaker.

"All right, honey. We're at the gate. Give us a minute or so and then call him, then call me back."

"Dad," she said. "I'm not feeling good about this. That place is dangerous. You really need to be careful."

"Don't worry. I got Steve with me."

Wolf heard her loud sigh.

"Great. I'm sure he'll be a lot of help since he still can't carry a gun. And now I've got two of you to worry about."

It's mildly surprising that she mentioned being worried about me, Wolf thought.

But then again, perhaps it wasn't that surprising. Despite the contentious relationship with Mac's daughter, slowly but surely, things had begun to get a little better. To say she didn't initially approve of him was a bit of an understatement, and was downright resentful when Mac had brought him back from his Leavenworth stint to live in the garage apartment, rent-free. Kasey and her son lived in the main house with Mac back then. The trouble he'd brought with him hadn't made things easy. But little by little, her opinion of him had improved. And her son, Chad, had taken a real shine to Wolf, calling him "Uncle Steve." After she'd remarried and moved out, things became a little more friendly between them. Of course, part of that was due to them not seeing each other that often. Familiarity bred contempt, while absence made the heart more tolerant.

"Just make the damn call in another minute, okay?" McNamara terminated the call, shifted into gear, and crept forward, cursing under his breath.

"I swear," he said. "That girl's just like my ex used to be. Marrying that FBI geek and moving my grandson out of my house." He sat and blew a couple of heavy breaths through his nostrils. "I don't think her momma whipped her enough when she was a young'un."

"It sounds to me like she takes after her daddy," Wolf said, smiling.

Mac chuckled. "Yeah, I guess you got that right."

The housing units were one-story townhouses with adobe roofs and cheap-looking tan aluminum siding all clustered on a series of cul-de-sacs. Two units sat next to each other, sharing a support wall, and the streets, which had the names of trees and flowers, were all pretty much indistinguishable with sparse patches of dry, brownish grass providing a small yard in front of each one. Each pair of joined units had a driveway on each side, leading to a back parking lot area. Beyond the lots, the pattern was repeated with other rows of small houses.

"What she going to say if he answers?" Wolf asked.

"If he does, fine. Kase will tell him the place is surrounded and to step out, or we'll be taking down his sister's door. But, the way I figure it, sister will probably answer, and when she hears that it's a white girl calling, she'll probably figure it's the police and hang up. Then she'll notify Willie, who will most likely book, in which case we'll grab his ass."

"Wishful thinking. These places have back doors, don't they?"

McNamara nodded.

"Which is why I'm gonna take the front and you take the back. In case he rabbits."

Wolf was suddenly more than a little concerned, thinking this was a little bit too ambitious for just the two of them. And Mac was no spring chicken anymore.

"That's the one," McNamara said, pulling onto the driveway and stopping so the vehicle was at the corner of the house.

His cell phone jangled, and McNamara answered and listened.

"Shit," he said. "Okay." He terminated the call and popped open the driver's door. "I'll make a show of getting the sledge. You head around back and Tase that son of a bitch when he runs out the back."

"Just don't get shot," Wolf said, pulling open the passenger door.

He slid out and moved rapidly to the rear of the residence. Pausing at the corner, he did a quick peek.

A big air-conditioning unit sat next to the back wall on a cement slab. There was a window on each side and a door in the middle. Four cars were parked in the back lot. Wolf moved quickly, bending down at the waist as he went past the window and then crouched next to the air-conditioning unit. On the other side of the house's thin wall, he could hear voices—a man and a woman's, yelling. The words were indistinguishable.

More jumbling noises came from inside.

Wolf caught the sound of Mac bellowing, followed by a sharp thumping sound.

He was taking down the door.

Wolf wished that he and Mac had prepared better for this one, maybe taking radios so they could communicate. Wolf had been in so much of a hurry that he hadn't even taken his cell phone.

He started to straighten up when he heard the sound of the inner rear door opening, followed by the screen door banging against the wall.

A Black man pushed through the open door, his arms flailing as he tried to slip on a loose blue shirt before starting to sprint toward the back parking area.

Wolf was up in a second and running on an intercept course, the Taser in his right hand.

"Bail enforcement agent," he yelled out. "Stop."

Without waiting for a reply, Wolf leveled the Taser at the fleeing suspect and centered the red dot of the laser sight on the man's right hip area.

It wasn't a real good spot, but it was either that or let Mr. Jones reach his stride. And from the looks of it, he wasn't that far away from it.

The Taser popped, and the prongs flew outward along with a burst of small confetti chips. Wolf saw one prong dig into Jones's side, but the other got knocked askew by his swinging arm.

Stripping off the cartridge, Wolf tossed it down and began an angled sprint of his own, trying to cut Brown off. The long copper wire trailed behind Jones for an instant and then his rapidly moving arm knocked it completely off. Wolf slowed for a moment so as not to get tangled in the wires and then increased his speed. He caught up to Jones seconds later and reached out to grab him. Jones, however, had other ideas and did a quick pivot, throwing a looping punch at Wolf. He blocked the blow with his left and it landed with marginal impact. Wolf was used to taking punches and this one barely registered. Simultaneously, his right fist shot out in instinctive retaliation. Wolf had been aiming at the other man's jaw, but Jones ducked with the acumen of an experienced street-fighter and Wolf's fist smashed against the upper part of Jones's head. Pain shot up Wolf's arm, feeling like he'd just shoved a metal fork into an electrical socket, but his adversary dropped to the ground. In the Octagon Wolf was always a tad reluctant to go after a downed opponent even though the rules allowed it. This time, however, he had no such compunction and settled on top of Jones, who was face-down on the asphalt. Straddling him, Wolf grabbed the other man's right arm and twisted it behind him in a hammer-locking Kimora.

Jones emitted a harsh sounding squeal.

"Get offa me," he screamed, followed by a litany of threats of which every other word was "motherfucker."

Wolf increased the pressure in the Kimora as he leaned forward.

"I can just as easily break your arm, asshole," he said. "Now shut the fuck up."

A rather hefty Black woman was running toward them now and she carried a long butcher knife. Wolf was just debating whether to break Jones's arm and then rise to meet this new threat when McNamara ran up beside the woman, grabbed the hand with the knife, and then flipped her to the ground. The knife bounced on the pavement and Mac pulled out his pepper spray and gave her face a quick blast.

The woman screamed and began rubbing her eyes.

McNamara bent and grabbed the errant knife, then headed over to Wolf.

"Here," McNamara said, handing Wolf some handcuffs.

Wolf reached out with his right hand to grab them and felt a sharp pain as his fingers extended. Working through the pain, he slipped the cuffs in place over Jones's wrists. As he lifted him up the man spit in Wolf's face.

"Do that again, and I'll give you a recto-cranial inversion," Wolf said, wiping the spittle off.

"What's that?" Jones said.

"He'll shove your head up your ass," McNamara said, stepping over to give Jones a powerful slap across the face. "And before he does that, I'll twist your head around backward. Got it?"

Jones said nothing but didn't spit again.

McNamara strode over to grab the crying woman, who was now on her knees. He helped her to her feet, securing her arms in his powerful grip.

"What's your name, sweetheart?" he asked.

She didn't reply.

"That's my sister, motherfucker," Jones said. "And if you hurt her, I'll kill your motherfucking ass."

"You'll have to get in line to get a shot at that," McNamara said. "And you also need to expand your vocabulary."

Jones replied with more profanity.

"That boy don't ever learn, does he?" McNamara smirked and took out his second pair of handcuffs. "So you're Confetti Jones, I take it?"

"Yeah, so what?" She spewed off a litany of profane name-calling that put her brother's to shame.

He ratcheted the cuffs over her wrists and steered her over toward the Hummer.

"Come on, darlin'," he said. "I got me a spray bottle in the car over there and I'll wash spray outta your eyes for you. And if you behave yourself, I'll lock up your house for you before we leave."

"We're taking her in too?" Wolf said, walking Jones toward the Hummer.

"The more, the merrier," McNamara said. "She did come at us with a knife, so I could make a citizen's arrest, but as it turns out she's got an outstanding warrant. Aggravated battery and attempted murder. Two bounties for the price of one. The luck of the Irish."

"Yeah," Wolf said. "Too bad I'm an Indian."

"Well, I'll tell you what. I'll make you an honorary Irishman for today."

Wolf shot him a half smile, trying to mask the pain that was now coursing through his right hand. He winced.

I don't feel so lucky, he thought.

McNamara's brow furrowed.

"You get hurt?"

Wolf nodded. "My hand."

"Shit," McNamara said. "Reno's gonna kill me. I guess some of my Irish luck already rubbed off on you. The real kind of Irish luck—all bad."

You got that right, Wolf thought, not wanting to think about having to tell Reno either.

CHAPTER 2

A IGREJA SANTA DOS ANJOS
RIO DE JANEIRO
BRAZIL

Sean Dylan Hawkins studied his reflection in the mirror of the church washroom and adjusted the gray wig and smoothed out the artificial mustache and false beard. He was wearing a baggy tan shirt and dark-colored pants that were a couple sizes too large, both of which had been difficult to find for a man with his large frame. A metal cane rested horizontally on the sink in front of him.

"How do I look?" he asked his waspish looking partner. Hawkins made no attempt to alter or subdue his rich, vigorous sounding Irish brogue.

Charles William Peregrine, who was dressed in a custodian's outfit that they'd purchased at a local supply shop, was busy checking the stalls in the facility to assure that no one else was in the room. He pushed open the last stall door with the toe of his finely polished shoe and then glanced at his partner.

"Like an atypical sinner," he said in his most assiduously proper English. "And you're sounding way too verve for a man of your apparent advanced years."

"And your shoes look way too highly shined to belong to some lowly church janitor."

Peregrine frowned and held up his cell phone. "Which is all the more reason for us to move quickly. I just received notification that the Bureau's account has been properly credited."

"Sounds as right as the mail," Hawkins said, remembering that old line from James Joyce's long short story, *The Dead.*

Which is particularly appropriate, he thought.

"Let's get it done then," Peregrine said. "I'll give you the whistle when the coast is clear."

"I'll be listening for the call of the falcon." Hawkins smiled and made sure that none of his reddish hair was visible under the disguise. He then plucked the metal cane from its perch on the sink, twirled it like a baton, did a little soft-shoe dance across the tiled floor, and finished by slapping the cane up under his right armpit with a brisk-sounding snap.

"Hadn't you best stay in character?" Peregrine said, frowning slightly. "With both your voice and your alacrity?"

"Just like a stuffy Brit to harangue his talented Irish partner with just the two of them in an empty shitter," Hawkins said. "Or would you rather I say, the loo."

Peregrine smirked as his head canted toward the door.

"And what, pray tell, if some poor soul had happened to come in at that very moment and saw the aged man you're supposed to be on his way to the confessional doing a little tap dance with such vigor?"

"We're in a house of God, for Christ's sake. The poor bastard would probably think he was in the presence of a blessed miracle."

Hawkins emitted a chuckle and immediately swiveled the tip of the cane to the floor and assumed a stooped position, his head hanging down solemnly.

"Better?"

"Much better," Peregrine said.

Hawkins barked a laugh.

They did work well together.

When they'd served together in Afghanistan with the International Security Assistance Front, Hawkins with his SAS detachment, and Peregrine an ace helicopter pilot who ferried them to and fro, the two of them found they had a lot in common, mostly a desire to get the hell out of there in one piece and not look back. Someone in the unit remarked that it was an odd combination of an Irishman and an Englishman, but both Hawkins and Peregrine laughed off such comments.

Two birds of prey, two raptors, ready for action. Him on the ground and Peregrine swooping in with those twin mini-guns blazing.

That they'd both been disgraced and tossed out on the ludicrous charge of conduct unbecoming still stuck in Hawkins's craw. Not that it was altogether ludicrous...but what did they expect being stuck in that miserable excuse for a country with all its ridiculous restrictions on dealing with a nondescript enemy. So what if a couple more damn Afghans had been knocked off?

He sighed. It made you wonder how the old guard like the Royal Marines had managed back in the day. No whiskey, no women, no prospects for a bit of R&R after a six-month stay…what the hell was a man supposed to do in a damn war, anyway? And if you can't enjoy yourself by stepping outside the rules to get the job done now and then, what was the use.

"Ah, but a man's reach must exceed his grasp," he said, remembering that quote from Robert Browning. "Or what's a heaven for?"

"Let's hope Father Ramirez finds out soon enough. If you're finally so obliged, that is." He grabbed the broom that was leaning against the wall.

Hawkins winked at his diminutive partner.

"Ready?"

"Most assuredly," Peregrine said. "As I advised you previously, the place is practically empty and he still has five more minutes to go in the booth."

"Ah, to confess one's sins. What a nice burden to be lifted off a reprobate's shoulders. You have to give the damn Catholics credit for that, even though one has to confess to a man who's sworn to celibacy and wants to be called 'father.'"

"Definitely a contradiction." Peregrine grinned. "And now, enter the Hawk."

In the informal circles they went by the sobriquets the Falcon and the Hawk. Peregrine gave himself top billing with their metaphorical professional title because he was the one who had thought it all up, stating their own selective International Bureau of Adjustments, and offering their services on the dark web to "fix any problem, with a minimum of complications, by whatever means deemed necessary, and for a most reasonable price." That wasn't totally correct because the prices they charged were anything but reasonable at times, however, they were always most appropriately prorated to whatever level the client was capable of paying. But the types of "adjustments" sought by their prospective clients did not lend themselves readily to an open public discourse. The Bureau had developed an impeccable reputation on the dark web. This particular one dealt with the elimination of a radical priest who was pushing the local constabulary to put more effort into the investigation of the year-old murder of an equally radical city assemblyman.

Things were so much more simple when sleeping dogs were left to lie.

They made their way out of the lavatory and moved down the hallway toward the main auditorium which was beyond the row of large oaken doors. The flourishes on the woodwork had probably been done more than a century ago, each one topped with a pinion-shaped flourish. Hawkins had adopted a limping, unsteady gait, leaning heavily on the metallic cane with each step. Peregrine was ahead of him now, and grasping the ornate handle and pulling the massive wooden door open to allow the "old man" entrance. Inside the opulence was stunning, with a long line of wooden pews on either side of a main aisle that led to a beautifully painted statue of the crucifixion in the center, flanked by the fourteen stations of the cross on the side walls. The twin pair of confessional booths sat off to the right side.

Hawkins stopped to cross himself as he got to the main aisle, his eyes darting from side to side to survey how many patrons were inside. He saw a pair of older women dressed in dark rags up front, their heads bowed in apparent prayer.

"Always room for the devout," he told himself and cast a quick look at Peregrine, who nodded and headed up front, broom in hand. By the time Hawkins had reached the confessional booth, the Falcon was upfront, working his broom and purposely stirring up some clouds of dust.

One of the kneeling women coughed.

Devoutness has its consequences, the Hawk told himself with a sly grin. We'll see how long they last.

He pulled open the door and settled himself on the narrow bench. Glancing upward, he saw the top was a variegated screen that allowed some light to be admitted, but was conducive to creating a shadowed obscurity. He placed the cane between his legs, reached up, and pulled back the small wooden slate. On the other side of the thin wall he could discern the profile of the priest. Unfolding the paper with the printed words, he began in a halting voice.

"*Abençoe -me o pai,*" Hawkins said with practiced efficiency, intentionally stumbling over the words and mispronouncing them badly as he added, "*Pois eu pecinei.*"

The priest's reply was hesitant.

"*O que você deseja confessar meu filho?*"

Hawkins hesitated again, clearing his throat before continuing with the same stumbling cadence. "*Perdoe -me, você fala Inglês?*"

The priest's reply was immediate and reassuring.

"Yes, I speak English."

Hawkins crumpled the paper with the Portuguese printing on it and slid it into his pocket. He then began twisting the handle of the cane.

"Ah, thank you, Father," he said. "May I start over?"

"Of course."

"Bless me, Father, for I have sinned. It has been many months—even longer…years perhaps, since my last confession."

"What is it you wish to confess, my son?"

My son?

Who did this son of a bitch think he was?

Hawkins could barely conceal a snort of laughter and tried his best to make it sound like a cough.

"Pardon me," he said, adding a few more subdued coughs.

"It is all right."

Hawkins was twirling the top of the cane now in a counterclockwise manner, the oiled threads responding well.

"I have led a very sinful life, Father. Very sinful." The handle released with a minute clicking sound as the last thread spun loose. Hawkins gripped the top portion of the handle, twisted it to the right, and pulled back on the solid black padding. As it released, the trigger slipped down into place.

"I've done some terrible things, father. Terrible things."

"The heavenly father forgives all who come to him."

"So I've been told." Hawkins rotated the handle back clockwise and then pulled it back an inch or so, chambering the round. It was a fully jacketed, nine millimeter cartridge. "But there's more, father."

He heard the priest inhale and exhale. "Go on."

I wonder if he's bored? Hawkins smirked. Listening to all these pathetic losers coming in, day after day, to pour out their shortcomings and wanting absolution.

The wig and false beard were starting to itch. It was time to end it. But he hadn't gotten the signal from the Falcon yet.

"I've lived a sinful life, Father."

"The Lord forgives those who admit their sins and repent."

Where the hell was that damn signal? His mouth was dry but he could feel the sweat forming on his hands.

"There's more," he muttered.

"Women, father," Hawkins said. "A lot of women. I've treated them badly. Used them for my own carnal pleasures, and then discarded them. And—"

The priest was silent.

Hawkins wondered if the fellow might be getting his rocks off listening to this last part.

Still no signal.

"I've...I've..."

Hawkins paused for maximum effect, buying some time. Even through the murkiness of the thin shrouded veil Hawkins could see the priest's head tilt to gaze at him.

"I've killed people, Father. Many people."

The priest was silent, but the shadow profile twitched ever-so-slightly again on the other side of the screen.

"You were in the military?" the priest asked.

Hawkins heaved a loud sigh. "Yes. I was." He listened, he heard nothing. "Yes. Yes, I was. It was in wartime."

"Sometimes such things cannot be avoided. It is understandable."

"But, is it God's will?"

"His ways are not always clear to us."

From outside the booth Hawkins finally heard it—the low, cooing whistle, like a bird's shrill call.

The signal.

He smiled.

"So, is there any hope for a sinner like me?"

"You are forgiven. Now perform an act of contrition. Say ten Our Fathers and ten hail Ma—"

"Wait," Hawkins said. He leaned back away from the

small window separating them. "I have one more thing to confess."

His voice was a whisper now.

"Please, father, come closer now. This last thing is very difficult for me to tell you."

He watched as the priest pressed his head closer to the opening.

"Yes, my son?"

"Father," Hawkins said, bringing the barrel of the weapon up to the small rectangular shrouded window. "All those people …"

His voice was barely audible.

After a long moment of silence between them, the priest's profile leaned closer to the small opening.

"Yes?"

"Those people I killed," Hawkins said, his voice rising a few decibels now to a grating whisper. "I actually enjoyed it."

He pulled the trigger and the blast reverberated in the confines of the booth, decimating his hearing, as the bullet and the flash perforated the wispy veil.

The priest's head jerked back and he slumped down against the opposite side of the booth. Hawkins peered through the opening and saw that the bullet had entered the priest's right temporal declivity adjacent to the orbital bone.

A cloud of smoke along with the acrid odor of burnt gunpowder hovered in the air. Hawkins lined up the threads on the end of the handle and began twisting in a clockwise rotation, all the while intently studying the body on the other side of the partition. Blood seeped not only from the dark, penetrating hole, but from the priest's nostrils and the twisted corner of his slack mouth. His eyes had the vacuous look of death.

The Hawk's distorted hearing was returning to normal and he heard the adjacent curtain in front of him being pulled open. Hawkins put the final twist on the handle of the cane, stood, and pushed the curtain on his side away.

The Falcon was leaning inside the other section of the confessional booth, checking the deceased priest. He then withdrew and pulled the curtain back in place. Hawkins did the same.

"So, I'm curious," Peregrine said, "did he grant you bloody absolution?"

"All except for the last part," Hawkins answered, his grin wide beneath the bushy, artificial hirsuteness. "I think that one knocked him for a loop. And I didn't even get to tell him I was a fucking Protestant."

"It's just as well," Peregrine said. "Time is of the essence. While you were in there confessing, we got a text. Another job offer."

"Oh?"

"It was from that fellow, Boulle. Our rich and eccentric friend on his little island has a new task for us."

"I wonder what that might be?" Hawkins said.

"Who the hell knows, with all the shit he has going on." Peregrine turned and started heading for the rear of the church. "I'll get the car so we can get out of this goddamned place."

"Now is that any way for a good Christian lad to be taking the Lord's name in vain inside of a church?" Hawkins grinned. "You could be jinxing us."

"Whatever it is," Peregrine said over his shoulder, "I doubt that this new job will have anything to do with confessing to a priest."

Hawkins barked a quick laugh and glanced back at the curtained booths.

"Most assuredly."

* * *

MIXED MARTIAL ARTS FIGHTING ACADEMY
RENO'S OFFICE
PHOENIX, ARIZONA

"Aw, dammit, Steve," Reno Garth said, the corners of his mouth twisting downward in a fierce scowl. "Why did it have to be *that* hand?"

Does it make any difference? Wolf asked himself as his trainer, Georgie Patton, wrapped the cold pack covering Wolf's right hand in place with an elastic bandage. Georgie's expression was dour as well. He looked plenty worried. So did Reno's steady girlfriend and personal assistance, Barbie. Her pretty face was glum. McNamara stood off to the side with an equally sour expression.

"Dammit, it's all my fault," he muttered.

Wolf was about to tell him not to take things so hard when Reno burst in with, "You're damn right it is. What the hell were you thinking, taking him on a bounty pick-up like that?"

McNamara didn't answer.

"Reno, it's not his fault," Wolf said. "It was just one of those things. Shit happens."

"Shit happens, all right," Reno repeated with derision. "But why does it always have to happen to us?"

There was that "us" again, Wolf thought. Wolf found it mildly amusing that Reno, once his and Mac's arch-competitor and rival, had now formed such an indelible bond with them. Much of it was the result of the life-changing events that had occurred down in Mexico those long months ago—how long was it now? Over a year and then some. Anyway, things had changed, and certainly for the better as far as he, Mac, and Reno were concerned.

"What am I always tellin' you, champ?" Georgie said in a low, calm voice. "When you ain't wearing no gloves, and don't have your hands wrapped, go for the body. It's safer, and them body shots…"

A hint of a smile traced over his lips as he let the rest of the sentence drift away.

Wolf took in a deep breath. He knew Georgie was right, but it wasn't like he'd planned it that way.

But again, he kept silent. He'd earned the rebukes.

"First those assholes hold up our damn purse using some namby-pamby bullshit," Reno said, his voice rising. "And then they withhold our belt, too. And our title. And now, after lucking out by getting this substitution match, we might have to pull out. Can things get any worse?"

Wolf felt like telling him that things could always get worse. It was the nature of the game. But he kept that to himself. No sense causing more consternation than he already had with his misapplied punch.

"Take it easy, Reno," Georgie said. "Maybe it ain't broke. Won't know till we get it x-rayed."

Reno stared down at Wolf's hand for several long seconds, then shook his head and looked directly at Wolf.

"It's broken all right," he said. "I can tell."

Wolf shrugged. "Maybe not."

"Anyway, this Dos Pastos guy ain't no pushover," Reno said. "No way I'm gonna let you fight with that hand in just a few days."

"Look—" Wolf started to say.

"No," Reno said, "you look. It's over. I'm canceling the fight."

"Reno, maybe we can get Digger to step in," Georgie said. "Or Leroy."

Reno shook his head. "Neither one of those two could put up a good fight." He blew out a breath. "They'd get creamed inside of one round. This Dos Pastos's a real contender in this league."

"At least let's go get that x-ray first," Georgie said.

Reno said nothing.

"Can't hurt to do that, baby," Barbie said.

Her voice sounded almost childlike, her presence an anomaly in the testosterone-laden office. But Wolf always appreciated her input as well as her ability to calm Reno down. She'd started out as his physical therapist after the shooting down in Mexico, and then their relationship developed into something more.

Almost like Wolf's relationship with his own lady love.

But that one was on permanent hold, at least for the moment.

"Okay," Reno said finally. "Run over to the hospital and get it x-rayed. I'll wait to call the promoters till you get back. They'll be pissed, and we ain't gonna be getting that purse, but an injury's an injury."

Wolf stood, thinking of yet another bill coming in. Going to the ER was going to cost a pretty penny unless...

"I'll just run by the VA and get it done," he said.

"Huh?" Reno said, his face contorting. "You'll be waiting all day in there."

Wolf shrugged. "Be easier on the wallet."

"Nah, nah, nah." Reno shook his head. "I'll cover it. We got insurance."

"I'll drive you," McNamara said, straightening up from his slouch.

"Honey," Barbie interceded. "The insurance isn't going to cover it if it didn't happen in the gym."

Reno emitted an exasperated sigh.

"So just lie about it," he said. "Nobody'll know."

"The way our luck's been running lately," Wolf said, "we'd better not chance it. Take me to the VA."

Besides, he thought. *I need some time to think.*

* * *

**THE ESTATE OF EDGAR VON TILLBERG
SAINT FRANCIS ISLAND
THE CARIBBEAN**

Pierre Boulle heaved a sigh as he fastened the towel around his waist and closed the door of the locker. Even though the air-conditioning in the huge mansion was set at a comfortable seventy degrees, he felt a distinct chill as he trod along on his bare feet along the tiled floor of the locker room toward the sauna bath, but he'd been through worse...much worse. As an ex-Legionnaire, he'd served his conscription in numerous hellholes around Europe, the Middle East, and Africa. His body was lean and hard and replete with the scars of numerous military engagements. Above all, he prided himself on being clever, strong, and adaptable. The Legion had taught him that. He was a survivor.

Despite his recent upgrade to the position of Von Tillberg's new executive assistant, Boulle still felt like a glorified gofer. The last one, a woman named Bridgette Swenstrom, had gotten arrested in the U. S. trying to take care of some of their rich boss's business. Boulle's ex

French Foreign Legion buddy, August Reign, had been killed during the same incident. All this contributed to Boulle's growing anxiety, and made him worry more than just a little. The executive assistant's position wasn't a job with a lot of long-term benefits and failure had severe consequences. And he did not have Bridgette's looks or seductive ability to offset any setbacks or short-comings with the rich bastard. It wasn't as if Boulle was bisexual, or anything, and even if he were, he doubted whether an offer to take care of Von Tillberg's needs in bed would have the same lascivious charm that Bridgette's had had. Sleeping with the boss—a smart businesswoman's best insurance. But maybe now that she'd been arrested, her luck and influence had started to run out.

Pablo Lopez, also nude except for the towel, walked beside him and it was the Mexican's first face-to-face meeting with Von Tillberg. He'd arrived the night before from Mexico City on the rich man's private jet. This heir-apparent to the Cortez Cartel looked like anything but a significant player. Lopez had come into the position by default when his boss, Esteban Cortez, had been killed in a shootout in Las Vegas back in July. With the senior Cortez and his son both suddenly out of the picture, the cartel's business leadership had gone through the usual inner circle power struggles until Lopez emerged as the dominant one. Middle-aged and flabby, Lopez was essentially a compromise candidate. What he lacked in brawn and charisma, he more than made up for with intelligence and guile. After years of keeping a low profile and establishing good professional relationships on the behalf of Cortez, he was essentially the only one with enough business acumen to take over the organization. And now in Mexico he always traveled with two bodyguards and had a distinct aversion to taking chances. Word had it that he seldom left the security of the fortress Cortez had constructed in Yucatan for fear of being bumped off by some would-be successor. Boulle wondered how long that might be, and couldn't blame Lopez for his agoraphobic practices.

But a summons from the big money boss, the man primarily funding the transportation of the human trafficking of the nubile young females to Mexico and the US could not be ignored.

"Why does he want to meet in *dere*?" Lopez asked, motioning toward the glass door of the sauna.

"*Dere* is his favorite place for a meeting," Boulle said.

Dere—There...Lopez's pronunciation of the troublesome English TH prefix wasn't any better than Boulle's own, but then again, neither of them were native speakers of the pathetic English language. Their own tongues, French and Spanish, were more sophisticated, but of little use in certain circles.

The Mexican's brow furrowed. "His favorite place? What does *dis* mean?"

"It means it is his favorite place for a meeting," Boulle said, offering no further comment on their boss's growing paranoia over being surreptitiously recorded. It had stemmed from the revelation that a tape of Von Tillberg's now deceased uncle was in the possession of the US Government. The royal nephew wasn't about to make the same mistake, hence he conducted all of his sensitive meetings in either the steam or sauna rooms.

Boulle saw the other man was growing suspicious and confused.

I had better head off any complications, he thought.

"No bugs," he whispered.

"Bugs?" Lopez repeated, his brow wrinkling. "*¿Los insectos?*"

"No. Listening and recording devices," Boulle said, keeping his voice just above a whisper. "*Para escuchar.*"

He kept his voice low, acutely aware of the two massive bodyguards who brought up the rear. The big black one was named Andre and he was fluent in both French and English. Boulle wasn't sure about Spanish, but the French verb, *écouter*, was somewhat similar and the context and tone spoke volumes. Dressed in a black T-shirt and accompanying black cargo pants, Andre's huge arms were covered with a network of ropy veins. A large pistol of some sort was holstered on his right hip. The equally massive white one whose name Boulle didn't know, was equally well-muscled. He was similarly attired and also had a big gun on his hip. Boulle knew that both of them were skilled at hand-to-hand combat as well. Von Tillberg had made sure that Boulle sat through one of the bodyguards' training sessions, watching them break boards and bricks with karate blows. Von Tillberg had monitored Boulle's reactions as a homeless reprobate whom the roving security force had apprehended on the section of private beach behind the estate was brought in and mercilessly beaten to death.

"Trespassing on my estate has its consequences," Von Tillberg had said, his thin lips curling into a devious-looking smile.

His estate. It was more like a military compound.

Boulle didn't dare ask what would become of the reprobate's body.

The poor son of a bitch no doubt now sleeps with the fishes, he thought.

"*Mecanismos de eschchar de excondidas*," Lopez whispered back. "*Qué ridículo.*"

"Shhh," Boulle hissed, tipping his head toward the bodyguards bringing up the rear.

Lopez glanced back over his shoulder at the two giants trailing them and muttered something that sounded even more disparaging under his breath.

Please don't let Andre or the other one hears that, Boulle thought.

There was no telling how Von Tillberg would react to an insult, real or imagined, in his little fiefdom. The man's behavior had taken a distinctive turn for the bizarre in the last three months. The news of Esteban Cortez's death, as well as the lawyer, Jason Abraham and Von Tillberg's fixer, August Reign all contributed to a feeling that the Von Tillberg empire was in danger of collapsing. The two B's, Robert Bray and Bridgette Swenstrom, now being in federal custody, had pushed the rich man a bit over the edge of sanity.

Not that he needed that much of a push.

Boulle suspected Von Tillberg's enhanced paranoia was a byproduct of some escalating drug use. He'd seen him consuming numerous pills and occasionally injecting himself with something.

Better living through chemistry, he thought and blew out a long breath as they got to the door of the sauna.

He pulled it open and stood back, allowing the Mexican to enter first.

The waves of dry, super-charged heat engulfed him as he then entered.

Andre caught the door and stepped in right behind them.

* * *

VETERANS AFFAIRS HOSPITAL
EMERGENCY ROOM
PHOENIX, ARIZONA

Although the price was right, the wait took a while. Finally, Wolf had been ushered into a room and a technician took two pictures. He didn't ask why they needed two, but this was the VA, and thus an offshoot of the military.

Ours is not to question why, Wolf thought.

He knew the score.

After another protracted wait in the huge waiting room, a pretty nurse came to the door and called his name, referring to him as "Sergeant Wolf," which surprised him. It had been a while since anyone had called him that and he figured someone in the Veterans Administration had reposted his old 201 file reinstating his pre-court martial rank of E-6 and pasting it over his former separation rank of E-1. He'd had slick sleeves when he'd gone to Leavenworth, and now, apparently, he had his chevrons back. At least the Great Oz had accomplished something.

"It's been a while since anybody's called me that," he said.

The nurse smiled. "Well, you still have the look of a sergeant."

Inside the small, box-like room, the attending doctor slapped the x-ray onto the lighted, horizontal glass plate fixed inside a metal box suspended on a retractable rack on the left side of the bench. The thick photographic plate stayed there as he studied it, as if it were magnetized or something. Wolf was fully clothed but had his arm elevated with a plastic ice pack wrapped over the top of his right hand. He wondered if the doctor was a veteran. The guy was young and black and looked like he didn't even have to shave every day, but that didn't really matter. He thought for a moment of all the young GIs he'd served with in Iraq and Afghanistan back in the day. Some of them looked pretty young, too, but they did all right when the chips were down. Age meant little. Experience was the rider, education the horse. But in a combat zone luck often superseded both.

"You've got a lot of calcium buildup on your knuckles, sir," the doctor said.

The nametag on his white lab coat said Dr. Bell.

"He's an MMA fighter," McNamara said. "World champion, too. In two weight classes."

Wolf didn't bother correcting him that it was only one world championship. The other was just a USA title.

The VA staff had allowed Mac to accompany Wolf into the small, curtained examination room.

"No kidding?" the doctor said, his eyebrows rising in unison. "That's pretty impressive." He glanced from the x-ray to Wolf and then back again. "Well, the good news is that I don't see any fractures."

Wolf felt a surge of relief.

"The bad news is that it looks to be a pretty severe sprain and accompanying hematoma. I'd suggest keeping it ice-wrapped for the next twelve hours and then limited activity for a week or so."

Reduced activity wouldn't cut it. Not only did he have to train, but he had to drop the weight too.

"Doc," Wolf said. "I can't do that. I've got a fight in seven days."

The edges of Dr. Bell's mouth twisted downward.

"I really wouldn't advise that. I can prescribe a steroid treatment to make it heal faster."

Wolf wondered how that would affect his urine

sample. With this ongoing lawsuit over the Rakhimanov fight, last thing he needed would be to fail the post-fight urinalysis.

"But he's got to take a piss test after the fight, Doc," McNamara chimed in. From the expression on his face, he was as concerned as Wolf was.

"I'll give you a five-pack," the doctor said. "It should be out of your system by fight time. But again, I'm advising you to reconsider fighting at all."

Wolf blew out a slow breath.

Not fighting at all wasn't an option, unless he wanted to declare bankruptcy, and that wasn't an option either. He needed money, and he needed time, neither of which was in the hand he'd been dealt.

Pardon the pun, he thought.

They were out of the building a few minutes later and trudging back to the Hummer. At least the fading autumn weather was nice. It was now closing in on mid-afternoon and the temperature was hovering at a comfortable seventy degrees. As they walked, McNamara's head hung down.

"Aw, dammit, Steve," he said. "I'm real sorry I messed things up for you."

"What are you talking about? You didn't mess up nothing."

"If I wouldn't have asked you to come back me up this morning—"

"Then you would've been facing those two jokers alone in the briar patch. And that guy's sister was built like an Abrams tank."

McNamara smiled for a moment.

"Yeah, she was a great warrior, all right." His expression got serious again. "But look, you should really consider postponing the fight."

"I can't. I got it because the original fighter backed out. I'm a replacement."

"Is it worth it?"

"It is if you've got the bills coming due that I do." He mentally started to list them.

McNamara's lips compressed. "Well then, I'm giving you that whole bounty fee that we got this morning. "

"Mac—"

"Don't argue with me. It's a done deal."

Wolf blew out a slow breath. "Mac, I'm the one that owes you. You picked me up when I was at the lowest point in my life, brought me to live at your own house, and gave me a new start. Everything I've gotten, I owe to you."

McNamara said nothing, but Wolf couldn't tell if his words had had the desired effect.

After flicking the key fob to unlock the monstrous vehicle, they climbed in their respective sides and McNamara asked, "So you're sure about fighting? I mean, you and me could mosey on down to the border again and join up with Buck and the boys."

Their friend Buck Mason had his group of hard-core vets down there working private security for the farmers who were being overrun by illegal aliens swarming across the border. They'd both put in some time down there and Wolf found it dangerous, taxing, and miserable. There were no clear-cut legal boundaries on how far the security patrols could go, what they were authorized to do, and little or no support from the authorities. It was a loser's job, all the way around. He remembered that recent news story about a homeowner who'd shot to death an intruder he claimed was threatening him and wound up being charged with murder. Wolf didn't know the exact particulars of the case, but it reeked with similarities of the type of things he and Mac had experienced down there.

No winners, he thought. Only losers all the way around.

"No thanks," he said. "I'd rather take my chances in the Octagon with this."

He held up his swollen hand, which was now hurting with a persistent, rhythmic aching.

McNamara heaved a sigh.

"So what you gonna do now?"

He twisted the key and started the vehicle. The motor roared to life like a sleeping lion suddenly awoken.

"Train like hell one-handed," Wolf said. "It's all about adapting and overcoming. Just like the army."

"Think it'll work?" McNamara shifted into gear and the big Hummer lurched forward.

Wolf was pushed back in the seat by the sudden acceleration.

"It did wonders for James Braddock back in the day," he said. The Cinderella Man broke his right hand in a boxing match. It was his power hand, and it was in a cast all the while he worked on the docks, so he developed more strength in his left to overcompensate. Then he came back to beat Max Baer for the championship."

"Yeah, but that didn't help him much against Joe Louis, did it?"

"They cracked the mold when they made him," Wolf said. "And this guy I'm fighting is no Brown Bomber."

"Who's the guy again?"

"Juan Dos Pastos. He's out of Brazil."

"He any good?"

"All those Brazilians are tough as hell," Wolf said.

"Hell, a lot of guys are tough," McNamara said. "But is he good?"

"They're all good at this stage of the game, so I'm sure he is."

They came to a red light and coasted to a stop.

McNamara glanced over at him.

"Look, all I'm saying is, maybe you should think about canceling or postponing this one. There's no sense risking getting hurt."

"The risk is there every time I step into the Octagon, Mac. And there is no canceling or postponing."

McNamara blew out a long breath.

"Dammit, this is all my fault."

"Knock that shit off," Wolf said. "I can take this guy. No problem."

It sounded positive, but the truth was that he didn't know that much about his opponent, nor did he want to think too much about him at the moment. He'd taken the fight on short notice because it was essentially all about the money. He wondered if Dos Pastos guy was as good as Reno had said?

But did it matter?

It wasn't like Wolf had much of a choice if he wanted to stay one step ahead of the bill collector. He took his own advice to Mac and pushed the negativity out of his head. Georgie was supposed to be reviewing some videos of the guy's last couple of fights and was going to come up with a quick game plan so they could train accordingly.

Wolf took in a deep breath.

But at least I'm going into it all of it with my name cleared, he thought. First time in a long time.

He saw Mac still staring at him.

A horn sounded behind them.

"The light's green," Wolf said.

"I know, I know."

The Hummer shot forward again.

"Mac."

"What?" McNamara's head turned toward him.

Wolf grinned and held up his left hand in a thumbs-up gesture.

"It's gonna be okay. And it wasn't your fault."

McNamara gave his head a quick shake as he weaved the big vehicle through the traffic.

Wolf remained silent but thought about how much he owed the man who was sitting right beside him.

More than I can ever pay back, he thought.

So there wasn't a lot of choice. Things were pretty much laid out before him with little room for variance. His course was clear. He had to face whatever was thrown at him and overcome it.

* * *

THE ESTATE OF EDGAR VON TILLBERG
SAINT FRANCIS ISLAND
THE CARIBBEAN

Von Tillberg was nestled on the uppermost tier of the redwood benches with a fluffy towel draped over his waist. Two naked young dark-skinned women sat on either side of him, one massaging his back and the other his thighs. All three of them were slick with sweat and the rich man's body looked thin and wiry, his ultra-white flesh looking like alabaster beneath their dark, kneading fingers. Both of them were pretty and Boulle knew them to be underage and African. The lighting was a bit subdued, but still bright enough to discern the slight but steady twitching of Von Tillberg's irises.

Boulle wondered if that was a result of some recent pleasurable chemical enhancement.

Von Tillberg made a hissing sound, tapped the girl seated on the tier below him, and made a dismissive gesture. She stopped her rhythmic massaging of his legs as did the other girl working on his back.

"Go," he said. "Both of you. Clean yourselves up."

The two girls scampered down from their perches, their breasts bobbling, their tight buttocks barely jiggling. The sight gave Boulle a bit of physical arousal, which he quickly tried to subdue. He had to admit that despite their young ages, their figures were already aesthetically pleasing, in a nubile sort of way. Lopez, whose smile was stretched across his narrow, lupine face was also appraising them. Out of the corner of his eye Boulle saw that the big bodyguard showed no reaction as they brushed past him and out the door.

He wondered if the big monster was gay? That might be a way to assure that none of the young females could corrupt him and turn him against their boss. There was clearly a lot more to be learned now that Boulle was stepping up to the exalted personal assistant position. And much to prepare for.

As the door swung closed behind the two females, Von Tillberg gestured toward the lower sections.

"Do sit down. We have much to discuss." His gaze went to the giant. "Andre, go fetch me another bottle of water."

Without a word, the big man turned and stepped out of the hot box. As the door whooshed closed with pneumatic precision Boulle noticed four empty plastic bottles haphazardly strewn about on the uppermost level.

It would have been nice for him to offer us some, he

thought but cynically added that niceness was not in the rich man's DNA.

Boulle's thirst increased exponentially as he sat on the lower wooden tier, the separation between the wooden planks noticeable against his bare ass. But the comfort of those considered beneath him was not in Von Tillberg's DNA either.

"May I reintroduce *Señor* Pablo Lopez," Boulle said. He'd made the introduction the previous evening when the Mexican had arrived, but Von Tillberg had made no effort at acknowledgment at that time.

This time the rich man nodded and smiled.

Lopez extended his open palm but Von Tillberg ignored it.

"I trust your flight on my Learjet was pleasant?" he asked.

"Oh, *sí*, ah, yes," Lopez said. "Very nice."

"And did Pierre fix you up with some feminine companionship last night."

Lopez grinned and gave his head a vigorous nod.

"Muy bien." Very nice.

Von Tillberg's smile broadened and he cast a quick glance at Boulle, who wondered if the amusement was in appreciation of the Mexican drug lord getting laid last night, or the fact that the entire interlude had been caught on video. In all probability, Von Tillberg had been watching and controlling the camera movements himself.

"Fine," the rich man said. "Ask Pierre if you want the same girl back again, or some variance. Your predecessor had some very distinctive tastes, as I recall." He inhaled deeply, as if recalling those visits. "And I want you to enjoy your stay here."

Lopez muttered something about being very appreciative of the hospitality.

The door opened and Andre stepped in holding out a frosty bottle of water. Von Tillberg accepted it, popped the cap with a deft twist, and drank copiously. After he lowered the bottle he raised an eyebrow.

"Oh, how thoughtless of me. Would either of you two like something?"

Boulle was surprised at this inquiry. In past meetings, Von Tilberg had never so much as given the comfort of the others a thought.

"It's good to stay hydrated," the rich man said. "Andre, two more."

The giant turned and left.

The opening of the door had reduced the oppressive electronic heat for a moment, but the cloying, pervasive heat quickly engulfed Boulle's body again. It was an uncomfortable feeling, like being forced to wear a wool sweater on a sweltering summer day. He hoped this session wouldn't last too long.

"Your predecessor, Mr. Cortez, and I had a rather successful business arrangement," Von Tillberg said, pausing to take another drink. "And he proved helpful to me in trying to settle a few troublesome nuisances."

"I know," Lopez said. "After his son was killed, I handled everything."

"Everything? Then you're familiar with the situation? Mr. Cortez was less than successful."

Lopez's face twitched with obvious embarrassment. "Oh, *pardone*. What I was trying to say was that I made all of the arrangements for Esteban to travel to *los estados unidos*, as was his wish…his ah, how you say, obsession? He wished to…no, he demanded to be present at the execution of *los dos hombres* he blamed for killing his son."

Boulle noticed that the more nervous Lopez became, the more the Spanish words crept into his English.

Von Tillberg raised an eyebrow. "To say it was unsatisfactorily executed is an understatement."

Lopez flashed a weak smile and continued. "You are referring to *de* two *Americanos* you want killed?" Lopez shrugged self-effacingly. "It was regrettable, but in the end, I am afraid that Esteban let his grief for his son interfere with what should have been a better plan. Rest assured, *señor*, I can do better. I will not make that mistake."

"I hope so," Von Tillberg said. "But let's get one thing straight. I've already taken steps to assure that you will. And those two *Americanos*, as you put it, are no longer my first priority."

"Oh no?"

Lopez's brow furrowed. Before he could say anything more, the door of the sauna opened again and Andre entered with two bottles of water. He held them both in his left hand, leaving his gun hand free of any encumbrances. The man's hands were enormous and Boulle wondered if the rest of him was just as large.

"Best to keep my mind of the task ahead," he told himself.

Neither he nor Lopez made a move to open their bottles.

Andre looked to his boss, who waggled his fingers dismissively. The big man left again.

"I'm bringing in a pair of professionals I've used before," Von Tillberg said. "They should be arriving later tonight." He glanced at Boulle, who gave his head a fractional nod.

"I am looking forward to meeting them," Lopez said.

"No mistakes," Von Tillberg said. "I want this matter taken care of expeditiously and successfully this time."

"*Por supresto*. Of course."

"One other thing." The rich man brought his water bottle to his lips and drank again. "I'm suspending my supply of chattel for the time being. Until I get some matters settled."

Lopez's brow furrowed again.

"Chattel," Boulle said. "Meaning no more new girls, or boys, until this matter is settled."

"I'm lowering my profile, so to speak," Von Tillberg said. "Temporarily, of course."

Lopez grunted.

"I understand."

"What I will need from you," Von Tillberg said, "is to quickly assemble a contingent of secondary personnel to supply my two new employees with weapons and direct them to certain locations within the United States. Can you manage that?"

"*Por supuesto*—ah, certainly. As you wish, it will be done, *señor*."

"Good," Von Tillberg said. "Regarding those individuals I want dealt with, I have a particular sequence that needs to be adhered to. Strictly adhered to." He paused and gave a five-second stare at Lopez. "Expect to be leaving for the U.S. tomorrow afternoon. Pierre will give you some burner phones so you can start setting things up. This must be done quickly. There is a limited time frame in which it must be accomplished."

Boulle knew he was referring to the official date when the federal grand jury was going to be called back into session. It was not yet set, but according to their source, it was going to be soon. There wasn't a lot of time.

Lopez nodded.

"*Dis es de* two *Americanos* that Esteban tried to kill?"

"No," Von Tillberg said. "There are two others. These new targets must be located and dealt with first. And, as I said, this must be done quickly."

"Quickly," Lopez repeated.

Boulle knew the rich man was referring to the two ex-employees who were in the custody of the authorities, Robert Bray, the PI and Von Tillberg's former chief assistant, Bridgette Swenstrom.

The second name sent a chill down his spine since he'd now taken her place in the pecking order. It reminded him of the perpetual delicacy and peril of his current situation.

If I mess this up, he thought, *the rich bastard will be sending someone after me next.*

CHAPTER 3

OUTSIDE THE MIXED MARTIAL ARTS FIGHTING ACADEMY
PHOENIX, ARIZONA

As they were getting out of the fortified Hummer Wolf heard a voice call out from behind them.

"Hey, what the hell happened to your goddamned hand?"

Wolf turned and saw the large figure of Lucien Pike strolling toward them looking even more deeply tanned than usual. He had a camo-colored bandana tied over his head in blanket-fashion and his long blond hair was hanging down from underneath it, touching the collar of his Desert Storm colored BDU blouse. The sleeves of the garment had been razor-bladed off, revealing Pike's well developed deltoids and heavily muscled upper arms. The "biker" look was compounded by his worn blue jeans and scuffed black engineer boots. The grin spreading over his face was infectious.

"Aw, hell," McNamara said in a loud voice. "Here comes trouble."

Pike affected a wounded expression and held both of his hands over his heart.

"I'm wounded," he said. "And it looks like I'm not the only one."

He pointed to Wolf's wrapped hand.

"I got caught reaching in the cookie jar when I wasn't supposed to be," Wolf said.

Pike's head tilted to the side accompanied by a squint on the right side of his face.

"The cookie jar? I hope you don't mean that your girlfriend did that to you." His grin widened. "How is the finest of Las Vegas Metro's finest?"

Yolanda...an image of her beautiful face and figure flashed into his mind's eye. He'd purposely been trying not to think about her too much, although he was finding that next to impossible. He couldn't afford any distractions, and he knew she'd be there for him at the fight. And hopefully afterward, too.

"Not hardly," Wolf said.

"So is it broken?" Pike raised one eyebrow. "The hand, I mean. Not the cookie jar."

Wolf shook his head.

Pike blew out a quick breath. "That's good. I heard you had a fight coming up and I was planning on betting some money on you."

"What do you want, Pike?" McNamara asked.

The big fed's grin widened.

"Can't an old buddy show up to wish his best friend the best of luck on his upcoming fight?"

"Best friend?" Wolf said. "I'd hardly call us that."

"Now is that any way to talk about the guy who saved your life more times than you can count?"

Wolf frowned and rolled his eyes.

"And made more trouble for him each time than a whole team of sappers," McNamara said. "Plus, I think you're forgetting that it was me and Steve that pulled your fat out of the fire more than just a couple of times."

"No argument there," Pike said. "We're all blood brothers, that's for sure. Airborne."

Wolf and McNamara exchange glances. It was true that all three shared that common bond.

"How far?" Pike said with a grin.

"All the way," Wolf said. "Now what do you want?"

Pike held up his open palms and waggled his fingers. "I just wanted to give you a little update on the VT situation."

The VT situation...the two letters hit Wolf like a pair of body blows.

Von Tillberg—another rich man he'd never met who was trying to kill him, and McNamara too.

"Is this what that cryptic text message was about?" Wolf asked as the text still loomed in his memory.

HEY, WE GOTTA TALK. IMPORTANT. BE IN TOUCH SOON.

Pike pointed a pair of extended index fingers toward him.

"You got it. I figured it was getting time for a pow-wow." He smirked. "No offense."

"Very funny," Wolf said as he set his gym bag down on the ground. "Okay, I'm listening."

"Well," Pike said, pausing to give his next words plenty of lead time. "There's no need to worry too much —yet."

"Meaning what?" Wolf asked.

Pike shrugged his big shoulders and canted his head to the side.

"Even though the weather's kind of nice," he said. "Standing around in a parking lot is not the best place to be discussing things of a sensitive nature."

Wolf glared at him.

"You got a better place in mind?"

"Sure do. I'll just drop by your place tonight. After dinner, we can watch the football game."

Wolf and McNamara exchanged glances.

"Nice of you to invite yourself," McNamara said.

"Hey, I'm from the G, remember," Pike said. "We're always insinuating ourselves into your business. You know what they say: If we ain't crawling up your asshole every chance we get, we ain't doing our job. You know what time the game starts?"

"Not really," Wolf said. "I don't watch football, and even if I did, I'll be going to bed early. I'm in training. I've got a fight coming up in seven days."

"I know," Pike said. "In Vegas against some cat name Daspasso, or something, right?"

"It's Dos Pastos."

Pike shrugged. "All right then, No time for football. I'll be there at seven then." He directed his gaze at McNamara. "No offense, but your daughter's not going to be there, is she?"

McNamara shook his head.

"Good," Pike said. "I don't think she likes me, not to mention her being married to an FBI agent and all. Sometimes the less people knowing about stuff, the better. Know what I mean?"

Wolf glanced at Mac, who nodded.

"Be there at seven," McNamara said. "We'll set a place for you."

"Outstanding," Pike said. "I'll tell you what, I'll bring

the dessert. What do you got a taste for? I got a real yearning for some apple pie."

"I'm not eating dessert," Wolf said. "I'm in training. Remember?"

Pike made a show of swinging his hand while he snapped his fingers. "Aw, heck. I shoulda known. Tell you what, I'll eat some for both of us."

"You do that," Wolf said.

"Okay then." Pike turned and began walking away. "See ya tonight."

"And why do I have the feeling that there's something you're not telling us?"

"Probably because there is," McNamara said.

The big fed stopped and turned back around to face them. "There's a lot I'm not telling you. Just yet."

"Just yet?"

Pike blew out a heavy breath. "Like I told you, I'm not saying there's cause for worry. I just don't want either of you two guys to get caught with your drawers down. That's all I stopped by to say. Just a friendly reminder, one old airborne trooper to another, to keep an eye out and your powder dry." He raised and extended his index finger and shook it a few times at Wolf. "That reminds me, how's your little brother doing? He went airborne, right?"

"He did," Wolf said. "And as far as I know, he's all right. He's over in Europe with the hundred and first."

"Good to hear," Pike said. "I'm glad I was able to pull those strings to get him in."

So it's business as usual, Wolf thought. Remind us of how much we owe you and hint around at stuff enough to keep the pot stirred.

"Say, I forgot to ask," Pike said. "Now that I helped you get your name cleared, you applied for that concealed carry yet? I got a couple nice guns I can sell you."

The fact that he was asking that set off another alarm inside Wolf's head. What did it matter to him if Wolf was authorized to carry a weapon? Was the danger more imminent than the big fed was letting on?

"I'm working on it," Wolf said. "But nothing yet."

"Okay. Well, in the meantime..." Pike cleared his throat and puffed up his chest. "Concentrate on winning that damn fight, will ya? Like I said, I plan on betting some money on you."

"Don't tempt me." Wolf flashed him a sardonic grin. "You're giving me a lot of incentive to take a dive."

"You wouldn't dare." Pike turned again and headed toward his car, speaking once again over his shoulder. "Now go on and get in there so you can resume your one-handed training and win me some money."

Wolf watched him go and then picked up his gym bag with his left hand and started walking toward the entrance as he looked around. The parking lot had a sparse number of cars, and none appeared to be occupied. Wolf figured the tan, nondescript sedan was Pike's. It looked like a typical governmental vehicle. Other than that one, nothing else stood out. No prying eyes, no lurking covert assassins. But Pike showing up out of the blue was always a bad sign—like the ringing of some indistinct fire alarm somewhere deep within a building.

It could be nothing, or it could be danger.

Business as usual.

It was already shaping up to be a lousy workout, and Wolf had the feeling that in addition to Dos Pastos, a bigger fight might be waiting just over the horizon.

* * *

MAIN ROADWAY EAST
SAINT FRANCIS ISLAND
THE CARIBBEAN

As usual, the massive commercial 737 had swooped down low over the beach coming in for the landing. It had to be less than sixty or seventy feet off the ground. Hawkins had laughed thinking about the jet blast perhaps bowling over some of the beachgoers. Or at least maybe blowing off the tops of some of the bikinis. It had been a trifle bit too dark to catch a glimpse of the people on the beach, but what did it matter? A set of bare tits was hardly a novelty on the beaches around here, and there were usually plenty to be seen at the estate. Some guy named Boulle had been waiting for them in the airport and whisked them through customs. Said he'd taken over the position that Bridgette had before. Like a typical Frog, he murdered the Queen's English with his consistency in mispronouncing certain sounds. Hawkins had always found that a trifle bit irritating about the French.

If you're going to learn another man's tongue, he thought. *At least do your best to master the intricacies of it.*

He turned his thoughts to something more pleasant—about the missing femme fatale, Bridgette, and felt a rush of excitement. No doubt about it, she was one beautiful piece of ass, not that he'd had the opportunity to try her out. But he wondered if the big boss had. Lucky guy, if he did. Too bad she wasn't still around.

But things changed and the world was always in a state of flux and you had to adapt. He'd been a trifle bit saddened to have to leave his lethal metallic cane in a trash can at the airport in Rio de Janeiro, for instance, but it couldn't be helped. Now, a delightful shade of evening darkness had settled over the island as Hawkins watched the glowing lights from the major city fading into the eclipsing darkness as the limousine wound up the sinuous mountain road. They'd been to the huge estate of Edgar Von Tillberg twice before, both times receiving assignments for operations in Africa—Libya and Morocco. They'd been easy hit jobs. Local politicians who were making some kind of waves. Probably about not getting a big enough slice of the pie. He and Peregrine had scoped the targets out, figured out a plan, and dealt them the losing hand, just like they'd done in Rio. A few hits in places like that were nothing out of the ordinary. He wondered where they'd be going next, and if he was going to be able to get laid tonight.

Boulle had said virtually nothing to them on the ride from the airport. He'd merely met them inside the airport, got them whisked through customs in a hurry, and ushered them into a big, waiting limousine. They'd met the Frenchman a time or two before, but had previously dealt with Von Tillberg's gorgeous assistant, Bridgette. Man, she was a nice piece and he always wondered if the skinny rich brat was fucking her on the side. Hawkins smiled at the thought. That was something he wouldn't mind doing, on the side or not. Any position would do.

The tinted windows made the view to the outside world a bit murky and Hawkins wondered if it was already as dark as it appeared to be. He glanced at his watch. Nineteen-oh-five. They'd lost a bit of clock time flying back east from Brazil. Or was it west? Hawkins was feeling a bit hungry and horny. Hopefully, their host would be kind enough to provide them with some sustenance as well as some feminine company. Having been there before, he set about considering the type of female he'd choose for tonight. After being in Brazil for a spell, he'd grown a bit tired of the dark Latin types. On the last trip, Von Tillberg had offered them a couple of Scandinavians.

Maybe a bit of vanilla would go nice after all that caramel and chocolate...

The hilly mountain range leveled out substantially and in a few more minutes they were approaching the long bridge that separated Von Tillberg's estate from the rest of the island. The tires of the limo hummed as they traversed the two-lane bridge and headed for the lighted fortress that was just becoming visible. The estate was massive and surrounded by a huge stone fence, replete with a row of spikes along the top. The house itself resembled a feudal castle made of immense blocks of white limestone. It sat perhaps fifty yards or so from the iron gate that was sandwiched between two tall stone pillars. A guard shack was positioned immediately outside and a uniformed man stepped out. He was wearing a big semi-automatic pistol in a leather holster on his right hip. The other side of his belt held a sizable radio. After an inaudible exchange of words between the guard and the driver, the guard went into the gate shack and began talking on his radio. Presently, the two sections of the large gate rotated backward and the limo pulled through.

"You will *haf* approximately ten minutes or so to freshen up and attend to any necessary bodily functions," Pierre said. "*Zen* we will *haf* our meeting *wit* Mr. Von Tillberg."

"Ten minutes?" Hawkins said, cracking a smile to offset the tone of his complaint. "That's barely enough time to take a decent crap. What's this all about?"

Pierre's expression did change.

"We are on a very strict timetable," he said.

"Listen," Hawkins said. "We haven't had anything to eat since breakfast."

"You'll be provided with some amenities after *zee* meeting."

"After the meeting? What the hell kind of bullshit is this?"

"As I indicated to you on the phone," Pierre said, "*zee* matter is very delicate. And we are on a very strict timetable."

"We're used to delicate," Hawkins said. "But a timetable? What the hell does that mean?"

"Relax, old boy." Peregrine smiled. "I'm sure the amenities *Monsieur* Boulle here mentioned will be more than adequate. After all, this isn't our first rodeo here, is it?"

Hawkins smirked at the stupidity of the American cowboy analogy. Any time a Brit tried to imitate an American it sounded a trifle bit dumb and out of place.

"Not hardly. But I, for one, was hoping for a bit of professional courtesy and consideration. Namely, a bit of feminine companionship for the night. Or maybe even two."

Pierre frowned.

"You wouldn't send a couple of soldiers out to face the slings and arrows of outrageous fortune with allowing them to get laid first," Peregrine said. "Would you?"

"*Mon ami*, am I not a Frenchman at heart? I will see to it tonight. On *zat*, you have my word. But...I must also inform you, be ready to take off for *zee* United States in short order."

"The States?" Hawkins said.

He and Peregrine exchanged glances.

"And in short order?" Peregrine said.

"So what is so all-fired urgent?" Hawkins asked. "Hustling us over here by private jet from Rio, barely giving us time to take a piss before some meeting. Makes this Irish lad wonder what all you've got in store."

"Like who it is you wish us to kill?" Peregrine added. "And how many?"

The Frenchman smiled.

"Well, now *zat* you mention it," he said. "*Zere* is more *zan* one. Four, to be exact. And *everyting* must be done in a specially prescribed sequence and *wit zee* utmost discretion."

"A prescribed sequence," Hawkins repeated.

"With the utmost precision," Peregrine added.

"*Oui*. It will all be explained to you at *zee* meeting. But we must have your assurance of absolute secrecy and a pledge of fidelity."

"Fidelity?" Hawkins barked out a laugh. "Now that's an interesting choice of words."

"Perhaps loyalty would have been a better choice of words," Pierre said. He glanced at the thick, opaque sheet of Plexiglas that separated the rear section of the limousine from the driver's compartment. "And two of *zem*, *zee* first two, are in protective custody of *zee* government."

"The government?" Hawkins repeated. "Who? The FBI?"

"Among *utters*," Boulle said.

"Others?" Peregrine raised an eyebrow. "Such as?"

"I believe it is *zee* US Marshal Service at this time. And perhaps *zee* FBI as well."

"Sounds like the makings of what the Americans might call a cluster-fuck," Hawkins said.

Boulle raised an eyebrow.

"A tribute to *zeir* stupidity, brashness, and vulgarity."

"Most assuredly," Peregrine said. "But what my Irish partner is implying is that the difficulty factor seems to have increased exponentially."

"In other words," Hawkins said, "locating them might be a bit tricky."

"*Zat* will not be a problem," Boulle said. "We have a man on *zee* inside. I am going to contact him tonight."

"And getting to them could be problematic as well," Hawkins said.

"Which is why we *haf* sought to hire the best," Boulle said. "And *haf* made arrangements for you to be most adequately supplied and assisted."

"Supplied and assisted? By whom?" Hawkins's voice was gruff.

"A selection of cartel personnel," Boulle said. "Do you foresee *zat* as being a problem?"

"Not at all," Peregrine said. "So long as we're paid, and paid well."

"In advance," Hawkins added.

"But of course," Boulle said. "But once again, I must stress that this job is one of *zee* utmost importance."

"Which is why you're hiring the best," Hawkins said. "Just make sure you get us those two or three girls for the night."

* * *

THE MCNAMARA RANCH
PHOENIX, ARIZONA

Wolf took a sip from his bottled water and watched as Mac and Pike both shoveled another mouthful of apple pie from their respective dessert plates. The pie that Pike had brought looked good—a crumbly Dutch-apple-style topping over the appropriately baked apple interior, and laid upon a layer of golden baked crust. It made his mouth water, but he knew that if he wanted to have a chance of making weight, he couldn't afford to go off-diet now. He took another swallow of water and vowed that as soon as the fight was over it would be pie à la mode.

If my jaw isn't too sore to chew, that is, he thought.

Wolf caught a glimpse of Pike chomping down another copious bite and grinning.

Was there a hint of malevolent satisfaction in that malicious simper?

After the fight, he told himself.

McNamara had finished his portion and slid the saucer away. He picked up his coffee and drank, looking at Wolf over the rim.

"You all right, Steve?" he asked.

Wolf smiled. "Yeah, just thinking about how much sweating I'm going to have to do to make weight."

"I been meaning to ask you," Pike said, pausing to smack his tongue over his teeth. "How come you're fighting light-heavy again? I thought you were the heavyweight champ now."

"Only if we're inside Reno's gym," Wolf said. "The commission withheld my title due to the shootout after the fight in the triage and parking garage."

"Withheld his purse, too," McNamara said. "And the damn Golden Chip Casino's declined to hold any more fights there."

"No," Pike said. "Say it ain't so."

"I'm afraid it is," Wolf said. "So in answer to your original question, this was the only fight I could get, and the only reason I got it was that the original opponent got injured and bowed out, so in desperation, they asked me."

Pike started to say something, then stopped and emitted a long belch.

"*Pardonne-moi*," he said and then raised an eyebrow. "Now why didn't you call and tell me about this before?"

Wolf didn't answer immediately. He felt like telling Pike that it was because the whole thing was none of his business, and every time the big fed stuck his nose into something, it usually made things worse. Of course, Pike had apparently greased some wheels somewhere to get Wolf's appeal on the docket at the Military Court of Appeals. Or so he claimed. But the withheld title and purse had nothing to do with the G.

"Are you saying you coulda done something?" McNamara asked. His expression reflected dubiousness.

"Listen," Pike said. "I'm from the government and I can move mountains."

"We're talking the World Mixed Martial Arts Commission." Wolf's tone was laced with skepticism. "It's a civil contract matter. What's the government going to do?"

Pike used his fork to section off another piece of pie and elevated it to mouth level

"You'd be surprised what the threat of setting some of them eighty-eight thousand new IRS agents on their ass would do." He stuck the bit of pie into his mouth, chewed, and shifted it to his right cheek. "Lemme look into it for you."

"Steve's already got his lawyer looking into it," McNamara said. "Now quit messing with him. And tell us what you came here tonight to say and quit dancing around, will ya?"

Pike finished chewing the pie and chopped off another piece. His brow was furrowed.

"Dancing...did I ever tell you that joke about the guy and the girl at the single's resort?"

"Cut the crap," Wolf said. "Will you get to the point? I got to make a phone call."

The right side of Pike's big face wrinkled with something between a wink and a squint.

"Bet you're gonna call your sweetie, ain't ya?"

Wolf rolled his eyes and started to get up. The fact was that he was supposed to touch base with Yolanda.

"All right, all right, all right." Pike set the fork down next to the unfinished piece of pie and assumed what appeared to be a serious look. "You remember that private dick we saved from those renegade Mexican bikers? Robert Bray? That guy that was shadowing you? The one we ended up rescuing from that big Aussie fella in Vegas?"

Wolf remembered it, all right. They'd found the Bray character bound head to toe and hooked up to a Taser. Von Tillberg had bailed him out of jail only to abduct him for what looked like a one-way trip to the knackers, as George Orwell would have put it.

Wolf nodded.

"Well," Pike continued, "he's now seen the light and the US Attorney's prepping him to testify before a federal grand jury in ten days or so. His testimony, in conjunction with what his former gal-pal, Maureen, already testified to, is what we call building a rock-solid case. You remember Maureen, right?"

Wolf remembered her. Blonde, good looking, well built, and flirtatious as all hell. He'd rescued her from being raped by the Mexican gangbangers and killed Esteban Cortez Jr. in the process, which had set off the vendetta by Cortez Sr. Wolf suspected that Pike and she might have developed more than just a government agent to informant relationship, but that wasn't any of his business.

"How is Miss Squeeze Me Tender?" Wolf asked.

Pike clucked his tongue.

"She's great. Already got her set up in Wit-Sec. Can't tell you where, of course, but she's as happy as a robin in springtime."

"I'll bet," Wolf said.

"Anyway, with what her ex-boss, Bray's gonna be saying, and if and when we can get our other femme fatale, Bridgette, to play ball—"

"Bridgette?" McNamara said, "Ain't that the one that tried to slash you? And would have, too, if Steve hadn't knocked the damn blade outta her hand."

"She has assured me she didn't mean it," Pike said.

"Yeah, right," Wolf said. "And you're planning on getting her involved in this too?"

"Well," Pike said, opening his eyes and raising an eyebrow as he spoke. "Let's just say I'm working on that. Trying to get her to repent and see the evilness of her ways. Get her to sing a different tune. One of C-O-P-E-R-A-T-I-O-N."

Wolf frowned. "You mean cooperation? You spelled it wrong."

"No I didn't," Pike said. "It's *cop*-eration."

"Ha ha," Wolf said.

Pike winked. "She talking about maybe firing the attorney that Von Tillberg set up for her, but hasn't officially done it yet. I been sorta working things off the record, and I do mean totally off the record. I ran it by the US Attorney who's handling things but he's slower than an escargot crawling up a hill trying to see if we can re-initiate a conversation without first getting permission from the Pope, or something."

"The Pope?" McNamara said. "What's he got to do with this?"

"Figure of speech," Pike said. "Anyway, before she lawyered up, she originally told me that she can lead us to her treasure trove of incriminating videos on all kinds of people. According to her, some you wouldn't believe. With that kind of leverage, we'll not only be able to get an international arrest warrant for Von Tillberg and company, but we'll have the goods on a whole lot of really bad people."

"So you're saying you're close to being able to take that son of a bitch down for good?" McNamara asked.

"Like I said, it's complicated. We gotta go through the French with everything, but we're working on it."

"You're *working* on it?" Wolf said, letting the edge of skepticism tincture his voice.

"As we speak. Believe me, I think that eventually she'll come around."

"The operative word sounds like 'eventually.'"

"Yeah," Pike said. "*Eventually* we should have enough to take to the French authorities and have them eventually move on it."

"The French?" Mac said. "When the hell have they ever gotten their heads out of their damn asses long enough to do anything worth a damn?"

"Don't underestimate them," Pike said. "Didn't you ever heard of Inspector Maigreit?"

"Inspector Maigreit?" McNamara asked. "Who the hell's that?"

"He's a fictional character written by George Simenon," Wolf said. "Wrote books in the nineteen seventies and eighties about a Paris police detective."

"Right," Pike said. "You know, you're sounding more and more like a college professor all the time. Maybe you should consider going into teaching."

"Yeah, right," Wolf said. "Now what the hell's he got to do with anything?"

"Well," Pike said. "Simenon—he's French, ain't he?"

Wolf shook his head. "I think he was Belgian."

"Same thing," Pike said. "I read a lot of books by him when I was lounging on the beach."

"Never heard of him. And as far as authors," Mac said, "if you ain't talking about John D. MacDonald, forget it."

"Well, that Simenon guy's my idol," Pike said, grinning. "Supposed to have slept with over ten thousand women."

"Sounds like the guy probably had an overactive imagination," Wolf said. "When would he have had the time to write all those books?"

"Sounds like typical French bullshit," McNamara added.

"Yeah, most likely he enhanced the number," Pike said. "The guy's wife claimed the number was only like a couple of thousand."

"Sounds like a moot point to me," Wolf said. "Anyway, are you going to finish what you were saying?"

Pike extended his big arms and rotated them slowly, showing both sides.

"As you can see," he said. "I got one of those deep, tropical tans."

"So?"

"It's from the Caribbean."

"Big deal," McNamara said. "Back in the day, I had one of them too, courtesy of the Mekong Delta. Now why'd you come here telling us all this?"

"Because," Pike said. "I just wanted to let you know we're close."

"Close?" McNamara said. "Close to what?"

Pike lowered his arms and his grin widened.

"You know..." He picked up the fork once more. "If I was to stand up and drop my drawers, you'd see that I don't have any tan-lines at all. They got lots of nude beaches down where I was."

"Please, spare us. We'll just take your word for that." But something clicked for Wolf. "You were down on St. Francis?"

Pike canted his head slightly.

"You got it. Me and my team had your buddy, Von Tillberg, under sort of a half-assed surveillance, so to speak."

"And?" Wolf asked.

"And," Pike said. "He's got himself burrowed in his compound tighter than a Louisiana wood tick. Which ain't a good sign. I'm concerned he might be planning something."

"Like what?"

Pike placed another piece of pie into his mouth and began chewing.

"Don't know, but considering his past activities, I figured I'd better come over and give you a heads-up."

"When are you gonna finally get around to locking that son of a bitch up," McNamara said. He squinted at Pike. "I mean, how many times did they send a bunch of killers after Steve and me?"

Pike's breath came out with an exaggerated huff.

"It's like the line from that old joke about the man and the woman dancing at the single's resort, and he says, 'I'm only here for the weekend,' and she says, 'I'm dancing as fast as I can.'"

So he finally got it in, Wolf thought.

He blew out an exasperated breath.

"Dumb jokes ain't gonna cut it," Wolf said. "Are we in danger again, or what?"

"Hard to say exactly." Pike took in a deep breath. "Like I said, we were down on the island seeing what we could find out," Pike said. "As it turns out, Interpol's been aware of Von Tillberg's bullshit and activities for a while now. They're just waiting for the right time."

"That's real nice." Mac snorted. "And I wonder how many pretty little girls will be sold into prostitution or killed while they stand twiddling their thumbs?"

Pike's expression changed, losing any trace of mirth.

"You're preaching to the choir, Mac," he said. "Believe me, they want him as bad as we do."

McNamara rolled his eyes. "You talk a good game, Pike. But when it comes right down to it, that son of a bitch has put American lives in jeopardy here within our own borders, and you gotta admit that nobody, not you or the French, has done shit about it."

Wolf thought Mac was being a little too hard on the big fed but said nothing.

"There ain't a lot we, as in the G, can do," Pike said. "We're dealing with foreign governments. That's plural. St. Francis is half-owned by the French, and half owned by the Dutch. They got different laws than we do, and let's just say that Von Tillberg, who's got dual or triple citizenship, has a lot of influence. Bridgette says that he's got everybody from a couple of the past presidents to half the royal family on videos doing the nasty. And some of it with kids nowhere near the age of consent. Plus, he lives in a big, isolated compound that's almost like a separate island itself."

"Bridgette again," McNamara said. "I'm already tired of hearing about that broad."

"I got a feeling she's almost ready to cooperate, like I told you before." Pike grinned expansively. "And man, if she can deliver a quarter of what she says she can..." He emitted a low whistle. "It could really blow the lid off things."

"You still haven't told us why you're telling us all this?" Wolf asked.

Pike was slow to answer, his mouth framed with a lips-only smile.

"Just to keep you two updated," Pike said. "I still have hopes of you two and me flying a couple of kites down there someday."

"Fat chance of that," Wolf said. "Every time we get involved in one of your schemes, we end up getting beat up, shot at, or put on some gangster's hit list."

Pike raised an eyebrow.

"How do you know you're not already on one?"

Wolf thought about that.

How indeed?

CHAPTER 4

MIXED MARTIAL ARTS FIGHTING ACADEMY
PHOENIX, ARIZONA

Six more days, Wolf thought as he strained out another one-armed push-up using his left arm. Less than a week.

He was feeling less sure of himself with every work-out. The swelling on his right hand had shrunk considerably, but the tenderness and pain were still there. It hurt like hell to make a fist, but at this point it wasn't a devastating pain—just a severe reminder that it still hadn't completely healed yet.

"Okay, Steve, that's good," Georgie Patton said, standing over him. "Now let me see that hand."

Wolf jumped to his feet and held out his right arm. Georgie took the hand in both of his and studied it, his dark fingers occasionally massaging and causing Wolf to wince slightly. Each touch brought a new wave of pain.

"Still hurts, huh?" Georgie said.

Wolf nodded.

"Little bit."

Georgie glanced up at him, an expression of cynicism on his face. He brought both of his thumbs down hard on the swollen portion and Wolf emitted a grunt of pain.

"A little bit?" Georgie asked.

Wolf spoke through gritted teeth. "Well, maybe more than that."

Georgie released the pressure and patted Wolf's hand gently. "You is one tough white boy. I'll say that for you."

"I'm half Indian, remember?" He leaned closer to his trainer. "What do you think?"

"It means the nerves are still inflamed," Georgie said. "Got some blood collected in the tissues, too. But I'm thinking that in a few more days or so, it should be back pretty much to normal. If'n' we baby it a little."

Wolf nodded again, pretending to agree, but he got the feeling that Georgie was only whistling past the graveyard. The deep fissures lining his forehead and between his eyes were set in granite. Usually he was upbeat and positive during training. This time his game seemed a bit off.

"Let's hope," Wolf said. "You get those fight videos?"

"Still waiting on 'em. Most of this dude's fights have been down in Brazil, so getting films of them ain't easy." Georgie paused and grinned. "But I got my sources. Should be here soon."

Wolf knew little about Juan Dos Pastos, his upcoming opponent, nor had they had any common opponents. Dos Pastos fought in a separate and lesser-known organization than the one Wolf was in. But he knew that just because it wasn't as well-known, it didn't mean his opponent wasn't tough. Most Brazilian fighters were.

"Him being from down there," Georgie said, "makes me figure he's most likely primarily a grappler rather than a striker, which means we got to do some work on your ground techniques and staying in the guard. He takes you down to the mat, it's like fightin' one of them pythons. That happens, your best chance is to keep him tied up until the ref breaks you. That's one of the rules for this league. No action after thirty seconds or so, they call a break and stand you up."

Wolf knew his ground game wasn't as good as it should be, and his gripping strength was severely depleted by the hand injury.

This ain't going well, he thought and then pushed the negativity out of his mind.

"If you can keep things stand-up," Georgie continued, "we can catch him with a one-two and knock him out. If your hand's all healed up, that is."

Wolf flexed his fingers again and made a fist. The pain was there, not so much debilitating as it was constant and imminent, like a waiting adversary standing across the Octagon between rounds.

"You been getting your roadwork in every morning?" Georgie asked.

"As regular as clockwork," a voice said from behind them. Wolf recognized it.

Pike had reappeared.

Georgie frowned.

"Who let you in here? You know we're trainin'."

"Yeah," Pike said. "I just came by to see how it was going."

"It'd be going a lot better if'n' you didn't come by and be messin' with my man's mind," Georgie shot back. "We ain't got no time for negativity."

Pike held his hands palms outward and fluttered his fingers.

"I just came by for a quick minute. Got some news for Steve here."

Georgie started to say something but Wolf stopped him.

"It's okay," he said. "Just give us a minute, okay?"

Georgie turned his baleful gaze in Wolf's direction but said nothing.

Wolf placed his hand on his trainer's shoulder.

"Please," Wolf said.

Georgie compressed his lips, then gave his head a quick nod.

"All right," he said. "I'm gonna run over to the office and make a call about them fight videos. You got one minute to talk to Hulk Hogan here, and then I expect you to be working the tire by the time I get back."

Working the tire meant lifting up an immense tractor tire from the floor, setting it straight up on its tread, and then pushing it over. Then the process was repeated, over and over again. It was one of Wolf's least favorite parts of the training.

"Roger that, boss," Wolf said.

"Roger nothing," Georgie said, holding up his forearm and pointing to the watch on his wrist. "I'm gonna be timing you and listening for them big thumps once this second hand goes around and reaches sixty." The twin clefts between his eyebrows deepened. "Remember, Steve, you got to get down to that two-oh-six limit. This one's light-heavy."

Wolf didn't need any reminders. He was dreading that almost as much as picking up the tire.

Georgie's brown eyes stared at him for several seconds before he turned and walked toward the office.

"Better not let Reno see you over here, Pike," he said over his shoulder. "If'n you know what's good for you."

Pike waited until Georgie was out of earshot before snorting out a laugh.

"Man, I'm really persona non grata around this place," he said. "You think it'd help if I bought a lifetime membership or something?"

"Were you really shadowing me on my run this morning?"

Pike chuckled. "Let's just say I been keeping a close watch. From a distance."

"Is that a fact?" Wolf asked. "I haven't seen your government-issue sedan, and it's pretty easy to spot."

"Well, let's just say somebody's been keeping tabs on you. And they been keeping close enough for government work."

Wolf suddenly began to wonder about the veracity of the big fed. There'd been no sign of anybody this morning. He'd been keeping a close watch. So had Mac. And Pike had a propensity for grandstanding. But then again, Wolf hadn't been looking up. It could have been a drone watching from above. He decided to let it ride.

"So, what's up?" Wolf said. "I've got to get back to training. The fight's in six days."

"I know, I know," Pike said, his head bobbing up and down. "I just stopped by to tell you that—" He stopped talking and looked around. Apparently satisfied that no one was within listening distance, he began again. "Our buddy Bray's ready to be prepped at the US Attorney's office for his grand jury testimony."

"You going to take him?"

Pike shook his head. "I can't do everything. Gotta delegate. I got my good buddy Quincy doing it. He's with the US Marshal's Service. Good guy."

"Bray still in protection at a safe house?"

Pike winced.

"You know I can't tell you that," he said, "or I'd have to kill you. Well, seeing as how we're such good friends, I might just reconsider and just hurt you real bad."

"Yeah, right. So is that all you wanted to tell me?"

Pike glanced around again and then leaned closer, speaking in a whisper.

"We're guarding Bray round the clock in a hotel, don't ask me where. And he's set to testify before the federal grand jury in just a few days."

A few days, Wolf thought. Same as the fight.

"They got it set for a Friday," Pike said. "So they'll break for the weekend, and then hopefully we'll be able to get Bridgette to play ball that next week."

"The grand jury testimony's closed to the public, right?" Wolf asked.

"It is."

"So why you telling me all this?"

Pike grinned. "It's just my way of telling you not to worry. As far as I know, Von Tilberg's still holed up in his little castle, and there's no activity outta what's left of the Cortez Cartel, so things are looking good for you as far as any bad guys gunning for you."

"Good to know."

"And better still," Pike said, smiling. "With this grand jury testimony winding up, I might just be able to catch a flight up to Vegas and see your fight. Remember, I'm betting some money on you."

Wolf said nothing.

"So can you get me a couple of tickets?" Pike asked.

"A couple?"

"Yeah, I was figuring on maybe taking some of my team up there to see you fight. Ah, you are going to win, aren't you?"

"Not if I don't get back to training."

Pike was just starting to say something else when Georgie's loud yell floated toward them.

"Your minute's up, Pike. And, Steve, I don't hear no tire flopping."

Wolf turned and went to the big tire, squatted, and worked his fingers under the edge of the thick sidewall.

"Better get out of here," he said to Pike.

"But what about the tickets?"

Wolf lifted the heavy tire as he straightened up, lifting the huge rubber monstrosity upward.

"I'll see what I can do," he said, the strain obvious in his voice. "Now get the hell outta here."

"That's my man," Pike said with a grin and turned to go.

Your man? Wolf thought. *Not hardly.*

* * *

FEDERAL BUILDING
OFFICE OF US ATTORNEY BENJAMIN TURNER
PHOENIX, ARIZONA

Chester A. Loudermilk, second chair assistant to United States District Attorney Benjamin Turner, wiped the trickle of sweat from his forehead hoping that his boss wouldn't notice. He could feel the vibrating tingle of the burner phone in his right front pants pocket, picked up the sheaf of papers he'd been working on, and stood up. Why did they have to text him now, while he was still here at work? In another few hours or so he'd be at home and able to text them back immediately. Or was it just their way of maintaining dominance over him?

What the hell could they want now? Hadn't he given them enough already?

But the sad, desperation of his situation was like a specter hanging over his shoulder.

It'll never be enough, he told himself. *I'm in too deep.*

"Chester," Turner's voice called out on the intercom in his office. His room was adjacent to the larger section that Loudermilk shared with two other administrative assistants.

A second chair administrative assistant.

Even the title sounded pretentious. In reality, it was little more than a euphemism for the guy who went around the circus ring with a shovel and a bucket cleaning up the animal shit after the main performances. It was nothing more than a synonym for a mediocre career choice. And Turner always made sure to hand him the shit jobs.

"Yes, sir?"

"Have you finished going over those briefs?"

"I have, sir. Do you wish to review them?"

"No. Bring me the file on that Bray character," Turner's voice said. "I want to review the questions I'm going to ask him. And get hold of Lucien Pike. I want Bray brought in here so I can prep him. Make sure it's right before his scheduled date."

"Yes, sir," Loudermilk said, getting up and going to the rows of filing cabinets that lined the opposite wall.

I'm relegated to the job of a secretary, he thought. *I went to law school for this?*

As always, Turner's tone was aloof, impervious, demanding. Was it any wonder he commanded fear, rather than respect among his underlings?

But then again, Loudermilk thought, *is that really any excuse for getting myself into this damn mess?*

He opened the appropriate file drawer and removed the manila folder. Even though Turner did everything on his official government office computer, he always had a hard copy printed up as well and filed, which made it easy for a resourceful and enterprising individual like Chester A. Loudermilk to make the most of the situation. It was nothing for him to sneak a few surreptitious pictures with his cell phone now and again. Not enough to arouse suspicion, but enough to keep the inquiring bastards off his back. But now what had initially been a thrilling escapade into intrigue, adventure, and sexual fantasy, had become a lodestone around his neck.

If only he hadn't fallen for their original ploy.

If only...

He should have never gone to that damn island on vacation. It had been the brochure that piqued his interest—he wondered who had been responsible for that? But he'd been stupid enough to look up the website on his computer.

His work computer.

Fabulous fun in the sun at an exotic location. Come join us...

He should have tried his luck in Vegas instead.

Enjoy the fullest adult entertainment spectrum at Le Club Carousel...Exclusive adult nightlife.

The accompanying pictures were artfully arranged, the wording enticingly crafted.

And after your dinner and drinks, feel free to ask the ladies out on a date.

The array of beautiful, smiling faces had been the trigger. It was too damn tempting for a perpetual wallflower like him. Not that he didn't know deep-down what she was. She was a pro, and played him with the acumen of a concert violinist picking up a country fiddle. Flattering him, treating him like a heavy-duty stud or some kind of rock star.

Him, the one they'd called "Scarecrow" in high school. He'd hated it.

Tall, shy, gangly, rail-thin, bespectacled, prone to perpetual acne...a perennial wallflower at the school dances...they'd nicknamed him the Scarecrow back then, making every day a series of unending torments as the bullies took delight in making his adolescence a living hell.

So why shouldn't he have taken advantage of the once-in-a-lifetime opportunity that *Le Carousel* offered him?

And it wasn't like he'd paid her that much, or anything. It had all gone down so easily, fulfilling his every fantasy. It was like a dream come true.

A dream that subsequently turned into a nightmare.

They'd seen him coming a long way off.

The stunning invitation to come back on an all-expense-paid holiday a few months later. The opportunity to spend time with Calypso again—*She misses you, mon ami.*

He'd fallen for it, just like a mouse being lured into the sophisticated trap by some exotic cheese. They'd obviously been tracking him. Perhaps they somehow traced the IP address of his government computer. But he had bragged a bit to the bitch, elevating the status of his low-level administrative assistant position in his ramblings. And the offer of Calypso introducing him to her young girlfriend—very young. He didn't realize she was vastly underage until afterward. It had been way too tempting. And after all, he'd been out of the country and on vacation...

Then, a few months later, when he was back in Phoenix, it came time to pay the piper.

The phone call, the invitation to dinner, the beautiful

woman with a business proposition...it hadn't seemed quite right to him, but he went anyway.

His suspicions were confirmed when the woman showed up with some big Australian brute who played the video on his cell phone as they sat in a remote corner of the restaurant.

It felt like a big hand had reached down out of nowhere and grabbed hold of his balls.

"Not to worry," the big Aussie had said, sliding the burner phone and charging kit across the table toward him. "We're very discreet and you'll be rewarded. We won't ask much. But when we do, you will respond and do whatever we want. Understood?"

He understood all right.

And that was the start of it.

Not that it hadn't been lucrative, but he'd come to realize that the payments he'd received were just another way of digging their hooks in deeper and ensuring their ultimate dominance. They owned him, lock, stock, and barrel, as the saying went. He'd never be free of them. Not until—

He felt the electronic trickle of the damn burner phone's vibration again which signaled another incoming text. He didn't bother to look at it because he knew who it was from.

How had he gotten in so deep?

He mulled over that question as he went to his boss's office door and knocked gently on the opaque glass.

Turner always made a point of requiring that bit of decorum.

"Come in," the voice from beyond the glass said in an authoritative tone.

Loudermilk twisted the flat-black metallic knob and entered, holding the file out in front of him.

Turner sat behind his big, gunmetal gray desk like a disheveled Buddha wearing a white shirt, open at the collar, his necktie was slackly drawn, and discernible fields of wetness extended from under each arm. His suit jacket was hanging haphazardly on a nearby chair. To describe the man as heavy was an understatement. He was morbidly obese, to say the least. The top of the desk had an old-fashioned rectangular paper calendar covering a fifteen by thirty-two space. Written scribbles covered the surface in each outlined date section. Off to the side sat an opened box of some kind of flavored crackers, a bag of pretzels, a cylindrical can of Pringles potato chips, and the crumpled wrappers of three ice cream sandwiches. That the man hadn't keeled over from a heart attack by this time always astounded Loudermilk.

But as long as he was feeding his face, the less likely he'd be to grow suspicious of his administrative assistant's periodic "other endeavors."

Seeing the huge, half-moon sweat stains on his boss's shirt made Loudermilk feel the persistent trickle from his own armpits.

The wall behind them was covered with an array of photographs and plaques, all commemorating visits with VIPs and various awards for Turner's role in special assignments.

Turner looked up and reached across the desk, his right hand extended and open.

"You get a hold of Pike yet?" he asked.

How the hell could he expect that when he'd only asked a little while ago?

"No, sir."

Turner exhaled loudly, snapped the fingers of his

right hand for the file while shoving a bunch of pretzels into his mouth with his left.

"Well do it, dammit," he said, not bothering to keep his lips fully closed as he chewed. Tiny particles spewed forth and settled on the white paper of the desk calendar and others on the file. Loudermilk wasn't looking forward to handling that once Turner had finished with it. "That grand jury's coming up in ten days, and I've got to get him in here for prepping."

"Yes, sir."

"And where are we with arranging something with that other chick? What's her name again? Spencer?"

The man's usage of the word "chick" seemed as out of place as a wallflower at a bachelor's party.

"Swenstrom," Loudermilk said, thinking about the other target of concern in the rich bastard Von Tillberg's scheme of things.

The burner phone tickled Loudermilk's leg once again and he emitted a cough in hopes that it would cover any trace of the faint sound.

Turner's face crinkled.

"Jesus Christ," he said. "Cover your damn mouth when you cough, will ya? We're just coming outta that COVID bullshit."

"Sorry," Loudermilk said, bringing his hand up to his lips.

Turner dropped the file onto the desktop, opened it, and began flipping through the pages. He paused and looked up.

"Well," he said, "what are you waiting for? I told you to get hold of Pike, didn't I?"

It's time for me to be dismissed, Loudermilk thought. *And to answer my other master.*

"I'll get right on it, sir," he said. "Right after I run to the washroom."

* * *

PRIVATE HANGAR SECTION
ST. FRANCIS INTERNATIONAL AIRPORT

Boulle stood off to the side in the private hangar with Hawkins and Peregrine next to him and contemplated the complexities of what was to come as the pre-take-off preparations on the leased Learjet were being completed. As he mulled over the complex plan that the insistent rich man had constructed he couldn't help but think of the many things that could go wrong. And things were teetering on the brink already. Moments before, Pablo Lopez, who looked like he'd just rolled out of bed, had been directed out of the hangar when he'd placed a cigarette between his lips and taken out his gold-plated lighter.

One of the maintenance workers had shouted at him in French and pointed to the signs in French, Dutch, and English:

DANGER~GEVAAR
NE PAS FUME~NIET ROKEN~~NO SMOKING

Too bad there's not a third line in Spanish, Boulle thought. *Then the idiot might have realized the danger.*

"You must not smoke in here, *mon ami*," he said. "There is jet fuel being dispensed."

Despite his hung-over condition, Lopez apparently got the gist of the peril, slipped the lighter back into his pocket, and headed toward the exit.

"How do you spell S-T-U-P-I-D in Spanish?" Hawkins muttered in a loud voice.

He looked hung over too.

Lopez kept walking, but his movement slowed and stiffened fractionally at the Irishman's words.

He glanced back over his shoulder and glared at them as. Hawkins mimicked a puffing, explosive sound and jerked both of his hands outward with a semi-circular motion.

Lopez pulled open the door and went out.

After the door had closed, Peregrine said, "It seems the old boy almost lent a new meaning to the term, dying for a cigarette."

"He's a fucking moron," Hawkins said.

Boulle's head swiveled toward him, and his mouth formed into a scowl.

The man had absolutely no *savoir-faire*.

"That was not too smart," he said. "We will have need of him once we reach the United States."

Hawkins shrugged.

"He's right, you know," Peregrine said. "The old boy's a dunce, all right, but pointing it out as vociferously as you did, could put us in a bit of a pickle down the line. Please do your best to remain civil for the remainder of this flight."

Hawkins yawned and stretched.

"Aw, lay off. What's the use of being Irish if you can't be thick?" He rotated his head a bit. "Smooth things over for me with your inimitable and proper British charm then."

Peregrine chuckled at his partner's antics.

Boulle's frown deepened.

I have been thrust into the position of being the babysitter for three buffoons, he thought.

The buffoons' luggage was contained in five black duffel bags, one for Lopez, who had traveled light, and four more substantial packs for the Falcon and the Hawk. It was in stark contrast to Boulle's three large Louis Vuitton suitcases. But then again, since his promotion up the ladder he'd decided that everything from this point out was going to be first class. Additionally, the secret compartments of his suitcases contained a substantial amount of American currency needed for both the ops and the payoffs. Numerous expertly crafted passports and IDs were also in special compartments of the suitcases, although he had the first round of false IDs in his carry-on bag. No customs officer in the US was going to do any scratching at luggage that expensive.

Hawkins yawned loudly and rubbed his big hand over his face. He looked bleary-eyed and bored. Peregrine looked like he was on the verge of dozing off as well. These two seemed to have the attention spans of a couple of apes. But Boulle wondered if he was selling them short. They came highly recommended and had done work for Von Tillberg before.

Perhaps the parade of ladies he'd arranged for both of them the previous night had left them a bit drained, but how could it have not?

The big lout, Hawkins especially.

He'd grabbed three girls and hustled them, laughing and smiling, to his room. Peregrine had opted for only one, but then asked for another after about twenty minutes.

Impressive stamina. But a man's measure of professional talent was not measured by his appetites, and as he noted, neither of them had *savoir-faire*.

"Spoken by the poor Frenchman who had slept alone

last night," he told himself with an accompanying cynical laugh.

"They got any damn coffee around this place?" Hawkins asked.

Boulle figured the man probably hadn't gotten enough sleep.

I hope his performance was all that it was chalked up to be, he thought. *I'll have to review the video once we get back.*

Boulle was always careful about locating and blocking the camera lenses in his own room.

"There's a machine over there," Peregrine said, pointing to the large metal box with the picture of a steaming cup of coffee reposing among a sea of brown beans.

Hawkins snorted. "I'm looking for something a bit more substantial. Like a cup with a couple of shots of Baileys in it."

It was Peregrine's turn to laugh.

"Good luck with that, old boy," he said.

Boulle wasn't about to offer any assistance to that problem and stood in silence as he watched the maintenance crew prep Von Tillberg's private Learjet. He'd flown on the plane a few times before, but never as the primary executive assistant. Mostly the previous flights had been transporting a bunch of girls to the island, or other places for sale. Bridgette had handled those transactions, and Boulle was only the back-up. Most of the time August Reign had been along, too, pushing Boulle further into the background, and that had suited him just fine. His nickname in the Legion had been the mongoose —thus named after the innocuous little rodent that routinely routed and killed the mighty king cobras in India. Reign had often called him Rikki-Tikki-Tavi. He didn't understand the reference initially, but later found out it referred to some poem by an Englishman named Rudyard Kipling. Boulle tried to read it, but couldn't understand it and had no desire to try and find a French translation. Reign then explained that the poem was about a heroic mongoose defending a family against a pair of monstrous cobras. Boulle didn't particularly like being compared to a rodent, but he rolled with the punch, so to speak, and accepted the name. He earned it because of his prowess in the boxing ring on those lonely, edge-of-nowhere outposts in the Legion. Boredom and excess adrenaline gave way to contests of strength and skill, namely French boxing, or savate, and Boulle quickly established himself as an excellent counterpuncher. Let your opponent commit, evade his blow, and then pepper him with some of your own.

He'd always possessed lightning speed, and still considered himself a counter puncher, which was why he felt a bit uncomfortable at being the man in charge. He also felt ill at ease leading this dynamic duo, Hawkins and Peregrine. They had nicknames, too. The Falcon and the Hawk. Although he had second billing, it was apparent that Hawkins was the dominant one of the pair. The big Irishman was brash and loud, especially when he'd had a few drinks. His English counterpart was more subdued, more cerebral. Obviously, the planner of the two. Hawkins was the enforcer. The Falcon and the Hawk.

And I, the mongoose.

"Rikki-tikki-tavi," he repeated to himself.

This present alliance was a strange one indeed. A rodent and two birds of prey, all working together to do the bidding of a madman. But a rich madman. A very rich madman.

Boulle wondered how successful they would be.

The meeting the previous night had gone well. Von Tillberg appeared only long enough to brief the two of them on what he wanted done and in what order. Killing the two Americans was still on the agenda, but it had been pushed down as far as the main priority. It had been an obsession of the now deceased cartel boss, Cortez, more so than that of Von Tillberg. The over-riding number one priority for the rich man was now keeping Robert Bray from testifying in front of that federal grand jury in Phoenix. Second on the list was Bridgette. She was to be located and liberated and then brought back to the island. Boulle had already recontacted the lawyer that they'd been using—the one she'd supposedly fired, to reestablish contact with her. Boulle was certain that she had no intention of cooperating with the American authorities. All she really wanted was a way to procure her release. Firing the lawyer they'd arranged for her, and issuing a veiled threat of some type of rumored cooperation, was merely her way of flexing what little muscle she had left. An ultimatum to Von Tillberg that she wanted a get out of jail free card, or else.

"As for Bridgette," Von Tillberg had said the night before. "I'll deal with her when I have her here. She knows way too much to be abandoned."

Von Tillberg took it as an indication that the federal prosecutor was dangling some sort of deal in front of her, and that she was debating whether or not to take it.

It most likely was a signal to her rich boss saying, "Either you get me out of here, or I'll spill my guts." That didn't bode well in the grand scheme of things, and most of all it displeased Von Tillberg, who valued loyalty above all else. And, if she were on the verge of cooperating with the U.S. authorities, she could do a lot of damage in certain circles. Not only was Bridgette party to most of Von Tillberg's illicit activities as far as the human trafficking, the secret recording of his "guests," and his intimate relationship with the Mexican cartels, but the rich man was suspicious that she might have made copies of some of the illicit sexual peccadilloes of the rich and famous and politically connected through the course of their visits to the island.

After all, blackmail was traditionally a woman's gambit, was it not?

Plans for her liberation were already in the works, and Boulle himself was part of that. The Hawk and the Falcon would be needed for that venture as well. Boulle mentally reviewed the complex mission on which he was now being sent.

Lots of intricacies, he thought. *Perhaps too many.*

But, he reminded himself, as they used to say in the Legion, failure was not an option.

He was looking forward to seeing her again. Perhaps Von Tillberg would allow him to interrogate her, Legion style. He imagined taking a turn or two with her, before the rich man ordered Andre to break her pretty little neck. Concerns about his employer's mental stability also lingered. He'd demanded his usual meeting in the sauna and was naturally covered with perspiration, but his bodily movements seemed to exhibit a noticeable tremor. Like he was shivering at times, despite the excessive heat. Was this a sign of some sort of substance abuse? He certainly had enough money to purchase whatever pharmaceuticals he might desire.

Better living through chemistry?

No, Boulle thought. *Excessive living through chemistry.*

Lopez came strolling back into the hangar, and one

of the maintenance workers glanced up to make sure the Mexican wasn't smoking.

"We will be taking off soon?" he asked.

"I should damn well hope so," Hawkins said. "I'm getting a bit antsy already."

"Let them do their jobs and complete the safety inspection," Peregrine said. "It doesn't pay to rush."

Hawkins laughed and glanced at Lopez and Boulle.

"He's right. He used to fly helicopters in the SAS, you know."

Boulle knew, all right. Appropriate for a falcon.

That damn, overly complicated, intricate plan. And it was conceived by a pampered, rich sociopath who might very well have stepped over the edge with his possible substance abuse. The signs were all there, and ominously distinct. Not what you wanted in terms of future stability. But what other choice was there?

The maintenance technician descended the ladder by the side of the plane as another one removed the fuel nozzle and began retracting the hose.

"The plane has been refueled and we will load your baggage now," the technician said to Boulle in French. "You may board now."

Boulle replied in kind and turned to the others.

"We are to board now," he said in English.

"About bloody time," Peregrine muttered.

The smaller bird of prey looked and sounded a bit hungover too.

Hawkins slapped him on the back. "Time for you to pull one of your stiff upper lips out of your pocket, Falcon."

Lopez said nothing as he shuffled toward the plane's extended staircase. The other two stagger-stepped after him.

I am in charge of three buffoons who must work together to carry out a very complex plan devised by a rich drug addict, Boulle thought as he swung the carry-on bag over his shoulder. Hawkins almost bumped into him.

"*Sacre bleu,*" he muttered to himself.

"Eh?" Hawkins said, whirling toward him. "What was that remark?"

"Nothing," Boulle said. "It is a French expression. Nothing more."

The big Irishman raised one eyebrow, smirked, and started up the stairs, reaching up to smack Peregrine on the behind.

It made Boulle wonder about the relationship between those two.

But did it really matter?

The Legion motto came floating back to him: Failure is not an option.

* * *

FEDERAL BUILDING
OFFICE OF US ATTORNEY BENJAMIN TURNER
PHOENIX, ARIZONA

Chester A. Loudermilk sat at his desk in the outer office and strained his ears trying to listen to the conversation going on in the next room. The wraith-like federal agent, Lucien Pike, had arrived about ten minutes ago and was in there briefing Turner now. The solid pane of thick, frosted glass that separated Turner's inner office from Loudermilk was proving impenetrable as far as any sounds. All Loudermilk could discern was an occasional loud laugh from the big agent.

What a lout. The man always came sauntering in,

dressed like some fugitive from a motorcycle gang in a sleeveless army shirt and blue jeans. Even the boots he wore looked ridiculous. But Turner ate it up. Deep down, he must have been as intimidated as Loudermilk was by Pike, and covered it by pretending to be the agent's good buddy.

The intercom on his desk crackled.

"Chester," Turner said. "Go get us a couple of cans of soda from the vending machine." His boss's voice faded slightly and Loudermilk heard him ask the other man what kind he wanted.

Pike's brash voice was distinct. "The only thing I drink in cans is a nice cold beer. Make it a coffee instead. Hot, sweet, and black, just like my women." This was followed by a hearty chuckle.

Turner's grating laugh mixed in with Pike's.

Two Neanderthals sharing a joke, although Turner could hardly be considered that rugged. Intelligence-wise, he was probably a bit higher on the evolutionary plane, but not by much.

"You get that, Chester?" Turner asked.

"Yes, sir. Coffee, hot, sweet, and black for Agent Pike." He made a point of not allowing any sarcasm to creep into his tone. "And for you, sir? Coffee or soda?"

Turner's expiration of a loud breath was audible, followed by a low, guttural sound.

"Coffee for me," he finally said. "And get me a candy bar, too. The usual."

The usual depended on if it was before or after lunch. A regular milk chocolate bar in the morning, with his coffee, and a bag of chocolate-covered raisins after lunch.

Loudermilk made a perfunctory reply and rose from his seat. He absolutely detested being treated like some bimbo-level gofer, but on the other hand, this might give him a chance to overhear some of the privileged conversation when he entered the inner office. Any slight hint would be useful since that bastard, Pierre Boulle, had been so insistent on the burner phone yesterday.

"We are coming to *zee* United States tomorrow," the Frenchman had said. "We will need *zee* information *zen*."

Stick et up your ass, Loudermilk thought, allowing his sub-vocal tone to mimic Boulle's imagined French pronunciation of the English words. Talking to him after work on the phone was almost as bad as dealing with his persistent texts. Loudermilk had done his best to sound calm and placid, but in reality, he was nervous as hell. They wanted him to find out the location of a soon-to-be government witness in an ongoing investigation. He didn't need to wonder why. The cartel had already tried to take out that Bray fellow once. Maybe even twice. The guy was a target, that was for sure.

And, he thought, *these are the kind of people I'm dealing with. And once they hit him, there would be an investigation that would surely be traced back to him.*

But what other choice did he have?

As long as they had that incriminating video of him, he was in their pocket. A puppet.

Despite the high level of air-conditioning comfort, Loudermilk realized that he was starting to sweat and hoped it wouldn't be too noticeable. The big idiot Pike seemed to have a predator's feral sense of regular human emotions. It was like the big goon could smell nervousness and fear.

Loudermilk swallowed hard and pushed his glasses up on his nose as he strode out of the office. It was about a hundred feet or so to the break room where the vending machines were and as soon as he got there, he grabbed some napkins out of the metal receptacle and wiped his face and hands. One of the other assistants was in the room dumping coins into the slot and pressing the buttons. She nodded to him as the machine went through its grinding and humming cycle.

He reached in his pocket and felt for any change. There was none.

Swearing under his breath, he pulled out his billfold and sorted through his currency. Luckily, the machine accepted bills and gave back change. The prices, however, seemed to go up on a weekly basis.

More expenditures that I'll never get reimbursed for, he thought.

Moving to the candy machine, he fitted a five-dollar bill into the slot and pressed the button for the chocolate bar. It dropped down with a thud into the metal tray as the machine continued to dispense, one-by-one, the change in coinage.

The woman smiled at him as she lifted the little plastic door and removed her cup of steaming liquid.

"Where would we be without that morning cup of coffee?" she said, turning and walking out of the room.

He didn't reply. As far as he was concerned, she was just another retard in the maze of offices around here.

A toadie.

As he moved over to the coffee machine, he debated on how to handle the trek back to Turner's office with the two cups of coffee and the candy bar. After rotating his arms in small semicircles, he finally decided to put the candy bar in his shirt pocket. His fingers brushed his shirt, and he felt the dampness, which reminded him of how much he was sweating. Wrapping the candy bar in a napkin, he gingerly placed it in his shirt pocket and started to drop some quarters into the slot. Pressing the buttons, he selected the first coffee.

Hot, sweet, and black, he thought, imagining Special Agent Pike screwing a Black woman.

The fantasy momentarily excited him, and he was a bit careless as he removed the cup. Some of the hot liquid splashed onto his hand.

It was hot, at least.

Setting Pike's coffee on the nearby counter, he dumped more change into the machine and pressed the selector buttons again. Just as he did so the burner phone in his pants pocket vibrated with an incoming text. Loudermilk's eyes raced back and forth, surveying the room.

He was alone.

Why did they have to text him now?

Rotating his shoulders in a gesture of feigned relaxation, he reached into the pocket of his baggy pants, pulled out the burner, and read the text.

All is well?

He frowned. It was their usual summoning message indicating that he should reply with a time that he could call back.

He decided to ignore it and slipped the phone back into his pocket.

They could wait until later. He had nothing new to tell them anyway. He hadn't had a chance to find out much besides Bray being prepped for testimony in nine days.

Then his other phone chimed with a text. This one was his government phone and he always kept the ringtone activated. His fumbling fingers had a hard time extricating this phone from his pocket. Glancing at the screen, he saw it was from Turner.

You get lost?

That son of a bitch, Loudermilk thought.

He punched in his boss's usual coffee preference with a series of vigorous punches.

One coffee, cream and extra sugar.

It wasn't easy serving two masters, one a fat, incompetent asshole who was riding on the backs of his assistants, and the other a ruthless, blood-sucking vampire who had the ability to drain him dry.

"No choice," he told himself. Two masters. For the time being at least.

He slammed the palm of his hand against the front of the machine to punctuate the selection.

The coffee cup descended at a misaligned angle and got hung up on the brackets. Instead of the spray filling the cup, it poured over the edge and into the metallic drain at the bottom of the slot.

Swearing, Loudermilk pushed the plastic shield upward and managed to right the cup, but not in time. The hot liquid burned his fingers. The flow stopped seconds later, having only filled about a quarter of the paper cup.

Swearing, he removed the scantily-filled cup and set it on the counter.

Another bit of money for which he'd never be reimbursed.

Dropping more coins into the slot, he pushed the sequence of buttons again, more carefully this time.

The paper cup slid down into place perfectly and the liquid poured from the spout.

After the cycle was completed, he slammed up the plastic shield and pulled out the cup once more, glancing around as he did so.

Nobody else was in the break room.

Acting quickly and with alacrity, he drew some saliva into the front of his mouth and then held the cup up close to his chin, opening his lips to release his spittle into the light brown liquid.

No, asshole, he thought. *I didn't get lost. And I hope you enjoy your coffee.*

His only regret was that he couldn't do something more to debase it, like dipping his penis into it.

Too hot to consider, he thought with a sly grin and he couldn't wait to watch fat ass Turner take his first sip.

It was going to be a real pleasure to betray that son of a bitch.

* * *

MIXED MARTIAL ARTS FIGHTING ACADEMY
PHOENIX, ARIZONA

A day late and a dollar short, Wolf thought as he missed with a left hook and failed to follow up with a right.

More like a week late and ten dollars short. His timing was way off.

Or more like five days late, Wolf thought.

That was how long he had before fight night.

His opponent sent a counter right zinging into Wolf's face.

Georgie, who was right outside the gym Octagon, yelled loudly. "Keep your right up, Steve. You shouldn't be getting tagged like that."

Tell me what I don't know, Wolf thought.

"You the champ, dammit," Georgie added.

Wolf didn't feel very much like a champ as he backpedaled away, knowing that he should have pivoted and sent a right hand sailing into his opponent's unguarded face. If he had a right hand, that is. Instead, he'd pulled the punch, leery of re-injury, and had paid the price.

Hesitation was a deadly foe for any fighter. It eroded instinct, threw off timing.

Dancing away, he let his sparring partner, Rolando Villa, tall guy with an accompanying leanness and very quick hands, follow him. Wolf caught a peripheral glimpse of Reno standing next to Georgie.

Villa shot out a jab and Wolf blocked it with his left.

Stepping forward pivoting, his opponent tried to deliver an overhand right to Wolf's head, but this time Wolf slipped the punch, crouched, and slammed two left hooks into Villa's abdomen. They were wearing heavier than normal sparring gloves to muffle the impact, but just the same Villa crumbled to his knees after a two second delay.

For a moment, Wolf thought about delivering a follow-up right cross to the side of Villa's head. Instead, he merely checked the half-thrown punch and did a skip-step away.

Despite the lack of restrictions in MMA about hitting an opponent when he was down, Wolf always refrained from doing it, much to the chagrin of both Reno and Georgie.

This time was no exception.

"Goddammit, Steve," Reno shouted. "You shoulda finished him with a right."

"My right's injured," Wolf muttered, his mouthpiece making the words almost unintelligible. "Remember?"

That didn't matter. Reno got the drift. He knew Wolf too well.

"Yeah, right. But you try that against Dos Pastos and

you'll be getting your ass handed to you," Reno shot back. "Christ, we only got five fucking days."

Tell me something I don't know, Wolf thought.

He bounced around the Octagon as Villa slowly made his way to his feet, raised his hands to guard position, and held out his glove as a show of respect and acknowledgment.

Wolf slapped it with his left and then resumed the sparring session.

The two of them circled warily, but Wolf sensed that Villa hadn't quite recovered. Wolf danced away.

"What the fuck?" Reno yelled at the top of his voice. "You fucking playing Peter Pan, or something."

At the moment, Wolf wished he were in Neverland. He ignored Reno's taunt.

Villa shook his arms a bit and seemed to be fully recovered.

Wolf's left jab shot out once, twice, three times, peppering the other man's face. Momentarily befuddled, Villa stumbled ever-so-slightly, and Wolf angled in and delivered a triple left hook to the abdomen twice before bringing it upstairs.

The other man staggered, lurching around on stiff legs.

Once again, Wolf imagined delivering the overhand right that would no doubt end it, but he held off, did a stutter-step closer, and shoved Villa to the mat.

From the look of him, he was exhausted and spent.

"You going down to follow up with ground and pound, or what?" Georgie said.

Instead of replying, Wolf turned around and popped the mouthpiece out of his mouth.

"Round's over," he said, more clearly this time.

Georgie glanced at his stopwatch, blinked, and then

frowned.

"Like hell it is," he said. "You only been at it four minutes and forty-three seconds."

Close enough for government work, Wolf thought, paraphrasing Pike's off-hand remark earlier that morning.

"Aw, hell," Reno said, a sour expression twisting his mouth. "Let him go, Georgie. He ain't accomplishing nothing in there anyway." He glanced over at Wolf and shook his head. "I'm gonna cancel this damn fight."

Georgie looked at him, his eyebrows elevated like twin caterpillars.

"Damn straight," Reno said. "He's just setting himself up for a fall."

Wolf knew this was merely Reno's way of motivating Wolf to work harder, but it had been an exhausting day's training and he was in no mood for games or bullshit.

"Maybe you should do that," he said.

Reno's head swiveled around and his eyes widened. His mouth was gaping.

Georgie came to the rescue, holding up his open palm.

"All righty," he said. "Let's everybody take a deep breath now. Okay?"

Neither Wolf nor Reno said anything.

"We got five days left," Georgie continued. "I'm supposed to get them videos of this Dos Pastos dude tonight or tomorrow. Steve's always in good shape, and except for the hand, he's mostly ready. Reno, you know how hard you worked getting this fight set up. All the phone calls you made, all the favors you used up. Don't make sense to pull out now, 'lessin' it's because of the injury." He stepped forward and pointed to Wolf's right hand. "Get that glove off a there and let me take a look. Then we'll decide if'n' we're gonna quit or not."

Wolf extended his arm and Georgie stripped off the band of tape, undid the laces, and pulled off the glove with unusual care.

Wolf felt a surge of pain as the thick, padded material slid off his hand. It was still taped, and the pain was like a thousand needles being pressed in and out.

Georgie pulled a pair of scissors with a flattened end on one of the blades. He slipped the flat portion under the wrapped gauze and began cutting. The blades made a crisp sound cutting through the material ending each time with a sharp click. After a few deft strokes, the padding separated and Georgie pulled it off.

"Make a fist for me," he said.

Wolf did, feeling the pain intensify.

"How's it feel?" Georgie asked.

Wolf hesitated. He didn't want to say it still hurt like hell, but he knew he'd better not try to lay on the bullshit.

"It feels better than it did."

Georgie's lips drew back into a smile.

"It's lookin' better than it did, too." He glanced at Reno who was scrutinizing the hand now. "What you think, boss?"

Reno blew out a slow breath.

"I don't know." He stared straight at Wolf. "You're the one that's gonna be stepping into the cage. You tell me. Can you fight, or do you want me to cancel?"

Wolf's thoughts turned to the load of bills that he knew would be coming due by the end of the month. If they canceled, he'd get nothing in the way of payment. Plus, his reputation and marketability were also on the line. He was suing one organization to get his money and title back, and he knew that Reno had gone the extra yard getting him this fight with the rival MMA organization. If he couldn't deliver, or at least show up and make a good fight of it, what he had left of an MMA career would be over, plain and simple.

"I don't want to send you in there if you're not one hundred percent," Reno said.

I'll never be back to that in five days, Wolf thought.

But on the other hand, his mind flashed back to the just-completed workout. He'd almost managed to put Villa down for the count using just his left. While traditionally a sparring partner is nothing more than a man who's hired to take a beating, Villa was also a tough guy.

Would it be vanity speaking if he said he thought he could take out Dos Pastos using only one hand? And his right was feeling better and better with each passing day.

Five days.

Well, four really. Today was pretty much shot.

The weight was still a significant hurdle, too.

"Well," Reno said. "You gonna answer me, or what?"

"Let's do it," Wolf said.

Reno grinned and clapped him on the shoulder.

"That's why you're the champ," he said.

This one wasn't a title match, but Wolf felt like it was. He had a lot riding on it.

A big fight's coming, he told himself. And I'd better be ready.

"Okay," Georgie said. "Let's call it a day as far as sparring is concerned. Step on over to the locker room and get on the scale and we'll see how we doing on that particular factor."

Wolf was wearing a sweatsuit and had padding around his legs. He knew he'd have to strip down to get weighed.

The three of them walked into the locker room. Inside there were a few guys in various stages of undress.

Wolf quickly stripped off his sweats and then the leg pads and his plastic groin protector. After laying the sweaty mass on the long wooden bench between the rows of lockers he walked barefoot over to the scale. It was an old-fashioned model with a metal platform at the bottom of the scale. The T-shaped upper portion had two connected balance bars, each containing poise weights, with a larger one on the bottom going up to 300 pounds and the smaller one from one to fifty.

Wolf was completely naked and felt a sudden chill as he stepped onto the metal platform.

The pointed, needle-like end smacked against the top of the metal square with a definitive click.

Georgie first set the large poise weight on the lower balance beam bar at two hundred.

No movement from the indicator, but Wolf didn't expect any. He knew he was way over two hundred.

Georgie moved the smaller poise-weight counterbalance to the ten-pound increment on the upper portion of the balance bar.

The needle still didn't move.

Two hundred ten and counting, Wolf thought.

Georgie's finger pushed along the smaller poise weight to the next graduated increments.

Eleven, twelve, thirteen...

No movement yet.

Taking in a deep breath, Georgie moved the smaller weight a few more notches.

Still no movement.

What the hell?

Sighing, Georgie kept tapping the smaller one along to the fifteen-pound indicator.

Two fifteen, Wolf thought. *And it's going to get worse.*

Georgie gave his head a quick shake, like he was

shooing off a pesky insect, and advanced the smaller poise weight two more increments. The indicator needle finally drifted downward to balance in the middle of the square indicator window.

Georgie whistled.

"Two-seventeen," he said, and blew out a heavy breath.

"What?" Wolf said. "That can't be right."

"I thought you was supposed to be dieting?" Reno said.

"I have been," Wolf said, thinking that three months ago he'd weighed in at a rock-solid two-twenty-five for his heavyweight title bout with Dimitri Rakhimanov. It had been a real pleasure not to have to lose any weight for that fight. But what bothered him was that on his scale at home this morning he'd registered at two-twelve. Of course, it was just a regular bathroom model and not as sophisticated as this one, but what the hell. How could there be that much variance?

But regardless, it was looking like now he'd have to drop eleven pounds, and in a hurry.

"Two-seventeen's what Muhammad Ali used to weigh during his prime," Georgie said, his tone admonishing. "When he was fightin' for the *heavyweight* championship."

His emphasis on the weight class wasn't lost on Wolf. Things were turning to shit faster than he expected today.

"We gonna have to go some," Reno said. "Can you get down to two-oh-six for the weigh-in?"

Wolf stepped down onto the tiled floor and felt the chill rise up through the soles of his feet. "Got to."

"Five days," Reno said.

Four after tonight, Wolf reminded himself. But the

weigh-in was twenty-four hours before the fight, so that reduced it to three. But if he didn't make weight at the weigh-in, they'd give him another hour or so to drop some more pounds. Then, if he didn't make it, he'd be fined.

"Well now, let's not get ahead of ourselves," Georgie said. "We gotta think this thing through. We can do this. If'n' you can drop a pound or two a day up until the day of the weigh-in, and then spend a bunch of time in the sauna, it shouldn't be a problem."

More easily said than done. Wolf had gone through "the drought" before a couple times when he was fighting at light-heavy. Since he'd gotten out of prison, his weight had continued to creep upward. He attributed that to his eating better and the rigorous training routine. He'd come to feel that two-twenty-five was his optimal weight. Sweating off those pounds the day before the fight was always rough. Not only wasn't it a pleasant experience, but it tended to weaken the body. Even rehydrating after the weigh-in could leave you feeling weak and depleted.

"How much is the fine if I don't make weight?"

Reno shrugged. "I'll have to look at the contract, but hell, the weight's the least of our problems. I'm more worried about that hand."

Me too, Wolf thought.

"At least we got more than one thing to worry about," he said.

Reno frowned. "True that. But if that hand ain't looking no better by Friday, I'm gonna have to think real hard about canceling the whole thing."

It looked like there was going to be more than one battle on the horizon.

CHAPTER 5

THE HIGHWAY NEAR THE MCNAMARA RANCH
PHOENIX, ARIZONA

Three days till the weigh-in and ten pounds.

Those two things kept echoing in Wolf's mind as he ran along in the early morning darkness. He'd increased the hand weights to eight pounds each, sixteen pounds total.

Sixteen...his unlucky number of late. Or was it more appropriate to make it a three?

Last night after finishing up at the gym he'd felt almost too tired to eat. He'd thought about skipping the evening meal altogether, but Georgie convinced him to have something light. Instead of his usual sit down meal with Mac, Wolf had opted to nuke a couple of frozen chicken breasts that Barbi had given him at the gym along with a bottle of water. By the time he'd finished eating, his appetite returned with a vengeance later in the evening. He grabbed his jump rope and skipped out three five-minute rounds. After that, he was ready to hit the shower again. He resisted the temptation to hop on the bathroom scale, afraid of what it might show.

This morning, however, he did step on it and it read 216.

That meant that he'd succeeded in dropping one pound overnight, if this scale was to be believed. And only ten to go.

But the only one that counted was the scale at the weigh-in. He kept his sights set on the two hundred and six pounds mark. Right now, it was just between him and his roadwork. The old boxer's adage from the great Joe Frazier was that nobody'll know if you cut those dark, early morning runs a bit short. Nobody but you, that is. It'll come to you in those late rounds of the fight, when you're body's hurting, and it's all you can do to get up off of that stool, and you look across the ring, and the other guy's already standing and bouncing up and down on his toes…and then you realize you should never have cheated on those runs, and now it was your turn to pay the piper.

Yeah, right, he thought. *Nobody'll know but me.*

Wolf's reverie was interrupted as he saw a pair of headlights in the adjacent lane heading toward him.

Passenger car, moving at a pretty good clip.

No way to tell how many occupants.

Pike's warning played like the unforgettable refrain of an irritating old song.

No need to worry—yet.

He felt for the hardness of the Glock in the shoulder rig and veered farther over on the shoulder. The crown of the road slopped slightly which made running a tad awkward, but the angle would help if he had to hit the dirt and roll to avoid an attack.

The oncoming car didn't seem to be slowing at all.

Was that a good sign or a bad sign?

Good if the occupants in the vehicle were intending on sticking some guns out the window. Trying to hit a moving target with accuracy, even one as slow as a runner, when you were traveling at around fifty or sixty, would be problematic. It was a smallish sedan, dark colored, no license plate on the front.

Wolf averted his gaze from the car for a split-second to survey the terrain. If he had to make an evasive move there was nothing in the way of cover.

If anything untoward happened in the next few seconds, he mentally rehearsed tossing both of the weights at the car and doing a diving roll down the sloping surface of the highway's shoulder.

Hit the ground and roll, he told himself, Then pull out the Glock and return fire.

The car, a Chevy Malibu of indeterminate color, whooshed past him, appearing to have only one occupant, a female.

Threat over, he thought, turning his head to glance back over his shoulder to ensure that the vehicle had kept going.

Edging up closer to the roadway again, he picked up his pace, feeling frustrated at the constant wariness that he had to carry around. It almost reminded him of the instinctive circumspection of his days at Leavenworth—always watching, keeping thick magazines inside your shirt to serve as make-shift body armor, checking to see if the man moving toward you had his hand cupped.

Would it ever get to the point where he could just relax?

He longed to just be able to go for a leisurely run and not worry about some unknown adversary out to maybe get him.

He threw out a quick combination of punches. Hampered down by the weights, he felt slow and ineffective just like in the dreams that plagued his nights.

He came to the dirt path that signaled the trail up the mountain and veered off onto the soft surface.

Once again his eyes scanned the area.

Nobody in sight.

The sun was just starting to peep over the craggy landscape. There were also plenty of places to hide, and if it was a sniper, he was dead meat anyway.

A sniper.

Memories of his military service came back to him.

Being on patrol, watching for IEDs, indigenous personnel with cell phones, rooftops, and buildings that could hold the enemy.

Life on the edge, he thought. But at least then he knew what to expect. It was what he'd signed up for.

"You fuckers are going to *earn* your CIBs," his platoon sergeant had told him with they'd first been deployed.

And the old sarge was right. They had.

But that was overseas in a combat zone.

Now he was back home and that kind of stuff wasn't supposed to happen here.

Seeing no one on his trek up the mountain, Wolf concentrated on increasing his pace and soon rounded the marker and headed back down.

No suspicious cars appeared, but he did have another surprise when he came down off the mountain and got to the highway.

Lucien Pike sat on a bicycle at the juncture dressed in his usual sleeveless black sweat shirt and yellow tights. He wore a backpack that Wolf knew was stuffed with an MP-5 submachine gun—a welcome addition to any possible gunfight.

"Anybody ever tell you that you look like an over-sized bumblebee in that outfit?" Wolf asked as he came up on the big fed and trotted on past him.

Pike muttered for him to slow down as he tried to turn the bike around. That made Wolf speed up.

It took him a bit, but Pike finally came abreast and said,

"Why do you have to get up so damn early to do these runs?" Pike said, panting a bit.

Wolf didn't bother to answer.

"Man," Pike continued, pedaling at a faster rate and adjusting the gears on his bicycle. "I wasn't sure you'd even be out here this morning."

"Where the hell else would I be?"

"I meant that I was afraid that I mighta missed you."

"I should be so lucky," Wolf said. "You got some news?"

The big fed shrugged. "No news is good news. All's quiet on the western front."

"Interesting book. I had to read it in one of my lit classes. So what's up?"

"Just the usual. I just dropped by to see how your training was going and if the fight's still on."

"As of this morning, it is."

"Great," Pike said. "You get me them tickets yet?"

Wolf had completely forgotten about that. He made a mental note to ask Barbie to look into it.

"Does a bear shit in the woods?" he said.

Pike was huffing and puffing a bit now keeping up with his pedaling. A couple more cars whizzed by in the other lanes. Both Wolf and Pike remained silent and ready.

"Great. Thanks," Pike said. "And just so you know, we're gonna be transporting Mr. Bray to the US Attorney's office today sometime. They'll be prepping him for his grand jury testimony."

"When's that gonna be?"

"Soon." Pike grinned. "Real soon."

"And what about that blonde chick?" Wolf asked. He realized he'd slowed a bit and picked up his speed. "What's her name? Bridgette?"

"Still working on her, but I think she'll be coming around soon. As I told you, the wheels of justice move slowly."

"Or not at all." Wolf sped away from him.

Swearing, Pike's legs pumped a little faster to keep up. "Damn, you're going fast."

"Got to drop ten pounds by the weigh-in."

"Ten pounds." Pike emitted something between a grunt and a snort. "Maybe I'd better hold off on making that bet then."

"Maybe you'd better," Wolf said. "I'll just tell Barbie to forget about getting any tickets for you, too."

"Aw, please, don't go doing that. I still want to come and see you open up a can of whoop-ass and maybe make some money." His wide grin flashed again. "Only now I'm thinking of maybe betting on the other guy."

It was Wolf's turn to snort. "That might not be such a bad idea."

Three days till the weigh-in, he thought. Ten pounds.

* * *

BAGGAGE CLAIM AREA
PHOENIX INTERNATIONAL AIRPORT
PHOENIX, ARIZONA

Boulle had arranged for Lopez to take separate flights from Orlando to Phoenix so the three of them would avoid any possibility of attracting attention or being seen together on some airport video footage. It was more apropos if Lopez arrived in Arizona first. Hopefully, he had gotten there and was now gone. He had to make his connections with the branch of the cartel gangsters who would be supplying the weapons and other equipment. Boulle and his two birds of prey could rendezvous with the Mexican later.

The first leg of their journey from St. Francis had gone smoothly, and the fake passports had obscured all of their identities upon landing and going through customs in Orlando, Florida. When the customs official asked the purpose of their visit, Hawkins had burst forth with an exuberant, "We're going to Disney World." That got a laugh all around. Once inside the airport with their luggage, they'd all gone their separate ways. Boulle, and particularly Von Tillberg, had been paranoid about the possibility of the FBI or some other government organization being on his trail.

"Make sure you all wear disguises," the rich man had said. "To throw off any facial recognition software they might be using."

Boulle assured him they would, but he knew a poorly designed disguise would attract more suspicion, not less. Once they'd deplaned from Von Tillberg's private jet, he'd given them all large straw hats to wear with large brims and told them to keep their heads at a downward angle. Hopefully, that would suffice. He'd heard they'd made great advances on that facial recognition software. Who knew if one, or possibly all of their faces might be on some government data bank? Boulle assumed it was dubious that the Falcon and the Hawk would be known in the United States. Neither would he. In Europe, it might be a distinct possibility, but not here. Now Lopez was more of a possibility, but Boulle was counting on the aversion to any type of racial profiling currently in effect in America. They wouldn't check a middle-aged traveler who looked like a Hispanic. They were more concerned with maintaining their "woke" political correctness than singling out any real potential threats.

He smirked.

They were due for another terrorist attack here, and rightly so.

His subterfuge seemed to work like a charm. They walked toward their respective gates independent of one another, except for Hawkins and Peregrine. Lopez had a passport identifying him as Enrique Alvarez of Tucson, Arizona. Both Hawkins and Peregrine were listed as Edwin Hanks and Carl Lewis, "husband and wife," out of London, England. That had gotten a good laugh from the two of them on the Learjet when the IDs were distributed and Boulle gave out the information. It was a foregone conclusion that the pair of mercenaries masquerading as a gay couple was another perfect bit of cover. Political correctness again. Certain groups were untouchable. Boulle had come up with that himself, and Hawkins had put it best, in his own inimitable way: "The security will be treating us with such deference, we'd have to pull down our britches and take a shit on the middle of the terminal floor to attract any attention."

Crudely put, Boulle thought. *But essentially accurate.*

And he himself was Jean Paul Dumas, out of Montreal, Canada, in the US on a business trip. Americans loved Canadians, didn't they?

In all, there were no ties at all that could be traced back to St. Francis Island.

The gate was just up ahead and Boulle saw Hawkins and Peregrine heading for a pair of unoccupied seats. He veered off and went into a nearby washroom. Once inside, he went to one of the closeted stalls, shut the door, and checked his watch. It was 0850. That meant in Phoenix it was perhaps three hours earlier. Certainly an appropriate time for a dedicated civil servant of the American criminal justice system to be rolling out of bed. Boulle grinned sardonically. It was time to tweak the inside man, the patsy. Pulling the special burner phone from his pocket, he pulled up the appropriate screen and began texting.

Arrived on time. Will contact you later for a meeting. Stay available.

He waited for a response.

When none came, he typed in and sent another text:

Are you there? RESPOND NOW.

After sending it, he replaced the burner phone in his pocket, unzipped his pants, and leisurely urinated, not bothering to lift the toilet seat.

By the time his stream was subsiding, he felt the tickling vibration of the returning text.

Shaking his penis a few times and replacing it in his pants, Boulle zipped up and then checked the acknowledging text.

Sorry. I am here. Will wait for your call tonight.

Boulle smiled.

Obedient, prompt, and concise, just like Boulle had been told. Bridgette and her friend had done an excellent job grooming him.

This part of it was going to be easy.

* * *

PARKING GARAGE
FEDERAL BUILDING
PHOENIX, ARIZONA

Chester A. Loudermilk had just pulled into the space in the parking garage and now sat behind the wheel of his gray Nissan Sentra and stared at the text that remained on the screen of his burner phone. It had come in when he was driving which was why he hadn't been able to respond initially. And then the son of a bitch had to send that admonishment:

RESPOND NOW.

I was driving, for Christ's sake, he thought. *Did he want me to have a damn accident? Or he even care?*

He found himself starting to hyperventilate.

The stress was getting to him, that was for sure.

Boulle had told him he'd be coming to Phoenix and to be ready for a meeting.

He could easily guess what that would be about.

Loudermilk had already assumed that they were going to want more information about Bray's whereabouts. Plus, they'd want to know what the status was with that broad, too. For all he knew, she was playing all them for suckers, working one side against the other. Turner was certain she'd flip, but Loudermilk wasn't so sure. And if she did, he'd be in big trouble. She'd been the one who'd originally set him up and began the blackmail. Not that she'd wanted money. No, she demanded something much more severe—information. He thought about how cleverly she'd entrapped him and then subtly twisted the blade. She was a monster.

All of them were.

His mouth felt exceptionally dry, and at the same

time, he felt the sweat forming on his hands. He took a few deep breaths trying to compose himself.

Assess the situation, he thought.

He'd already given them the info about Bray and the plan to have him testify before the federal grand jury in little more than a week. What more did they want? And now Boulle was in town, no doubt with a hit squad. Bray was being guarded around the clock at some hotel. Boulle would expect him to find out where and when the son of a bitch was being transported. That was a given, since they'd tried to kill him before, that they couldn't afford to let him testify. If they were going to try some end run to take Bray out, it would no doubt be messy, and an investigation would immediately be launched. It wouldn't take them long to pinpoint the source of the leak.

The broad was a wild card. At this point she was still incarcerated, which put her out of reach by Boulle and his buddies, unless they could engineer another jailhouse assassination like they had with that one Mexican gangbanger.

What was his name?

Loudermilk prided himself on his memory. It's what made him a great attorney, or what would make him one, if he ever got elevated to the courtroom here to show what he could do.

He thought for a minute and the name came to him: Europa. Albert Europa.

Of course the little rat bastard had been in general population and that made it pretty easy. Bridgette was supposedly in solitary confinement and protective custody. It wouldn't do to lose another defendant in this same, convoluted case. But if Boulle and company could somehow get to her, that would keep him off the hook.

But regardless, it was apparent that the noose around his neck was getting tighter all the time. What he needed was to start formulating an exit strategy. Whatever information Boulle wanted, getting out would have to be part of it.

Another car pulled into the spot next to him and Loudermilk looked to the left.

Christ, it was Turner.

His fat boss's head turned to look at him, that judgmental, censuring smile plastered all over his round face.

The passenger window of Turner's Lexus lowered with electronic proficiency.

Loudermilk had already shut off his car, but the keys were still in the ignition. He switched the ignition to the on position and lowered his window as well.

"You all right, Chester?"

Loudermilk tried to get his panting under control. He nodded as he swallowed.

"Yeah," he said. "I was just feeling a little lightheaded, is all."

Turner's brow wrinkled.

"Lightheaded? What? Did you go out drinking or something last night?"

Loudermilk shook his head.

"No, no, nothing like that." The words came out quickly. He swallowed again and added in a calmer tone, "I've been thinking of making a doctor's appointment."

Turner's grin transformed into something that resembled a smirk.

"Well, don't schedule for company time," he said. "We've got a shit-ton of work to do this morning."

Without waiting for a reply, the window on the Lexus zoomed upward and into place.

Turner didn't look at him as he got out of the car,

retrieved his suit jacket from the hanger in the rear compartment, slipped it on, adjusted his shirt sleeves, and slammed the car door.

Asshole, Loudermilk thought. *Don't schedule it for company time.*

Yeah, it was almost going to be a pleasure messing up that fat prick's steadily building case.

Even if I won't be around to see it, he thought.

He started thinking about that exit strategy.

* * *

MIXED MARTIAL ARTS FIGHTING ACADEMY
PHOENIX, ARIZONA

"So you still going through with the fight, honey?" Yolanda asked him over the phone.

He'd finally managed to connect with her after playing phone tag last night and this morning. "I been on nights and then I have court this morning," she'd told him.

"I'm gonna do my best," he said. "Just hoping this hand heals up a little beforehand."

"How bad is it?"

He could hear the concern in her voice and didn't want to worry her.

"Ah, it's getting better all the time," he lied.

"Un-huh."

From the tone of her voice, his mendacity must have been easily detectable.

Deciding to change the subject, he asked, "You get the night off of the fight?"

"I did. And Miss Dolly and Brenda are coming, too."

Marvelous, he thought. *If I end up getting my ass handed to me, I'll have all my friends there to see it firsthand.*

"And I've got it arranged that I'll have a couple of days afterward off, too," she said. "So I can spoil my boo."

He just hoped there'd be enough of him left to spoil.

"That sounds good," he said as he slowed down, shifted into second, and made the right turn into the lot of the gym. "Well, I'm pulling into Reno's now, babe. Gotta go."

"Okay," she said. "I got to get moving myself." After a moment's hesitation, she added, "Steve, if your hand's not a hundred percent, don't fight, okay?"

Doubts began to flash in his mind's eye.

"I won't," he said. Another lie. "But I'm sure it'll be okay. It's practically healed now."

She said nothing for several seconds, then asked, "You sure?"

It was his turn to hesitate. "Hundred percent."

He steered over to an empty spot near the door. The lot was exceptionally empty this morning.

"Okay then, lover," she said. "See you in a couple of days."

A couple of days, two till the weigh-in, three till the fight, he thought as he terminated the call. And ten pounds.

After Wolf parked he jumped out of his Jeep and made a show of grabbing his stuff as his eyes scanned the lot. No one was about, and just a smattering of parked cars, all unoccupied. It seemed innocuous enough, but Pike's appearance this morning had made him more wary and on edge than usual.

Just what I needed, he thought. *Additional stress.*

He flexed the fingers of his right hand, and then made a fist. The stinging pain was instantly present, like a bunch of needles being jammed into his flesh. He'd identified the different pains and categorized them. This one was "the needles." There was also "the blowtorch," which was a more searing sensation over a broader, but non-specific area. It was a slow, radiating pain. And then there was the lightning bolt—that quick, sharp, excruciating sudden snap that could result in an involuntary jerking motion.

How much longer was this really going to take to heal?

With a sigh, he shouldered the gym bag and headed for the front door.

The sign in the plate glass window advertising him and his title was visible with full prominence

Steve Wolf, MMA Heavyweight Champ Trains Here.

Flattering, considering his title was being withheld from him at the present time.

Something else was present, too: heavy condensation all over the inside of the glass.

The poster sign looked like it was on the verge of getting waterlogged.

What the hell?

He noticed the temperature change inside the gym right away. Outside it had been rather mild. In the mid-to-high seventies, but inside it felt hot and stuffy. For some reason the air-conditioning wasn't working. It almost felt like he was walking into an oven. A real smelly oven. An odor of perspiration, laced with testosterone, hung in the air.

Wolf was frowning as he headed toward the locker room.

"Hey, Steve," a female voice called out.

It was Barbie, who was standing in the doorway of the office fanning herself with a paper folder.

He veered off toward her.

"What's up?" he asked, and then saw her face was covered with a sheen of perspiration. "And what's with the air-conditioning? It break down, or something?"

Barbie shook her head and scrunched up her nose.

"It was Georgie's idea," she said. "And Reno went along with it. For now, anyway, but hopefully not much longer."

"You got that right," one of the gym rats who was passing by muttered. "Give me a call when it's back on. I ain't working out in this shit."

Wolf noticed the man's baleful gaze seemed to be directed at him.

"Well," Barbie said. "It's a good thing I used extra deodorant this morning."

Wolf chuckled. "You're going to be disappointed if you get near me. I didn't."

"Mmmm, there's nothing like a sweaty man." She giggled and held her nose. "Or in this case, a whole gym full of them. Anyway, they want to see you."

She jerked her thumb toward Reno and Georgie, who were hunched over in two chairs and studying an open laptop on top of the desk. All Wolf could see was the back of the screen.

Reno glanced over toward the door, raised his left hand, and motioned for Wolf to come closer.

As he went over he heard Georgie, who was studying the screen with intensity, say, "Sheeit, this boy can deal."

"Good thing we won't be playing poker then," Wolf said, moving over behind Reno.

He assumed that the videos of Juan Dos Pastos had arrived and that was what Georgie and Reno were watching, and a second later this was confirmed. Two near-naked men circled one another on the small screen, both standing upright with their guards up.

One of them stepped forward and shot out a double jab, causing his opponent's head to snap back. The man instinctively retreated, his nose spouting a gusher of blood. The other man followed and shot out a couple more jabs, and then followed up with a flurry of rapid punches.

The shoe shine, Wolf thought.

Georgie confirmed it a moment later.

"Shoe shine," he muttered. "That boy's got some fast hands."

Reno let out a loud, derisive breath.

"I don't know, Steve," he said. "After seeing this, I'm not so sure taking this fight on short notice was such a good idea. I mean, this guy's got a big head start on us as far as training."

That was true, but Wolf told himself that he never let himself get that far out of condition. He'd been running every day and doing regular workouts. A lot of fighters take a month off after a match. He wondered if Dos Pastos did too.

Guess I'll find out soon enough, he thought.

Reno's expression was laden with concern.

In Wolf's mind-eye he imagined his escalating debts materializing into a huge anaconda which started to wrap itself around his inert body.

He was feeling the squeeze, and if the money for the fight fell through, it would be very tight. Plus, if he failed to show up for this fight and at least turn in a decent performance, who knew when or even if he'd get another one?

Reno's pungent body odor was growing noticeable. Huge sweat stains were plastering his shirt to his body. Georgie's hefty frame looked even worse.

"What the hell happened to the air-conditioning?"

Wolf asked. "You two guys smell worse than the finish line at the Boston Marathon."

Reno lifted his arm, sniffed, and grimaced.

"He's right, you know," he said to Georgie.

"What we got?" Georgie asked. "Two more days and how much weight to lose?"

Ten pounds, Wolf thought.

"Eleven pounds?" Georgie said, contradicting Wolf's mental estimate. "Air-conditioning, my black ass. I told you I trained some fighters in Puerto Rico, didn't I? Them gyms down there make this here feel like an igloo. That's how them Puerto Ricans never have no trouble making weight. They sweat it off."

If the Puerto Rican gyms were hotter than this, Wolf was glad that he didn't have to train in any of them.

"Lemme see the hand," Georgie said, hitting the pause button on the video and standing up. He walked around the desk to Wolf.

Georgie's body odor was even worse than Reno's.

Wolf held out his hand.

Georgie studied it and then said, "Make a fist."

Wolf did and felt the old, familiar pain come waltzing back.

He did his best to keep his expression neutral to give the appearance of being pain-free.

Georgie's dark eyes shot up to meet Wolf's and then narrowed slightly, like a big cat's once his prey is in sight. He reached out and grabbed Wolf's hand and squeezed.

Wolf emitted an involuntary grunt.

Georgie's lips puckered. He sighed as his head rocked back and forth with minute motions.

"What you think?" Reno asked.

"Reno," Wolf said, interrupting, "My hand'll be fine by

fight night. And we can't afford to miss this opportunity. Or this payday."

Reno turned his gaze on Wolf, who thought the other man's eyes were misting over a little.

"I just don't want to put you at risk," Reno said. "I feel like I been pushing you too hard to take this one. You're not one hundred percent, and I don't want you to fight. We can just wait for the court decision to get our title reinstated and for them to pay us our money."

"Who knows when that's going to be," Wolf said. "And we both know that court doesn't always go the way it should. This jailbird served four years, remember?"

Reno had called him "Jailbird" back in the day when they were rivals. That was ancient history, but the reference obviously was not lost on Reno. He lowered his gaze to the floor.

"But you is exonerated now," Georgie said. "Lemme see the hand again."

Wolf extended his arm once more and Georgie's dark fingers kneaded the flesh. The pain increased with each movement, but Wolf kept his face frozen.

Georgie's head rocked back and forth, and he said, "Yep."

"Yep what?" Wolf asked.

The two men locked eyes.

"Got me an idea," Georgie said, a slight grin tracing over his lips.

"What's that?" Wolf asked.

"Yeah," Reno said. "I'd like to hear this too."

Georgie released his grip on Wolf's hand and straightened up.

"Acupuncture," he said.

"Acupuncture?" Reno repeated.

"There an echo in here, or something?" Georgie said,

a triumphant grin stretching over his mouth as his gaze focused on Wolf. "I think that might do the trick. You game?"

Wolf had heard of the treatments but had never tried them. He was skeptical of a lot of unorthodox quasi-medical procedures, acupuncture included. The thought of someone jamming needles into him didn't do much to inspire confidence.

"Yeah," Reno said. "That might work. You game, Steve?"

Reno's agreement stunned Wolf almost as much as Georgie's suggestion. The blowtorch was starting to overtake the needlework in his hand once again. Still, at this point, what choice did he have?

He shrugged. "Why not?"

"Good man," Georgie said, clapping Wolf on the shoulder. "Just go through your regular strength-building workout now while I study the rest of these tapes. Then before lunch, you and me gonna take a little ride to Chinatown."

Wolf already felt the dread building, but he nodded in assent.

"Just one thing," said, waiting until he had both their undivided attention. "As of this morning, it's only ten pounds I got to lose, so can you please turn the air-conditioning back on?"

CHAPTER 6

THE MEDICAL OFFICER OF DR. YI, SON SHIN
DOBBS AVENUE
NEW CHINATOWN
MESA, ARIZONA

After Wolf consulted McNamara on the efficacy of acupuncture, he insisted he'd be right over. After arriving in the Escalade, Mac immediately engaged in an extended and hushed conversation with Georgie that Wolf couldn't quite discern. He was busy picking up the tractor tire, setting it upright, and then letting it slam down onto the floor. By the time he'd finished that, his sit-ups, his squats, and his one-armed push-ups—left arm only, it was almost time for lunch. McNamara stood by watching with a smile.

"Grab yourself a quick shower, champ," Georgie said. "Me and Mac gonna take you to Chinatown. You gonna have to eat in the car."

Now, about an hour later, Wolf, Georgie, and Mac all sat in the air-conditioned comfort of a sterile-looking medical office. Wolf silently hoped that Reno would have the air-conditioning turned back on when they got back. The morning session had been close to unbearable, but he'd dropped four pounds in water weight. He silently sipped from a plastic bottle and listened as McNamara extolled the virtues of acupuncture.

"This is the best idea you've had in a long while, Georgie," McNamara said. "I remember back in the Nam I twisted my ankle something fierce bailing out of a Huey. I could barely walk when all of a sudden, Charlie started chasing us. My team practically had to carry me. After playing tag for the better part of a day and a half, we hunkered down and waited for them and opened up for a good old-fashioned ambush and then gave them a little taste of some Claymores as they happened to come strolling by." He paused. "What was left of their bodies was scattered all over the trees and leaves. Flies were so thick walking back you woulda thought you were walking through a metallic haze."

"No shit?" Georgie said.

Wolf recalled some of the firefights he'd been in and thinking how he'd felt when he'd kicked in his first door in Iraq.

"Pretty soon we came to this little village," McNamara continued, "my leg hurting me so bad I didn't know if I was gonna make it back to the LZ. The Kit Carson—the Vietnamese scout we had told us that the village was friendly. They were a special tribe that hated the VC and liked Americans." He paused and his face got a sad look. "I reckon they're all gone now, after the US pulled out."

Nobody said anything.

"Sounds sort of like our recent debacle in Afghanistan," Wolf said.

McNamara gave a curt nod.

"Damn straight. This country doesn't learn nothing from its past mistakes." He blew out a long breath. "Anyway, to get back to what I was saying, one of them knew about acupuncture. Took one look at my swollen ankle and stuck a bunch of needles into it. Up my leg, too. The next thing I knew, the pain was all but gone and the swelling went way down. Couldn't believe it."

"Damn," Georgie said.

"Did it hurt?" Wolf asked.

"Only when I laughed," Mac said with a big smile. He snorted and shook his head. "Didn't even feel them needles going in. Of course I'm a helluva lot tougher than your average Joe. Plus, I was Special Forces."

"And what was you, Steve?" Georgie asked, looking at him.

"Oh, I was *just* a ranger," Wolf said, putting extra emphasis on the word 'just.'

McNamara's laugh was loud.

"He may only have been just a ranger," he said, "but he's still the best of the best."

Wolf smiled.

The door opened, and an elderly Asian man walked in. His hair was black but peppered with gray, and he wore a pair of delicate-looking wire-rimmed glasses. A much younger Asian woman dressed in a white nurse's uniform followed him in. The old man ducked his head in a quick bowing motion.

"This is Dr. Yi," the woman said. "I'm Nurse Han. I'll translate. What type of problem are you having?"

She was gorgeous, and her English was perfect and natural sounding.

Obviously American-born, thought Wolf.

The older guy, he figured wasn't. Or was this just part

of an elaborate act? He'd heard a lot of Asian medical techniques were steeped in century's old mysticism and sometimes even elaborate theatrics. What a person believed was an integral part of the treatment and possible healing process. Mac had once described seeing a "surgery" performed in the Philippines with no anesthesia and no scalpels. The "surgeon" merely manipulated the patient's skin and removed the "tumor."

"It was all a bunch of bullshit," McNamara had said. "The guy used a false thumb full of pig's blood and a bunch of wadded-up cotton. But people believed it."

Wolf wondered if he should try and get busy believing.

"It's his hand, Doc," Georgie said. "His right hand."

He nudged Wolf and gestured at him to hold up his hand.

Wolf did so as the pretty nurse spoke in a foreign language that wasn't unfamiliar to Wolf.

"What?" Georgie said, looking worried. "He only speak Chinese?"

"It's Korean," Mac said, and then added, *"Tong shonune han gook saremneka?"*

Dr. Yi smiled and nodded.

"You speak Korean?" the nurse asked, her eyes wide with amazement.

McNamara grinned. "Spent a couple of tours over the years on the DMZ. Plus, one of my exes was Korean."

The nurse said something to the doctor, and he responded. She smiled.

"Dr. Yi says thank you for your service."

"Chum marioh," McNamara replied. "Now what does he think about my buddy here? He's a professional fighter, and we need to get that hand healed up real quick."

The nurse translated as Dr. Yi ran his fingers over Wolf's hand and then his forearm. After about a minute, he said something to the girl, and she turned and left the room. He motioned for Wolf to sit on a nearby table.

"What they saying' now, Mac?" Georgie asked.

"Damned if I know. The only other things I know how to say are thanks and you're welcome and I came to get laid."

Wolf chuckled at that one. The firmness of the old man's grip had been painful, and it was all Wolf could do to keep from wincing.

"Concentrate on something positive," he told himself.

He'd felt good about dropping the four pounds but was sure he'd gained most of the weight back by drinking the water. Hopefully, he could do it again in the afternoon session, and he'd be at least a pound or so lighter in the morning.

Isn't it pretty to think so, he thought, recalling a line from one of Hemingway's old novels.

The nurse returned with a long leather case. She pulled over a metal stand and set the case on top. When she opened it, Wolf could see an array of needles of different lengths affixed in rows of plastic holders. He suddenly felt a trickle of sweat curling down from his right armpit.

"These things from China?" Georgie asked.

"Korea," the nurse replied. She continued to open the folds of the leather case.

"Nobody else has used them," Georgie asked. "Have they?"

The nurse shook her head.

Wolf found himself hoping she was right.

"Don't worry, Steve," McNamara said. "It won't hurt. Not even as bad as getting a tattoo."

Wolf had been through that before. Upon graduating jump school, he and several of his buddies had hit the downtown area of Fayetteville and gotten their airborne jump wings inscribed on their forearms.

Dr. Yi had washed his hands in a nearby sink and slipped on a pair of latex gloves and a cloth mask. He muttered something, and the nurse told Wolf to place his hand on the metal stand. She put on a mask, too.

After fitting two long needles into small, metallic handles, the doctor leaned over Wolf's arm and studied it for what seemed like a long time. Just when he was on the verge of asking what was going on, the old man flattened Wolf's hand down on the metal platform and stuck a needle into the space between his index and middle fingers.

Wolf was expecting pain but felt nothing. He stared at the needle sticking up perpendicular to the back of his hand. There was no pain and no blood.

The doctor took another needle.

"Please keep your hand as still as possible," the nurse said.

Wolf gave a minute nod of acknowledgment.

Another needle, this one in the fleshy part between the base of his thumb by the juncture to his hand.

Again, there was no blood and no pain.

This process continued for about four minutes, with the upright needles lining the back of Wolf's right hand, wrist, and forearm.

Dr. Yi straightened up and said something else.

"Please," the nurse said. "Sit absolutely still."

Wolf nodded again. He hadn't even been cognizant that he was moving.

Despite all the metal sticking into him, he felt no discomfort.

He looked at Georgie, whose eyes were closed. His fingers were pressed together, forming a steeple and his lips were moving in what must have been a silent prayer.

McNamara just sat there staring, but Wolf was sure his sentiments were similar to Georgie's.

He could feel their nervous hopefulness and it mingled with that of his own.

"This has to work," Wolf told himself.

Then he realized how pathetic that sounded.

I'm sitting in the small office of a foreign-born, non-traditional physician who spoke no English and who's just jammed half a dozen needles into my arm, he thought. And I've got the bill collector lurking on the other side of the door.

But at least he wasn't standing in the gym with no air-conditioning picking up a tractor tire and pushing it over with no end in sight.

* * *

CAR RENTAL FACILITY
PHOENIX INTERNATIONAL AIRPORT
PHOENIX, ARIZONA

Boulle stood at the counter with the false ID and credit card and waited as the girl behind the desk completed filling out the forms on her computer. The burner phone buzzed with an incoming text. This one was from Lopez, who had arrived about an hour earlier.

At my hotel. Text when you ready for meet.

Boulle took the time to craft an appropriate reply, putting in a bit of courtesy to offset the bit of belligerence Hawkins had displayed back at the island airport.

I will do that. Thanks for letting me know you have arrived safely.

The Falcon and the Hawk were certainly not diplomats. Lopez had hardly said two words to the pair during the flight on the Learjet. Once they'd separated at the airport, they'd all taken extreme measures not to be seen together. The flight to Phoenix was hardly the place to discuss business either. Now, with the pair of them standing in line behind him, Boulle felt a burning desire to admonish them to make sure they treated Lopez with more courtesy. That disrespectful comment the big Irishman had made ridiculing Lopez as stupid certainly had raised the man's ire. The big idiot should have used more discretion, but when were the Irish known for their tact? They were all three strangers in a strange land, so to speak, and they needed the Mexican gang/cartel's connections and cooperation here to get adequate supplies and assistance. He hoped the damage done was not irreparable. Boulle glanced over at the adjacent car rental booth to monitor the progress of the two of them. They appeared to be almost finished as well. Hawkins was leaning over the counter, engaged in some measure of flirtatious small talk with the pretty, young receptionist at that company.

And after I instructed them to remain low key, he thought.

He blew out a disgusted breath.

"Mr. Dumas," the girl at his booth asked. She was nice-looking as well, but Boulle had done his best to remain as bland and forgettable as possible. "Would you like to add insurance to your rental?"

"But of course," he said, thinking that the bill would end up not being paid anyway. Jean Paul Dumas was merely a figment of someone's imagination, and the car would end up being reported missing. But he would be long gone by then. All of them would be.

He signed the forms and handed her the credit card.

After she gave him the keys she smiled and said, "I hope you enjoy your trip to the United States. Is it business or pleasure?"

Boulle raised an eyebrow and returned her smile.

"Perhaps a bit of both," he said. "I hope."

He took the two large Louis Vuitton suitcases and began his slow walk toward the garage.

"I say," Peregrine said, "do you need some help, old top? My *wife* and I seem to be going your way."

The Falcon grinned, and he held his open hand toward the burly Hawkins, who strode beside him.

"Hey," Hawkins said with a grin. "I thought I was the husband?"

"Does it really matter?" Peregrine shot back, his grin wide as well. He reached for the extended handle of Boulle's suitcase and held it toward Hawkins.

The big Irishman, who already had both of their ditty bags slung over his shoulder, grabbed the suitcase and began walking with an exaggerated, skipping step.

"*Merde*," Boulle said. "Do you think you could do any more to attract unwanted attention?"

"Why certainly," Hawkins said, and continued his exaggerated, dance-like movements. "I always honor my audience's request."

Boulle emitted an exasperated breath and glanced around, worried that the big oaf's performance would be caught on a surveillance camera. He saw several, but at least the fool had the sense to keep his wide-brimmed hat on and his head mostly averted from the intrusive lens.

"The last thing we want to do is to be noticed," Boulle said, leaning toward Peregrine. He seemed to be the brains of the two of them, which wasn't saying much. "Or caught on some camera."

"Righto," the other man said, and then to his partner, "Do tone it done a tad, old chum. We are supposed to be circumspect."

Hawkins sighed heavily and ceased his exuberance. The three of them walked together toward the parking garage area and Boulle wondered how much damage might have been done.

Bring on the clowns, he thought.

And he still had another clown that he had to contact.

* * *

OFFICE OF THE US ATTORNEY
THE FEDERAL BUILDING
PHOENIX, ARIZONA

The four of them arrived like a herd of buffalo clamoring through the door and into the outer office. Loudermilk looked up in surprise as Special Agent Pike ushered in a man swathed in a hooded sweatshirt, baseball cap, and sunglasses who was flanked by two other good-sized men clad in blue windbreakers that said US Marshal Service across the back. Loudermilk assumed the man in the middle to be the protected witness, Robert Bray, who was due at the office sometime this morning. Pike had made it clear in his earlier meeting that they would be bringing Bray in, but the time would not be specified.

"We got to check out the route and make sure it's clear," Pike had said. "The poor bastard almost bought the farm the last time he was out in public."

Loudermilk recalled reading that in Pike's after-incident report. Von Tillberg's minions had captured Bray after the rich man had arranged for bond to be posted allowing Bray's release from incarceration. The poor SOB had been rescued after being bound and tortured by Bridgette Swenstrom and her cohorts. It had been enough to convince Bray to turn government witness with the promise of immunity and an eventual place in Wit-Sec. But first, he had to testify in front of the special federal grand jury that Turner was in the process of getting convened. The guy was no longer incarcerated, and they had him stashed in some luxury hotel of an undisclosed location.

Loudermilk shuddered. The exact location was what that bastard, Boulle, had been pressuring him about finding out. And he wasn't accepting any excuses or delays.

It was, Loudermilk knew, time to pay the piper.

The highly regarded and heavily protected witness didn't look like much, and the sunglasses, a baseball cap and a hooded sweatshirt, despite the rather agreeable temperatures this time of year, most likely made him more noticeable than if he were merely escorted in wearing regular garb. But that big idiot, Pike, seemed to thrive on theatrics. Turner did too.

Both of them self-aggrandizing morons more interested in basking in the limited limelight of government service, he thought, while leaving the grunt work to real men like me.

Loudermilk studied Bray. His face was drawn and haggard and he looked middle-aged and flabby. The two big guys on either side of him had expressionless faces, but their shoulder-holstered weapons were discernible under their garments. Each had a US Marshal badge affixed to the inner aspect of their belts. The procession stopped and Pike, who was similarly dressed as the marshals but without a blue windbreaker, paused and did a quick look up and down the hall before closing the door. He turned back toward the other three and nodded.

Bray was breathing hard, although whether it was from exertion or fear, Loudermilk didn't know.

"Hey Loudie," Pike said. "Do yourself a favor and tell your boss we're here."

A mockery of his name, with no greeting or acknowledgment...no attempt of even a modicum of courtesy. Loudermilk knew he was nothing more than another piece of the office furniture or a section of carpeting to be trodden upon by this big lout.

Screw you, asshole, his inner, sub-vocal voice screamed as he sat and stared at the top of his desk.

"Hey, pal," Pike said. "You hard of hearing or something?"

"The name's Loudermilk," he said and shot what he hoped passed for a baleful stare up at the big federal agent.

Pike affected a quivering shudder. "Well, *excuuoozse* me. Now just tell Turner we're here."

No apology, no attempt at civility...

Bray removed his sunglasses and hat and unzipped his sweatshirt and heaved a sigh. He shrugged it off and then fumbled with some Velcro straps on the front of a thick, blue panel of a bulletproof vest.

"Damn, these things are hot," he said. His mouth formed a nervous smile. "Get me some water, will ya?"

Pike smiled back.

"Yeah, but it beats the alternative." His head turned toward Loudermilk and he snapped his fingers. "Ah, go fetch my man a nice cool bottle of water. After you notify your boss of our arrival, that is."

Again, the tone was accusatory, belligerent. The big prick.

"Sorry." Loudermilk muttered as he pushed the call button on the inner-office intercom and said, "Excuse me, sir."

"Yeah, what is it?" Turner's voice was equally gruff, but that was business as usual for the smug son of a bitch.

Loudermilk gritted his teeth. Was there anyone around this place who regarded him with a little bit of respect? Just a little?

He swallowed and said, "Special Agent Pike's here, sir."

"With your soon-to-be star witness," Pike added in a loud voice.

Bray seemed to grimace at the big fed's brashness.

Turner's chuckle was audible over the intercom.

"Good, have them come in," he said. "And clear your slate. I'll want you to type up this interview and statement up afterward so I can review it."

Clear my slate. What a pompous ass.

"Yes, sir," Loudermilk said. Turner would no doubt record the interview on his tablet so that it could be accurately transcribed.

Loudermilk reflected on the possibilities of that. If he could make a duplicate of the recording, it might be something that he could use down the road. Something that he could dangle in front of Boulle in exchange for his freedom from this blackmail, and maybe even more…something like a nice, off-shore account in the Cayman Islands to augment his coming retirement.

Loudermilk turned and started toward the door to the inner office when he heard Pike making a tsking sound.

"I know the way in, *Loudie*," he said. "Just go get that water and bring it to us,"

The big son of a bitch stepped in front of him and gripped the doorknob, motioning Bray to follow as he pushed open the door.

"And make sure it's cold," Pike added, and then glanced at the two marshals. "You guys want something to drink too?"

The two big dullards shook their heads almost in unison.

As Loudermilk shuffled past them, one of them had what appeared to be a smirk plastered on his face.

Yeah, it was going to be a pleasure setting all of them up for the fall in the yet-to-be-seen finale, all right.

A real pleasure.

CHAPTER 7

MEN'S LOCKER ROOM
MIXED MARTIAL ARTS FIGHTING ACADEMY
PHOENIX, ARIZONA

Wolf stuffed his gym bag into the locker and closed and locked the door. He'd been amazed that his hand had felt so much better after the treatment yesterday afternoon that he'd resumed his training with a renewed exuberance. He knew now, the next morning, that it had been a mistake. He'd pounded both the bags and his sparring partners with a newfound exuberance, feeling almost as good as his old self. Now, some fourteen hours later, he was really regretting it. The old, familiar pain had returned with a bit of a vengeance. While the residual swelling had substantially diminished, the dull ache as he tried to make a fist this morning was as bad as it had been since the ill-timed punch. And to top it off, he seemed to have gained back the pound or so he'd lost.

One more day till the weigh-in, he thought, *and I'm still hovering at that stubborn ten pounds mark.*

He was stuck in a rut.

In little more than seventy-two hours or so, he'd be stepping into the Octagon to face Juan Dos Pastos. Georgie had promised to come up with a strategy, a fight plan, but Wolf had yet to hear it and they were almost at the eleventh hour. He'd answered the queries about his hand from both Georgie and Reno with a smile and a grunt. He didn't want to burst Georgie's bubble about acupuncture.

Chinese mysticism, he thought. *Or in this case, Korean.*

Either way, it had been little more than a diversion from his ongoing problems.

He went over to the scale, slipped off his shoes, and stepped on the metallic platform. The balance beam made a sudden click as the pointer indicator slammed against the top of the square metal measuring window and Wolf automatically winced. It was knowing you were touching something electrified and were going to get a shock. He worked the poise weights on the upper and lower beams and got the same result as he had earlier this morning on his own bathroom scale.

Two hundred sixteen.

"What's it say?" Georgie asked as he came up from behind.

"You really want to know?" Wolf said.

Georgie's eyes widened as he looked at the poise-weights on the twin balance beams, and then he looked at Wolf.

"What happened? I thought you was *losing* weight?"

"So did I."

Wolf readjusted the poise-weights back to zero and stepped off the scale. Georgie was counting off something on his fingers.

"Okay," he said. "We better face the facts. We got to

drop too much weight in too short a time. I'm telling Barbie to cut out all the carbs for tonight. Just broiled chicken before the drive tonight, and then nothing tomorrow all day long. After the weigh-in you can feast on protein shakes, steaks, and whatever you want. But we gotta concentrate on you droppin' that weight."

Wolf smirked. "Not even a protein shake tonight?"

"No way." Georgie shook his head. "You be drinking that stuff you be gainin', not losin'. And no fruit juices, neither."

"You're not giving me much to look forward to."

"What you got to look forward to is not having to lose all that much weight, maybe ten pounds at most before the weigh-in. You ain't eatin' all day, and you gonna be spending the rest of the time today in the sauna. We gonna give you something to make you shit real good, too."

"Marvelous," Wolf said. "That always gives me something to look forward to."

Wolf didn't have the heart to tell him that the acupuncture treatment didn't seem to have lasted.

"The thing we got to worry about now is you being too weak from all that dehydration. Now you got them twenty-four hours after the weigh-in to rehydrate, *if* we make weight on that first try."

There was that plural pronoun, "we," again. Wolf had to smile at how both Georgie and Reno vicariously experienced every setback and triumph in this training and fighting process.

Georgie shook his head slowly. "It's all because of you bulkin' up before when you fought that Russian dude. Your natural body weight and mass jumped up with all them muscles you built up."

"Yeah," Wolf said with a grin. "But it was worth it,

wasn't it? I won the title and that big purse. And maybe someday they'll give them to us."

"What you two in here jawing about?"

It was Reno.

Wolf turned and saw him hobbling toward them. His gait had never quite recovered from getting that 7.56 round that ripped through his leg down in Mexico. The smile on his face dissipated as he saw Georgie's expression.

"What's up?" Reno asked.

Georgie told him.

"Aw, shit." Reno's mouth worked. "Two sixteen? I thought you were down to two-thirteen last night?"

It was beginning to sound like a broken record.

"I thought I was."

Reno's frown deepened. "So how's the hand? It looked like you were working it pretty good last night after that acupuncture treatment."

Wolf thought about not telling him the truth but decided against it.

"Feeling a little bit stiff today," he said. "But I think I can work out the kinks."

Reno winced like he'd been slapped.

After exhaling, he looked directly into Wolf's eyes.

"Maybe we ought to think about canceling. I don't want you fighting if you're not one hundred percent. Whaddya think?"

Wolf thought about the pending bills and the future repercussions of a canceled fight. It would most likely be the end of his MMA career, and while that wasn't necessarily a devastating possibility, it also meant a substantial loss of future income. Despite winning his appeal and being awarded reinstatement of rank and benefits, the back pay he'd received had been eaten up by the medical expenses for his uncle and his lawyer fees. The Great Oz had done a great job, but at an equally great price. With everything else, his title and the previous match money being in limbo, he was back to being just this side of being broke.

The sad fact was that, ready or not, he couldn't afford financially not to go through with this fight.

"I think," Wolf said, "that we'd better get busy training and going over Georgie's new game plan. Forty-eight hours is still a long time."

He grinned.

Reno did too.

"Praise the Lord," Georgie shouted. "We gonna do this."

Let's hope He's listening, Wolf thought.

* * *

APEX TRANSPORTATION FACILITY
UNINCORPORATED MARICOPA COUNTY
ARIZONA

The huge overhead door rose slowly exposing the darkened interior of the large building. It was a cinder block structure, and the outside looked to be in fairly good condition. The inside appeared empty, from what Hawkins could tell as he sat behind the wheel of the olive-drab Lexus RX 350 SUV. He had the tinted windows rolled up and the air-conditioning going, so it was rather comfortable inside the vehicle. The steering wheel being on the left side rather than the right didn't really bother him. He'd driven vehicles in all parts of the world when he'd been in the SAS, and this particular car, with all its buttons and features, almost made him feel like he was flying in a helicopter. But that was the Falcon's gig.

"Maybe I should've let you drive," Hawkins said to him.

"I'd be glad to," Peregrine replied. He was sitting in the right front passenger seat. Boulle seemed content with the spacious back seat all to himself.

The overhead door jerked to a halt at the halfway point, and a skinny Mexican lad slid into view by the left side rail and motioned them to drive forward.

Hawkins shifted out of park and eased off the brake, immediately taking note of the construction and thickness of the big door as they passed underneath it, and calculating the amount of speed and force that might be necessary should he find it necessary to crash through it. Not that he expected he would need to do that, but his training had taught him to always figure a means of egress.

Again, credit the SAS, he thought.

"*Dere* he is," Boulle said with his French accent, his arm and pointing finger thrusting up between the front seats. "Pull up next to him."

Hawkins saw Lopez standing about twenty yards off to the right by two vehicles and a slew of motorcycles. One of the full-sized automobiles was a black Cadillac. The other was a tan and white van. Hawkins couldn't tell the make. Two younger men, both appearing to be Mexicans, stood next to Lopez. One was small and wiry looking, the other taller and lean. The second one looked like he could handle himself. A bunch of other young Mexicans, all dressed in leather vests and blue jeans with bandanas on top of their heads, were by the motorcycles.

"Looks like the gang's all here," Hawkins said as he edged the Lexus closer.

He didn't like being in what he considered hostile territory without any type of armament. A feeling of uneasiness began to creep up his spine but he did his best not to show any anxiety.

Keep cool under pressure.

Another bit of training that had been imbued into him in the SAS.

"I say," Peregrine said, "how well do you know these chaps?"

"Never met them," Boulle said. "They are friends of Lopez."

"That says a lot." Peregrine's voice betrayed a bit of edginess.

He was feeling the same as Hawkins, but that was standard operating procedure. They'd worked together so long that it was almost as if they were tuned in to each other's thoughts.

Hawkins recalled how Boulle had chastised him for his remark concerning the cartel man's ill-advised choice to light up a cigarette while the Learjet was being fueled.

How do you spell S-T-U-P-I-D in Spanish?

Hawkins had thought it quite a funny line back in the hangar when he'd said it. Peregrine had rebuked him as well, not wanting to cause problems down the line when they needed Lopez's connections and equipment.

Nobody seemed to have a sense of humor anymore, least of all the stinking Mexican.

But what the hell, he thought. *As I said before, what's the use of being Irish if you can't be thick?*

Hawkins pulled up next to them, shifted into park, and pressed the shut-off button. He intentionally drifted back and let Boulle take the lead. The cartel man smiled and shook hands with Boulle, introducing the two flunkies next to him as Pedro and Paco.

Two P's in a pod.

He also noticed that Lopez didn't even look at or acknowledge him.

Normally, Hawkins couldn't care less about the cartel man's slight, or the mundane appellations of the two underlings, but in this case he felt it best to make an exception. If they were going to follow the very elaborate and complex plan that the Frenchman had laid out to them on the plane, the Hawk and the Falcon were going to have to depend on these greasy little shits.

It all works better when we all work together, was the refrain one of his sergeants had extolled during training.

He watched as Peregrine stepped forward, smiled, and extended his open hand.

And normally the Brits weren't much for handshakes. In other words, it was time to schmooze a tad.

Hawkins swallowed his aloofness and stepped forward as well, extending his hand with an exaggerated smile on his face and said, "Any friend of Mr. Lopez here is a friend of mine. Top of the morning to ya."

It was still morning, more or less, wasn't it?

"*Es la tarde ahora*," Lopez muttered to the pair standing next to him, his voice laced with sarcasm. He subsequently nodded for them to shake hands with Hawkins.

Able to figure out what the cartel man had said from the little Spanish he knew, Hawkins widened his grin and said, "Well, it's morning somewhere, isn't it?"

The two Mexicans smiled and laughed as they shook

hands. Whether they understood or not, Hawkins had no idea.

Nor did he give a shit.

He'd made all the effort at civility that he was going to make.

"Let's see what hardware you've brought us," he said, deciding to take charge.

Lopez muttered a phrase in Spanish and the skinny Mexican next to him turned and said something to the one standing closest to the van. He reached up and opened one of the rear doors.

Hawkins felt his gut tighten. Vans were the perfect vehicles for surprise attacks.

With the door open, he could see an assortment of rifles and handguns lying on the vehicle's floorboards.

Clapping his hands together and rubbing them to demonstrate his anticipation, he strode over to the vehicle and began perusing the weapons. At the same time, he wondered how well-armed this little group watching him already was.

The weapons all looked to be in good condition. One of the rifles was an AR-15 with the bolt locked back exposing the empty ejection port. Two fully loaded banana mags had been placed just under the receiver. The ammunition was full metal jacketed .223 rounds. The other rifle was an Ithaca pump 12 gauge shotgun with extended magazine. The stock had an attachment where extra shells could be placed. Some boxes of double-ought buck and rifled slugs were nearby. Hawkins had fired both of those weapons before and liked them. The handguns were varied and also more plentiful: two little small snub-nosed revolvers—Smith & Wesson .38's, and two larger, .357 six-inch barreled models—again Smith & Wesson. The others were three

9mm semi-autos: a Sig Sauer P235, an FNX-Tactical, and a Beretta M9A3.the fist two had the protruding threaded barrels and Picatinny rails on top and below for a red dot attachment as well as a laser/flashlight. The Beretta, although a tried and true old battle horse that Hawkins had used and admired, also had a threaded barrel, but no suppressor height sights. Numerous boxes of 9mm ammunition were piled nearby, as were several loaded magazines for each gun. There were half a dozen smaller semi-autos for which Hawkins didn't know the brands, but they all appeared to be well made.

Not a Saturday night special in the bunch.

"What do you *tink?*" one of the Mexicans asked. His face had a sly grin, like he was showing his wares to a rube, and the dumb idiot pronounced "think" like "tink."

Hawkins picked up the Beretta and examined it.

"Do you have any suppressors?" he asked.

"Eh?" The Mexican's brow furrowed,

"Silencers," Hawkins said. "You know, *mucho siliento.*"

He made a pistol-like shape with his hand and said, "Ping. Ping."

"*Un silenciador,*" Lopez said, his tone pedantic.

The other Mexican grinned and nodded emphatically.

"Oh, *sí, sí.* I *haf dem.* You *wan?*"

"*Los quiere todos,*" Lopez said.

Hawkins cast a sideways glance at Lopez. He wasn't sure what that meant, but the haughty prick was starting to piss him off. All over a little off-the-wall humor.

Hawkins pointed to the Beretta's front and rear sights.

"The problem with this one is it doesn't have raised sights." He paused, letting that sink into the dunce. He looked at Lopez again. "You might want to translate, for this one's edification."

Lopez continued to glare at him.

"The problem with these," Hawkins continued, tapping the rear sight on the slide, "is that the cam of the silencer—the *silenciador*, is that once it's attached to the barrel, the cam prevents the shooter from acquiring an adequate sight picture. We'd need a red dot sight attachment for this one to go along with the suppressor."

Lopez made no effort to convey the words in Spanish.

The Mexican's brow accumulated a few more deepening wrinkles.

"Eh?"

"Never mind," Hawkins said, thinking if that was the way the cartel man wanted to play it, screw him. "Just bring us silencers for these two." He pointed to the FNX and the Sig Sauer, set down the Beretta, and picked up one of the smaller semi-autos.

The brand was an SCCY, and the caliber was .380. Single stack magazine. 10 round capacity.

Small, lethal, and very concealable. Not much use in their current scenario, but it caught Hawkins's eye and he pocketed it. Perhaps it would come in handy down the road.

"You want to try them out?" Lopez asked. "We own the building here." He pointed to the far end of the area to a stack of wooden boxes about twenty-five yards away in the center of the floor.

"Don't mind if I do," Hawkins said, and took out a pair of earplugs. Peregrine did the same and they both inserted them into their ear canals.

"Wait," Boulle said. "I have been in combat before and I do not wish to lose any more of my hearing."

"Tut tut, old chap," Peregrine said, reaching into the pocket of his pants and pulling out a plastic vial with another set of earplugs. "I always come prepared. The rest of you blokes will have to cover your ears, I'm afraid."

He tossed the vial to Boulle, who quickly unscrewed the top and jammed the plugs into his ears.

Hawkins strolled over to the stack of boxes, inspected them, and peered behind the stack. The wall was about fifty yards beyond and solid cement. Satisfied that the backstop was sufficient, he took a black marker out of his pocket and drew a circle approximately eight inches in circumference on the blank panel of the center box. He then strolled back and picked up the Sig P365, popped in a magazine, and yanked back on the slide, chambering a round.

"Ching-ching," he said, smirking. "My favorite martial art."

Without another word, he turned and assumed a modified Weaver stance, gripping the pistol with both hands. Peregrine had selected and loaded the Sig as well. He stepped beside his partner and assumed a firing stance.

Hawkins sighted in on the middle box. He squeezed the trigger and a split-second later a small round hole appeared in the middle of the front side of the box. The expended shell casing rolled on the concrete floor next to him.

Peregrine fired off two rounds, one on a line with Hawkins's first hit but about five inches to the left of it.

Hawkins grinned and fired again.

This round struck between the first two, but approximately three inches lower.

Peregrine then fired three more rounds, the holes in a

curve a few inches below the center shot. Hawkins then blasted off three more shots in rapid succession.

A haze of smoke hung in the air, and when it dissipated, everyone looked at the piercings on the side of the box. The pattern was easily distinct: a smiley face.

"Ah, chihauhau," one of the Mexicans said. "Estos hombres pueden fucilar muy bueno."

"No shit," said another in English.

"I guess the group is more bilingual than I assumed," Hawkins told himself with a grin. "But do you know what happens when you assume?"

Figuring he and his partner had demonstrated their prowess with aplomb and reestablished themselves as the apex predators of this motley group, Hawkins pressed the magazine release, dropped the mag, and pulled back the slide, catching the ejected round before it hit the floor.

Peregrine went through the same procedure, but cupped his hand over the ejection port to snare the expended bullet.

Hawkins then plucked the plugs out of his ears and replaced them in the small plastic vial. Peregrine did the same.

"I think we've about covered it all for now," Hawkins said, arching an eyebrow and stealing a glance at Boulle. "If you'd be so kind as to have your boys load these weapons and the ammo into our car, we'd be appreciative."

He pointed to the array of weapons he wanted.

"You want all of them?" Lopez said, his mouth twisting downward on each end.

"Certainly," Hawkins said. "Why not? As we used to say in Ireland, 'tis far better to be well prepared than to be left standing holding your privates in the lurch."

He smirked.

"A horse, a horse," Peregrine said. "My kingdom for a horse."

Lopez looked totally befuddled. "A horse?"

"It's Shakespeare," Hawkins said. "My friend here's enamored by his British roots."

Boulle had removed the extra earplugs and handed them back to Peregrine.

"If *dere* is nothing else for today," he said. "We'll be going back to our hotel. I have another meeting *dat* I must attend."

His pronunciation of the TH sound wasn't any better than that of the Mexicans, Hawkins noted. Pathetic.

After concluding a lengthy conversation in Spanish during which the younger Mexican kept bobbing his head in agreement, several of them went to the van and began packing the weapons into black canvas bags of various sizes. Hawkins took out the key fob and pressed the button raising the back tailgate. It popped open and rose with slow deliberation.

Lopez turned to them and said in perfect English, "It will all be done. We will meet tomorrow and he will have the silencers."

"That's bloody good news," Peregrine said. He then looked at the younger Mexican and said, *"Muchas gracias."*

His pronunciation sounded stiff and artificial and very British.

"*De nada*," the other man said, his voice a whisper. He strolled over and began issuing orders and pointing toward the Lexus. They began carrying the bags of weapons toward the vehicle.

"Well, I guess that just about does it for today," Hawkins said, still assuming the dominant role.

Boulle stared at him but said nothing. It was clear that he was a bit irritated with the big Irishman's brassiness.

Hawkins started to turn toward the Lexus, but Lopez raised an index finger.

"Oh, by *de* way," he said, now distorting his voice so that it took on the tone of a badly done caricature, "In regard to your question in *de* hangar, *et es espelled*, E-S-T-U-P-E-D-O, *wit una acento* over *de* U."

His dark brown eyes were intense, his expression confrontational.

Hawkins returned his stare.

It appeared there was a test of machismo brewing and wondered how this was going to affect the rest of the mission.

He thought about smacking the greasy son of a bitch right here and there but decided that might not be prudent, considering that he, Peregrine, and Boulle were all unarmed and in the belly of the beast. Nor could he afford to let this challenge go unanswered. That was how things worked in these Latin cultures.

It was all about *machismo*, *cajones*, or whatever else they wanted to call it.

A challenge unanswered was to embrace subservience, and he wasn't about to drop to his knees and service this son of a bitch.

Hawkins instead merely handled it with a smile and a light slap on the other man's shoulder.

"Thanks for the Spanish lesson, *amigo*," he said. "Perhaps next time, but at the moment, our mutual associates and I have a mission to run."

He turned and strode toward the Lexus, whistling a merry tune and not looking back, assuming that Peregrine and Boulle would be following. The Mexican lackeys had finished piling the array of gun-laden bags into the back of the SUV. Hawkins punched the button on the elevated tailgate to lower the door, and then leisurely strolled to the driver's door and got in, pausing to wave at Lopez and his boys.

A couple of them grinned and waved back, initiating a rebuke in Spanish from Lopez.

Hawkins kept the grin on his face as he slammed the door and pushed the start button.

Peregrine heaved a sigh.

"That was a bit tense," he said. "Wouldn't you say so?"

"I say whatever the hell I please," Hawkins said, shifting the vehicle into drive and pressing down on the accelerator.

The overhead door began to start its ascent.

"Not too smart, Boulle said. "We will need him and his men before this is over."

"Just establishing the ground rules," Hawkins said. "Like the dominant lion in the pack pissing on a couple of bushes to mark his territory."

Boulle shook his head in obvious disgust.

Peregrine laughed. "For a moment back there, I thought you two were going to pull down your britches and measure which of you was the bigger man."

"Britches?" Hawkins laughed. "In his case, it's probably knickers, as you Brits would say." His eyes went to the rearview mirror and focused on Boulle in the back seat. "And believe me, *Monsieur*, I'll never come up short in that department. Want to see?"

"Spare me, *s'il vous plaît*. We have much to do. Let us get on with it. Drop me in my car. I have an appointment to keep, and you must go to check out the prison, *n'est pa?*"

"Whatever," Hawkins said. He hit the gas harder and shot through the open aperture and onto the street.

Things were moving fast, he reflected. Just the way he liked it.

* * *

FEDERAL CORRECTIONAL INSTITUTE
SATELLITE FACILITY BETA
PHOENIX, ARIZONA

Hawkins drummed his fingers on the steering wheel of the Lexus RX 350 and watched his partner in the rearview mirror. Peregrine was in the back seat of the big SUV with a pair of binoculars. The windows of the vehicle were all heavily tinted so there was little danger of anyone catching a glimpse of him. The street surveillance cameras were a problem, but the Hawk doubted a view of the rear seat area would be feasible.

"How's it looking?" he said.

"If this one is their minimum facility, I'd hate to see the maximum." Peregrine exhaled with a huff. "Looks like a bloody fortress. Getting her out of there is going to take a bit of finesse."

"More like a lot of it," Hawkins said, looking at the imposing, multi-sectional group of triangular brick structures. It was the size of a small neighborhood and had a formidable wall surrounding the entire place. And he surmised that it was well staffed with all kinds of guards, most of whom would be armed and on the ready. Sneaking into this thing to get the woman was absolutely out of the question. They didn't even know what floor she was on or where she was being housed.

One thing was certain: to get her out, as Von Tillberg demanded, would require someone on the inside somewhere. Someone who could be bribed, and even if they could quickly find and groom somebody, the chances of pulling off an extraction that complicated within the time frame the rich man had laid out would be fraught with way too many what-ifs and problems. And if the clock was ticking at the rate the rich bastard seemed to think it was, mounting a successful op would literally be mission impossible, like something out of one of those stupid American movies.

Still, he did have an idea.

"How many women do they have in this place?" he asked.

"A couple hundred."

"What about doing something like we pulled off down in Columbia?" Hawkins said. "Looks like there's plenty of places to land a helicopter."

"Give me a break," Peregrine said. The police department probably has its own small air force around here."

"Well, there was that one in the Bahamas."

Peregrine had lowered his binoculars and was leaning back in his seat.

"You mean the Great Switcheroo?" he asked.

"Exactly," Hawkins said.

"I don't know. We had a lot longer to work out a plan on that one. And as it went, we took some God-awful chances and almost didn't pull it off. Plus..." He opened the folder that Boulle had given him earlier, flipped to the picture of Bridgette Swenstrom, and held it up. "Even if we could get in under some pretext, where would we find a bird this smashing who'd be willing to take her place?"

Hawkins silently agreed but wasn't ready to give up yet.

"Maybe we could find one of those trannie girls that are in the news over here. We could bring the bastard in with us as a male, have the two of them switch places in the loo, and then smuggle Bridgette out with us."

"What about the trannie?"

"He could melt into the general population and revert back to his male side from the waist down, and no one would be the wiser. The fellow would probably be in seventh heaven, and so would the female prisoners. Didn't you hear about that lucky bastard in Scotland who identified as a female and was put in a women's prison? He impregnated a bunch of them before somebody caught on to his game."

Peregrine snorted a laugh as he studied the photo.

"If you could find a trannie who looked as good as this bird," he said, "I'd marry him myself. Or at least consider taking him for a roll in the hay."

"She's a looker, all right," Hawkins said. "I do hope we have some time to get acquainted if and when we get her out of there. After all, he did say to bring her back alive, didn't he?"

"Right again. All so he can apparently torture her to death."

Hawkins shook his head. "Seems like a waste of a good tart, all right. But maybe he'll let us sample the goods first."

"I think the old boy's a bit off his rocker if you ask

me. Did you catch a glimpse of his face? And how he was sweating?"

"We were in a sauna bath, for Christ's sake," Hawkins said. "We were all sweating like a bunch of missionaries in line for the cannibal's stew pot."

"Not as much as that bugger was. If I had to guess, I'd say our employer has been trying to live better through chemistry."

Drugs?

Hawkins hadn't considered that particular wrinkle, but now that the Falcon had mentioned it, it did make a lot of sense.

Could go a long way toward explaining Von Tillberg's rather outlandish and extreme measures, he thought. Holding a meeting virtually naked in a fucking sauna room, for instance.

The son of a bitch may be rich, Hawkins thought, *but the fellow's elevator doesn't go all the way to the top floor.*

"As long as the money's good," he said.

"I'm sure it is, but we had still better be figuring some kind of way to beat a hasty retreat off his bloody estate when the time comes."

"Agreed." Hawkins smiled. "That's why God created men who can fly helicopters."

Peregrine smiled too.

He held up his burner phone.

"Well, we did our due diligence in reconnoitering," he said. "Let's check with Frenchie and see what he wants us to do next. He did say he was working on a plan for all this, didn't he?"

"He did," Hawkins said. "But I'm not so sure we'll want to follow it."

"Strangers in a strange land," Peregrine said. "What choice do we have?"

Hawkins managed a fractional nod of agreement but silently swore an oath to himself that he was nobody's pigeon.

"We'll have to wait and see," he said and shifted the Lexus into drive.

* * *

THE OFFICE OF JOHN H. MOORE & ASSOCIATES
ATTORNEY AT LAW
PHOENIX, ARIZONA

Boulle watched as the attorney closed the door separating his private office from the exterior office section which housed a secretarial pool and the offices for several other attorneys. The facilities were very impressive. The man was obviously highly successful and his prompt response to Boulle's short-notice request for an immediate meeting demonstrated that the large amount of money that they'd paid him already, ferreted through several shell companies and LLCs, had done the trick. When money called, this one jumped.

John H. Moore looked a bit soft and plump in his dark tan suit. His hair was thinning at the hairline and at the crown as well. Not only that, but he wore a pair of glasses with thick lenses. Obviously a man whose vigor was best suited for the courtroom rather than the battlefield. He motioned for Boulle to take a seat in front of the desk and then seated himself in what appeared to be an ergonomic office chair. Boulle did so and set the specially designed briefcase on the carpeted floor next to him.

Leaning forward and placing his elbows on the desktop, Moore brought his hands together in a gesture resembling a church steeple so that the tips of his index fingers touched his chin as if to obscure the dollop of fat that hung underneath.

"So good to finally meet you face to face," he said and smiled.

Boulle merely nodded an acknowledgment.

"What is the latest with our client?" he asked.

"She seems to be holding up well enough," Moore said. "Her spirits definitely improved once I mentioned that you would be arriving. I take it that you two worked together for a while?"

Boulle didn't reply to that query either. He had hired this Moore character three months ago at the behest of Von Tillberg, who had been advised through Lopez of the disastrous shootout in the Las Vegas hotel that had killed Reign and resulted in Bridgette and Bray being picked up by the authorities. Bray quickly scurried over to the other side, but Bridgette, slinky cat that she was, had demurred, demanding a lawyer and assuming that Von Tillberg, with all his money, would be able to get her released.

That had proved problematic, and Moore advised them that she was being held on numerous felony charges, including kidnapping, unlawful restraint, and the attempted murder of a federal officer. They'd been able to get Robert Bray out of custody before by posting a hefty bail amount, but the authorities had learned their lesson and got Bridgette remanded without bond. Things had dragged out, and she'd made it clear to Boulle and Von Tillberg, through her attorney, Moore, that if they didn't get her out soon, she was going to fire the attorney and cooperate with the federal authorities. Boulle had no doubt that this current ploy was just a veiled threat to shake things up. Regardless, they had one shot to get her out, and they had to move quickly but also cautiously.

"There's still no movement on getting her bond reduced," Moore said. "As per your instructions, we've waived the right to a speedy trial, but that's also working in the government's favor. They're keeping her locked up in a federal facility where they can keep pressuring her to flip."

"To flip?" Boulle was almost certain he understood the meaning of the word in this particular context but wanted to be sure.

"To cooperate with the authorities in exchange for a sweet deal. So far they haven't suggested what this might be, but they'll have to go through me first. I've advised them that she's not to be questioned without me present, and I've told her the same thing. It's against the rules for them to initiate any further conversation with her without me being there."

Boulle already knew this too, but, knowing Bridgette like he did, he had another concern.

"And what if she initiates the conversation? Can she not waive her right to counsel?"

"Well," Moore said, his lower lip creeping up over his upper. "I suppose she could, if she gave me notice that my services were no longer desired. But I don't see that happening."

Boulle did see it, however, knowing Bridgette like he did. And also knowing her penchant for luxury, he was all but certain she was close to forging a deal to get out of the American prison, one way or another. They were caught in a quagmire, and his Legion training told him some bold measure was needed. He would need to review the report of the facility with the Falcon and the

Hawk before he made any final plan, but things had to be set in motion soon.

"This is what I want you to do," he said, reaching into his pocket and withdrawing the special, preprogrammed burner phone. "You will go to see her today."

Before he could go on, Moore made a huffing sound.

"I'm afraid that's quite impossible," Moore said, interrupting. "I've got a deposition scheduled, and I—"

"I said you will go to see her today." It was Boulle's turn to interrupt. He kept his voice firm.

The lawyer's mouth twitched with a nervous grin.

"You don't seem to understand," he said. "Ms. Swenstrom isn't my only client. I have many, many client needs that need to be addressed. I can, however, send one of my associates to—"

"Have one of your associates take the disposition," Boulle said. Interruptions were ruling the day. He placed the burner phone on the desk and tapped it with his index finger. "You will give her this phone. It is preprogrammed to dial only one number. My number. Tell her to call me tonight for instructions. Tell her I have arrived and will be getting her released."

"But..." Moore's lips sputtered. "I can't give her a phone. It's totally against the rules. If I should get caught—"

"Do not get caught, then." Boulle briefly considered going with the lawyer to assure success, but Von Tillberg had strictly forbidden doing anything that might lead the authorities back to him, and Boulle was now a known employee. "When you speak with her, are you not in a room by yourselves?"

"We are, but it's monitored. There's no audio, but there are cameras. And I'm checked thoroughly beforehand. If I get caught smuggling contraband into the facility…" He paused and his head quivered. "Or if she gets caught with it—"

"She will not," Boulle said. "And neither will you."

He waited and directed one of his solid stares at the other man. In the Legion, they had called it the feral stare, that of the mongoose circling his prey.

Moore's tongue flicked out over his lips.

Before the lawyer could say anything else, Boulle lifted the briefcase up onto the desk and came around to stand beside it.

"Take a look at this," he said. He adjusted the top snaps and opened the briefcase, displaying that it was empty and had open-ended slotted portions in which to store various papers.

Moore's eyes swept over it.

"It is a nice, professional carrier," Boulle said. "Is it not?"

Moore nodded.

Boulle smiled. He could see a thin patina of sweat forming on the man's high forehead.

Closing the briefcase, Boulle then twisted the top snapping mechanism so that it was now parallel, rather than perpendicular, to the top edge of the briefcase lid. He positioned the case so that it was flat on the desktop, the rear portion facing Moore. After unsnapping the fasteners once more, Boulle raised the top lid to the open position, and then, with his left hand, pressed a squared-off section on the side edge. A small trap door of the bottom part of the briefcase popped open revealing an empty three-by-five-inch compartment that was perhaps an inch in depth. Boulle picked up the burner phone and placed it in the compartment. He pressed the square button on the side of the case and the trapdoor silently slid back into place. Waiting what he felt was an appropriate length of time, perhaps five seconds, he pressed the button again and the burner phone was displayed.

"You see," he said, "it will be a simple matter of bringing the phone into the interview room. Your privacy, as you say, is ensured. You need only to slip the phone to Bridgette under the pretext of having her sign some papers. She will know how to conceal it, believe me. Explain to her that it is preset with only one number, mine, and to call me when she is assured of some privacy. I will then give her whatever instructions I deem necessary."

Moore's mouth twisted down at the edges and his head began shaking minutely.

"I—I—I can't do that," he managed to say.

"Of course you can." Boulle smiled. "I will send a pair of my associates with you to assure success. They will assist you in blocking the view of any guards or cameras."

Moore's face was covered with a brocade of perspiration now. He removed his glasses and wiped at his eyes.

"I'm telling you I can't do it," he said.

"No, no, no," Boulle said quickly. "You do not understand. I am not giving you a choice in this matter. There is no such choice. It is, as we say in France, a *fait accompli.*" He fixed the lawyer with the feral stare again. "You will either comply and do as I say, or you will die."

Boulle saw the other man shiver and cast his eyes down at the desktop. Slowly, Moore's head nodded.

I have him now, Boulle thought. And it is too bad that he does not know that when he has outlived his usefulness, he shall meet with a very unfortunate mishap.

He reached out and gently laid his hand on Moore's shoulder.

"Do not despair, *mon ami*. In a short time, it will be over, and you will never see me or my associates again."

He smiled and the irony.

Nor will you be seeing anything at all, Boulle added mentally.

CHAPTER 8

NORTHBOUND ON ROUTE 93
SOMEWHERE NEAR ALAMO LAKE

As McNamara's Escalade sped along the ribbon of highway, Wolf reviewed the prospects of what was to come in little more than thirty hours or so when he'd have to step on that official scale at the weigh-in and see how much weight he'd have to lose in crunch time. He'd already resigned himself to the fact that he was going to be over the limit initially. He'd lost a good five pounds yesterday after his all-day workout, but it was mostly all water weight. It was back as soon as he finished quenching his thirst, which was a necessity. He'd even used water instead of Gatorade. And it hadn't been a particularly strenuous workout either. Most of the time had been spent going over Georgie's hastily conceived battle plan of straight, stand-up boxing, emphasizing his left jab and hook and deemphasizing his right. He'd also worked on initiating arm locks and guillotine chokes.

"You can use your kicks, too," Georgie said, "but only

to the legs. You try to go high, and this boy might be able to sweep you. He'll be looking for a chance to take this to the mat."

"That might not be such a bad thing," Reno had chimed in. "Steve's got to be a lot stronger than this guy."

"That's true," Georgie said. "But it's best to avoid grappling with this dude. He is supposed to be good at Brazilian jiu jitsu."

He wondered if they were still debating the plan in the white van that was just up ahead. It contained Reno, Georgie, Barbie, and Clancy, Wolf's expert cut man. He hoped he wouldn't need him.

Confusion reigned, Wolf thought.

It all felt like too little, too late, and he'd have to adapt and improvise after the initial bell rang. He also realized now that taking the fight on such short notice had been a mistake, but it was the only choice he'd had because of the pending legal action and near-desperate monetary situation.

Despite having finally succeeded in clearing his name, he was still tainted goods, for the time being anyway.

A sign came into view stating to take the next right if you wanted to go to Bagdad or Skull Valley, and Wolf smiled. There was no way he wanted to go to either one.

Especially a place called Bagdad. The name sounded way too similar to the original.

He watched as the green sign with the white letters whizzed by and then turned around the other way to glance over his shoulder. Nobody was behind them.

"There ain't nobody following us," McNamara said. "I been keeping watch. Besides..." He patted the Glock 19 on his right hip, "I got three extra magazines on me."

Wolf smiled, but the uneasiness persisted. He was

really getting tired of constantly looking over his shoulder. It was almost as bad as being on patrol in a combat zone, but then again, he'd been armed during that time. Now he wasn't, and he certainly wouldn't be once he stepped into the Octagon. The sudden and unexpected horror of the attack last time loomed large in his memory. If it hadn't been for that Kevlar robe that Mac and Pike had draped over him, he would've been wounded. But it had still cost him a lot. The hotel had forced the organization to procure an additional insurance policy in the event of any unforeseen violence occurring.

Unforeseen violence, he thought. An ironic choice of words considering the entire event consisted of various pairs of fighters trying to knock each other's blocks off.

"Why don't you put that seat back and try to get some rest?" McNamara said. "We got a ways to go yet."

Wolf pressed the button to recline the seat and closed his eyes. After a few minutes of trying, he straightened up and said, "It's no use."

Mac grunted an acknowledgment.

Wolf watched the bleak scenery zooming by on the other side of the window.

Miles to go before I sleep, he thought, and then added, *and pounds to lose as well.*

* * *

THIRD FLOOR
PARKING GARAGE STRUCTURE
MEADOWS SHOPPING MALL
PHOENIX, ARIZONA

Boulle flashed the lights of his Cadillac as soon as he saw the gray Nissan pull off of the elevated ramp leading up from the second floor. The Nissan jerked to a stop and then slowly made its way toward him.

The pigeon is nervous, Boulle thought. *Perhaps some reassurance will be needed.*

Either that, or a bit of other incentive.

Boulle was backed into a parking space against the outer wall. The solid barrier extended up perhaps four feet leaving an open expanse between it and the floor of the next level. Loudermilk's car lurched forward and jerked to a halt. He then proceeded very cautiously forward until their driver's doors were side-by-side.

Boulle's window was already down, but he waited while Loudermilk lowered his. The man's face looked pale and sweaty, his breathing noticeably ragged, even though Boulle could only see a small portion of him from the neck and shoulders up.

"Bonjour, *mon ami,*" Boulle said, flashing his most disarming smile.

Better not to use the stick on the nervous dog just yet.

Loudermilk nodded and quickly glanced around.

Theirs were the only two vehicles on the entire floor.

"We'll have to make this quick," Loudermilk said. "I'm due in at nine, and I don't want to be late."

"Heaven forbid," Boulle said, extending his hand out his window. "Do you have it?"

Loudermilk's lips compressed inward and for a moment he was motionless, as if deciding that taking this step was a very fateful one.

But what other choice did he have?

Boulle snapped the fingers on his extended hand.

"*Vite, vite,*" he said. "Give it to me now if you are so pressed for time."

Loudermilk's mouth twisted into a frown and he still sat motionless. Finally he spoke, and when he did, his voice came out with a tremor.

"I hope you realize that this is tantamount to me signing my own resignation." He paused and pursed his lips. "You know. If this comes to light, I could end up in prison."

Perhaps you should have thought about that before engaging in your little dalliances on the island, Boulle thought. But what he said was, "Mr. Von Tilberg is very appreciative of your loyalty and your cooperation in this matter. And he always rewards those who assist him."

Loudermilk swallowed hard. If Boulle's words reassured him, then it was not evident.

"That's not good enough," he blurted out.

Boulle arched an eyebrow. His arm was still extended out the window.

"Not good enough?" he asked.

The other man's chin trembled like quivering gelatin.

"Once they discover that there's a leak," he said, his voice now sounding like a sorrowful pig's squeal. "It could be traced back to me."

"Then we must be certain that does not happen," Boulle said. "For both our sakes."

He studied the pathetic government worker. Adding that last sentence to make it seem that they were both in this together seemed to have the desired effect. Loudermilk's breathing slowed.

"Listen," he said. looking Boulle straight in the eyes. "You saying that is all well and good, but if I'm going to give this to you, I want something in return."

"And what may that be?"

"Simple," Loudermilk said. "An exit strategy."

Boulle used the thumb and forefinger of his right hand to trace over the stubble growing on either side of his mouth. He hadn't shaved this morning and had thought about regrowing his goatee.

"An exit strategy?" he said.

Loudermilk nodded.

"Do you think I don't know what you want this address for?" he said. "You're planning on sending somebody to kill Bray, aren't you?"

"Well," Boulle said. "We are very concerned about him testifying in front of this, how do you say, grand jury?"

Loudermilk's head bobbed up and down.

"It is still set for tomorrow, no?" Boulle asked.

Loudermilk shook his head.

"They've moved it to Monday."

Boulle felt reassured hearing that. It meant that the buffoon Moore had delivered the false notification that Bridgette was ready to cooperate.

"Ah, all the better. It gives us more time to plan our next moves, no?" His smile widened. "Just like moving pieces on a chessboard. It must be done with both circumspection and deliberation. Do you not think so?"

Loudermilk's head shook. Or was it another tremble? His tongue shot out over his lips, which looked dry, and then slid back into his mouth.

"I want money," he said, almost tripping over the words as if it had been an effort to utter them. "A lot of money. Enough to retire and live comfortably somewhere."

"But of course," Boulle said. "Such a thing is already in the works."

Loudermilk's eyes widened.

"It is?"

"*Oui, mon ami*. Rest assured. You will be well taken care of." He smiled at the irony of his word choice, then reached into his inside jacket pocket and removed his phone. He swiped it to open the Wi-Fi, and after punching in the password and a few other sequences, the space appeared to enter the bank account number of one of Von Tillberg's throwaway accounts.

"You are, how do you say, on the payroll now."

Boulle handed the phone to Loudermilk, who accepted it.

He studied the screen and then looked back to Boulle. "What's this?"

"That," Boulle said, "is your new off-shore account in the Cayman Islands. Enter the following password." He repeated the familiar sequence of numbers and letters.

Loudermilk's thumbs worked on the screen, and then his eyes widened.

"That's a lot of money."

"It is," Boulle replied. "I will email you the proper access information shortly."

Loudermilk blinked a few times and then his jaw muscles bunched up.

"How do I know this is on the level?"

"*Monsieur* Von Tillberg is a businessman. He is not one to leave loose ends dangling. It is in his best interests to make sure you are well provided for." This seemed to have the desired effect." He intentionally cleared his throat. "But now, if you please, I must have that address. My associates have much reconnoitering to do."

Loudermilk studied the screen for a few moments more and then handed the phone back to Boulle.

"I'll be needing safe passage out of here too," he said. "Should I fly directly to the island?"

Boulle kept the disarming smile on his face as he shook his head.

"I shall email you the information for a ticket that will be purchased in your name. You will fly to Mexico first, and then you will be given a new identity and a very large amount of money to disappear." He paused and let the word sink in. After all, he was dealing with a dunce. "That sounds good, does it not?"

Loudermilk's lips twisted with a simpleton's simper. He nodded.

"Very good," Boulle said. "Now, the address where *Monsieur* Bray is being kept."

Loudermilk reached into a briefcase on the seat next to him and pulled out a folder. He started to hand it through the window but stopped.

"Here it is," he said. "But they're planning on moving him after the grand jury testimony on Monday. I don't know where."

"Then time is of the essence, is it not?" Boulle said.

Loudermilk didn't move and Boulle snapped his fingers again.

The other man handed the folder through the window.

Boulle opened it and examined the contents.

"Very good," he said. "As I told you, everything has been set. You will be getting the flight information very soon." He placed the folder on the seat beside him and regarded the other man once more. "You have done well, *mon ami*. However, there is one more small matter but of great importance that he wishes you to do."

"What's that?" Loudermilk's upper lip was wet with perspiration.

Boulle flashed the man another lips-only smile.

Dealing with a simpleton and fool made things so much easier.

"It is a very simple task but an important one," he said. "And then, you will be all through."

* * *

THE WINTHROP HOTEL
ROOM 645
PHOENIX, ARIZONA

It was the part that Hawkins liked least—the tediousness of the preparation, but he knew from past experience that it couldn't be avoided. And you had to do a thorough job. Besides, he had a reward coming soon. They both did. He and Peregrine had checked into the hotel under the assumed names and using the ersatz credit cards from Boulle that would soon be rendered useless. But for the time being, they had no limit. Hawkins requested a room on the sixth floor and Peregrine one on the fourth. Above and below their intended target on the fifth. The one above would be used for the pre-operation equipment storage, while the fourth would be for their change of clothes and quick departure.

Now they were both comfortably ensconced in the sixth-floor room with the mid-afternoon sunlight streaming in through the gossamer-like screen draped in front of the window. It was sumptuous and well-situated, only about ten yards from the corridor to the freight elevator. It required a special key to operate it, but that was just one more minor task that had to be addressed. Peregrine was seated at the desk adjusting the transmitter and modem on the miniature camera so that it coincided with the open laptop on the desk. He held up the mini-cam in his latex-gloved hand and aimed it at Hawkins, who sat across the room on the bed with a roll of highly adhesive double-sided tape and the elongated selfie stick.

"Wave for the camera, please," the Falcon said.

The Hawk complied, making a funny face, and giving him an extended, latex-encased middle finger.

"Can't say much for the subject matter," Peregrine said, "but the camera transmission is spot on."

"How's it recording?"

Peregrine's fingers danced over the laptop's keyboard and the screen went dark for a moment, then relit with a sharp image of Hawkins saying, "How's it recording."

"See?" Peregrine said, tapping the flash drive protruding from the USB slot. "All in here."

"Good." Hawkins looked at his watch. "Now all we have to do is hope she's as good-looking in person as she is in her pictures on the Internet."

"What's that old joke? If she isn't, just put a paper bag over her head?"

Hawkins grinned. "And a bag over yours as well. In case the one over hers breaks."

"Let's hope that it doesn't." Peregrine frowned and looked at his watch. "Dammit, I wish she'd bloody call."

"She will," Hawkins said. "She's not going to pass up a couple of easy scores this early in the day. And I did tell her it was a double. Let's get ready."

He got up, accepted the small camera/transmitter from Peregrine and wedged it between the two right-angle bars on the end of the selfie stick. After using his knife to slice off a section of the double-sided tape, he affixed the adhesive to the back of the mini-cam.

The phone rang as if on cue.

Hawkins picked it up and answered with a somewhat slurred, "Hello."

"Did you call for entertainment?" the female voice asked.

"We certainly did," Hawkins said, continuing his best imitation of a slightly tipsy prospective john. "My friend and I will be right down. We want to get a look at you. What are you wearing? Something sexy, I hope."

"Of course I am," she said. "I've got blonde hair, and I'm in a tan skirt and a white top."

"White? For virginal?" Hawkins said and then followed with a guttural laugh.

"Don't scare her off now," Peregrine muttered.

"Heaven forbid," Hawkins said.

"What did you say?" she asked.

"I was just talking to my friend," Hawkins said, allowing his Irish accent to come into prominence a bit more. "We'll meet you in the bar to buy you a drink and discuss terms. All right"

"Fine," she said and hung up.

Hawkins hung up the phone and handed the selfie stick with the camera attached to Peregrine.

"Let's go get it done," he said and peeled off his latex gloves and jammed them into his pocket.

* * *

MILO'S MIXED MARTIAL ARTS TRAINING CENTER
LAS VEGAS, NEVADA

Wolf knew that this would be his last hard workout before the fight, and it was mostly about working punching combinations, kicks, and a bit of the ground game. They were using the square boxing ring at Milo's gym, since the Octagon was in use with a couple of fighters who were also on the card on Saturday night and in the main event. Georgie held the focus mitts up and moved around the ring with the grace of a much slimmer man. Wolf always marveled at his trainer's nimbleness. He held up his left mitt horizontally, which was a cue for Wolf to use his jab.

He double-jabbed it with his left and then followed up with a right cross to the other one.

The pain shot through his right hand like an electrical shock, but he tried hard not to show the pain lacing his hand and wrist.

It didn't fool Georgie at all.

The big man grimaced.

"How bad?" he asked.

"Bad enough," Wolf said. He felt very disappointed. He'd been hoping against his better judgment that everything would be fine by fight time. Now, that seemed like a wishful dream.

"Shit," Georgie said. "I shoulda known that damn Chinese bullshit acupuncture wasn't worth nothing."

"Ah, it helped a little bit," Wolf said.

"But not enough." Georgie glanced over at Reno, who stood ringside watching. He'd apparently caught the conversation.

"Time," he said and pressed the button on his stopwatch.

Wolf dropped his guard stance and stepped over to the ring post.

Reno used the towel to wipe down Wolf's face, arms, and chest.

"We'd be in a pickle if we canceled now," Reno said. "But I got no qualms about doing it."

Wolf was feeling the fatigue. He leaned forward, placing both forearms on the top rope.

"We do that; we're out a lot of money," he said. "Not to mention all the expense money we already spent training and getting here."

Reno snorted.

"Hell, we been on a shoestring budget anyway," he said. "Only a few weeks and a half's worth of training and we drove here instead of flying. We ain't out that much." He paused and took in a deep breath. "It's like I said, I don't want you fighting if you're not a hundred percent."

"Listen to him," Georgie added. "You get hurt in there could ruin you."

Wolf smirked.

"Nothing like a united front of optimism from my corner."

"Steve," Reno said. "That's not the point."

But for Wolf, it was. The point was all monetary. He thought back just a few months ago, after winning the championship and being vindicated at the Military Court of Appeals. He'd been on top of the world, all set to start rolling around in lots of new money, just like that old cartoon character Scrooge McDuck, swimming around in his bathtub full of cash. Then, in an instant, it was all gone, and he was back behind the eight-ball, broke again and hoping for some kind of a miraculous windfall. He still had high hopes with the ongoing lawsuit to get his championship and frozen purse back, and, if he could make a good showing in this fight, a shot at redemption.

At least he was moving toward something now. He had a goal.

"I'm more worried about making weight than I am the fight," Wolf said.

"Yeah," Reno said. "Where are we on that front?"

Wolf and Georgie exchanged glances.

"Holding steady at ten." Georgie raised an eyebrow. "You want to try a laxative?"

The thought of getting hit in the gut and losing control of his bowels on a nationwide television broadcast made Wolf cringe. He shook his head.

"Let's do it the old-fashioned way," he said.

Georgie grinned. "That is the old-fashioned way. How you think Roberto Duran used to make weight after blowing up like he did between fights?"

"Didn't you also tell me that the reason he quit against Leonard in their second fight was that after using a laxative and then getting hit in the gut, he almost shit his pants?"

Georgie chuckled. "Well, that's the rumor. But nobody knows for sure."

"That might weaken him too much," Reno said. "I never did that when I was fighting light-heavy. Too risky. Anyway, let's knock off for now and have you spend some time in Milo's steam room."

Wolf thought about a scene in that old movie about Jake LaMotta where he was trying to drop weight by running in place in the steam room and begging for a sliver of ice for his tongue. The trainer shakes his head and says, "Ten more pounds."

"Let's do it," Wolf said.

Ten more pounds.

He felt like things were moving really fast—an accelerated pace over which he had no control. It gave him the feeling of running full speed through a dark tunnel toward a light at the other end. He just hoped it wasn't the glowing beam of a runaway locomotive heading toward him at full speed.

* * *

THE WINTHROP HOTEL
FIFTH FLOOR
PHOENIX, ARIZONA

"I thought you said your room was on the *sixth* floor," the call girl said, twin creases forming between her perfectly tweaked and accented eyebrows. "This is the fifth."

"Fifth, sixth, what's the difference?" Hawkins said, still slurring his words and pretending to be slightly inebriated. It was all part of the act. "All you have to worry about is two happy endings."

The girl frowned. She looked to be in her late twenties or maybe early thirties with blonde hair and a tight dress that emphasized her killer figure. Peregrine held the selfie stick with the camera elevated in front of them, as if recording for posterity. He still wore his latex gloves.

The call girl opened her purse and put on a pair of dark glasses, and then ducked her head.

"Didn't I tell you I didn't want to be filmed?" she said.

"Not a problem," Peregrine said. "I don't even know how to turn the bloody thing on."

Hawkins glanced down the hallway. It was fairly wide, with rooms on both sides. The room where they had Robert Bray stashed was number 526. Their target room would be the one right across from it, 527. The three of them began a slow amble down the corridor.

Hawkins surveyed the room numbers.

510, 511, 512…

Even numbers on the left side, odds on the right.

"Here, milady." Hawkins paused. "Let me carry you across the threshold."

"No, I don't think so."

"Aw, come on now, sweetmeat," Peregrine said. "I'll hold your little dolly bag for you."

The call girl clutched her purse closer against her.

"No thanks."

Peregrine shrugged and turned toward Hawkins.

They were at rooms 524/525 now.

"He's very strong, you know," Peregrine said. "He won't drop you."

"I won't drop you," Hawkins parroted.

The girl started to turn to walk back toward the elevators.

"Forget you two," she said.

"No," Peregrine said. "Please don't go. Here, watch."

Hawkins turned around and bent over. Peregrine took two quick steps and jumped up on his partner's back, then pushing himself up higher. As Hawkins straightened up to his full height, he staggered toward the right-side wall, knowing that his partner was poised to slap the adhesive-coated camera above the doorjamb of room 527. The thumping sound was hardly noticeable as Hawkins veered into the wall with controlled effort.

"Let me down," Peregrine said. "I'm getting a bit airsick."

Hawkins squatted, and Peregrine jumped off.

"Mission accomplished," he whispered and then ran down the hallway after the departing call girl crying out, "Ginger, my dear. Wait."

Hawkins stumbled down the hallway after them, stopped to lean against the left side wall and cast a quick look up at the mini-cam.

It was perfectly positioned by the edge of the door-jamb, high enough up that no one was likely to notice, especially two bored policemen on babysitting duty.

"We promise to be on our best behavior," Hawkins bellowed, figuring that if the coppers guarding Bray had heard anything and looked out the peephole, they would have just seen two drunks making fools of themselves over a hooker. He pulled out his wallet and removed a wad of cash.

The call girl had stopped by the elevators and pushed the down button. Her head tilted to the side and Hawkins knew she was obviously looking at the cash in his outstretched hand. The elevator doors opened with a pinging sound and the lighted down button blinked off. She didn't move, and Hawkins waved the cash again.

The elevator doors slid closed and after a moment she punched the up button and said, "You did say the sixth floor, didn't you."

The doors popped open again.

Hawkins and Peregrine exchanged glances and smiled as all three of them stepped into the empty elevator.

CHAPTER 9

THE FIGHT ARENA
THE LUCKY STAR CASINO
LAS VEGAS, NEVADA

It was a new setting, but it smelled and sounded the same.

"Ladies and gentlemen," the ring announcer's voice echoed. "It's time to *rummmble*."

The lights above the Octagon obscured everything else in the subdued lighting of the huge auditorium. Wolf knew there were people out there in the dark beyond, as he called it, but they mercifully remained unseen. He knew that somewhere out there Yolanda was sitting there watching. So were Mac, Miss Dolly, and Brenda. He and Reno had consented to let Dos Pastos enter the Octagon last, even though that was against tradition because Wolf had more prestige as a US and a World Champion. But with the latter on hold and both titles being in a separate MMA organization, they didn't make an issue of the violated protocol. It was a subtle slap in the face, but given that Wolf was a last-minute replacement facing a young up-and-comer, it hadn't seemed something to argue about. During the fighter introductions, however, the announcer listed both of Wolf's titles, building the hype, even though this was not a championship bout.

Three five-minute rounds, Wolf thought. *Fifteen minutes, with two-minute breaks in between.*

Seventeen more minutes and it would be over.

Across the expanse of mat, Dos Pastos looked incredibly sinewy and loose. He bounced up and down on his toes, his face showing total confidence as he stared at Wolf. He'd looked equally impressive at the weigh-in yesterday and didn't seem intimidated by Wolf at all, even though their size differential was obvious. Wolf was much bigger. He was heavier as well.

A little bit too heavy.

Despite having spent the better part of the day in the sauna sweating and flicking off perspiration, he'd come in five pounds over the limit. The officials gave him an hour to lose it, and despite another trip to the sauna and jogging in place the whole time, Wolf had still come in two-and-a-half pounds over. A fine was assessed, and the Dos Pastos camp was given the option of being awarded a forfeit. They'd declined, so the fight was on.

And now, after hours of trying to rehydrate himself and get ready, Wolf was still feeling weakened and depleted.

"Let him do his little fucking stare-down trying to look like a badass," Reno said. "He ain't nothing. You can take him."

"You bigger and better than him," Georgie added. "You a natural heavyweight now. And you is faster, too."

As if disputing that statement, across the mat, Dos

Pastos shot out a combination in the air in front of him. Each punch looked quick and powerful. His trainer's fingers massaged his fighter's neck, whose sullen expression on his face seemed to say, "All business."

Wolf took in a few deep breaths, clamping his teeth down on his mouthpiece. At least the hand felt pretty good. Georgie had wrapped it really tight, and it had fit snuggly, but not uncomfortably, into his glove. Wolf told himself he was as ready to go as he would ever be.

He almost believed it.

The announcer concluded his spiel and the ref stepped forward.

"Seconds out," he said.

Both Reno and Georgie gave Wolf a thumbs-up sign and they left the fenced-in ring. Dos Pastos's crew followed behind them, and the referee secured the gate and moved to the center of the mat.

"Are you ready here?" he said, glancing at Dos Pastos.

The Brazilian nodded.

The ref looked at Wolf. "Are you ready here?"

He nodded as well.

The air horn sounded.

* * *

FIFTH FLOOR MAINTENANCE AREA
THE FREIGHT ELEVATOR
THE WINTHROP HOTEL
PHOENIX, ARIZONA

Hawkins still held the bellman's neck in the crook of his arm, holding the limp body upright as he hit the STOP button, causing the freight elevator to lurch to a stop. They were between the fourth and fifth floors. The bellman had seemed surprised when the elevator had stopped and the doors automatically opened on the fourth floor and Hawkins and Peregrine had stepped inside. Hawkins nodded to him and stepped to one side of the cart, Peregrine to the other. The doors started closing and Hawkins had the bellman in a chokehold before they'd even finished moving. It only took him a few seconds of practiced technique to snap the man's neck.

To the best of their knowledge, no one had even noticed the little mini-cam they'd affixed to the door jamb across from room 526 two days ago. It was still in place transmitting flawlessly. Its mini transmitter and had provided videos giving them plenty of time to learn the routine of the group of US Marshals guarding the target. Room service three times a day at the same times, and nobody in or out of the room except at shift change. The poor bastards were working twelve-hour shifts, six to six. The housekeeping staff regularly delivered batches of clean towels and linen, but the occupants never left the room. The room service came and went with regularity, up and down the freight elevator three times a day, pushing the four-wheeled metallic little cart with the white cloth draped over it. The bellman was allowed to push the cart with the food inside, the door remaining open with one agent guarding the door, and then the bellman was dismissed after the one guarding the door signed something on the bellman's tablet. Hawkins had yet to see them give the poor fellows a decent tip, but perhaps that was included on the over-all computerized bill. That was the way things were done nowadays in this country, wasn't it? The copper who answered the door always had on a sports jacket, no doubt to cover his weapon. They were being careful, but not careful enough.

According to what Boulle's inside source had told them, the feds were once again getting ready to change locations, which meant that the timetable for the hit had to be moved up.

So tonight it was.

"Time?" Hawkins asked as he stooped down and picked up the limp form of the bellman.

"Seventeen-oh-seven," Peregrine said, checking his watch. "We're right on schedule."

Hawkins now dropped the body into the laundry cart, and the frame made a metallic squealing sound. Peregrine helped to cover the dead man with a few dirty sheets after slipping on the dead man's white jacket. The guy wasn't very big, and the kill had been clean and quick. A broken neck so there would be no worries about leakage.

Well, almost none, anyway.

Peregrine smiled and waved his hand in front of his nose.

Hawkins then caught the scent of feces and fresh urine lingering in the air. The poor bastard had been so scared he'd pissed and shit himself.

And all without a decent tip, he thought.

Hawkins was dressed very casually: a loose-fitting blue shirt with an emblem of a pizzeria emblazoned on the pocket, baggy jeans, and one of those ubiquitous baseball caps that Americans loved so much.

A perfect cover, he thought as he picked up the insulated nylon pizza delivery bag. It had an empty pizza carton inside to make sure it looked the part. Well, the box wasn't totally empty, just devoid of any pizza, but containing the FNX-Tactical 9mm, equipped with the sound suppressor and a red dot sighting system. Peregrine had the Sig Sauer, also equipped with a silencer, on the under-tray section of the cart. It would take him a moment longer to reach down and secure his weapon, so it was decided that Hawkins would fire first.

Peregrine rolled his shoulders and arms, trying to get used to the restrictive white bellman's jacket that he was now wearing.

"How's it fit?" the Hawk asked.

"Just like a tart's knickers," the Falcon said, slipping on a pair of latex gloves.

The Hawk slipped his on as well and reset the STOP button. The elevator continued its upward ascent to the fifth floor.

"Let's get to it," he said.

* * *

THE FIGHT ARENA
THE LUCKY STAR CASINO
LAS VEGAS, NEVADA

Wolf collapsed onto the stool and concentrated on getting his breathing back to normal as Georgie was massaging Wolf's arms and legs as the coolness of the ice pack against his neck began to revive him.

"You did good that round," Reno whispered into Wolf's ear. "You stayed away from his ground game and kept the stand-up going good. Keep it up."

"You the champ," Georgie said, rinsing off Wolf's mouthpiece and offering him the water bottle. "Just a little sip now."

Wolf felt a tiny bit of the liquid slide down his throat.

"Was it my round or his?" Wolf asked.

"I scored it pretty even," Reno said. "But you got to pick it up this round."

Wolf didn't take that as a good sign.

"Give me a little more water," he said.

"Huh-un." Georgie rubbed some more Vaseline over the contours of Wolf's face. "He ain't marked you up, but you caught him with some good ones. How's the hand?"

"It's good," Wolf lied. He was feeling a throbbing pain now after landing it a few times.

"Good," Georgie said. "Stay on your feet. You stronger than him."

Of that, Wolf wasn't quite so sure. He'd been surprised by the strength in the lean Brazilian's body. And he seemed fresh, bouncing up and down on his toes, not even sitting down between rounds. The taxing dehydration Wolf had gone through to try and make weight had drained him and he felt like he hadn't really recovered. He wondered if he had enough left in the tank to get through these next two rounds.

"It's tactical," Georgie said. "Outbox him. Don't go down to the mat unless you can take his back."

Wolf nodded at the instructions but knew as soon as the bell sounded he'd be going on instinct once again.

The whistle blew.

"Ten seconds," the referee yelled out. "Seconds out."

Georgie slipped the mouthpiece back in and Wolf adjusted it into place.

They all stood now and Reno and Georgie were moving toward the gate, as were Dos Pastos's corner crew. The Brazilian had a hint of a smile on his face, like he thought he was ahead.

Was he?

Wolf took a deep breath as the air horn sounded once

more and the ref dropped his outstretched arm, signaling that Round Two had begun.

* * *

FIFTH FLOOR HALLWAY AREA
THE WINTHROP HOTEL
PHOENIX, ARIZONA

The freight elevator stopped at the fifth floor and the elongated horizontal doors opened in clam-like fashion. Peregrine pushed the cart out into the corridor and Hawkins stepped out as well, carrying the insulated pizza bag. The elevator car would remain at this floor until someone pressed the button to manually close the doors. Hawkins didn't think the dead bellman would do that.

He gave Peregrine the lead, allowing him to get about twenty feet in front of him as they proceeded down the hallway toward room 526. The corridor was deserted.

So far, so good, Hawkins thought as he stopped in mid-step.

The empty pizza box gave the nylon bag a structured support. Hawkins's hand was inside the unzipped end of the bag holding the FNX.

This baby will remain hot without the bag, he thought with a smile. The only thing he was concerned about was the possibility of the gun jamming due to the cardboard lid interfering with the ejection of the spent cartridge. But he would deal with that if it happened. It wouldn't be the first time he'd cleared a malfunction.

"Room service," Peregrine announced in his best American accent as he knocked on the door. Hawkins was frozen in place about a dozen steps or so away, pretending to be looking at a paper on top of the insulated pizza bag. As soon as the door opened, he resumed his forward motion, coming to a stop right behind his partner.

"How's it going tonight?" Peregrine was saying. "Here's your order."

He sounded just like a Yank.

Hawkins stopped right in back of him and grinned as he looked at the US Marshal standing by the doorjamb, his sport jacket obviously covering a shoulder rig with his weapon.

No need to tip anyone off on the hotel staff that they were police guarding a special witness.

A special, soon-to-be-dead witness, he told himself.

"Hey, you guys order a pizza," Hawkins said in a loud voice, taking a step closer. It was a statement rather than a question.

He was right behind Peregrine now.

"Huh?" the guard said, shaking his head. "No. Wrong room."

Peregrine was past the doorway now and into the room, still pushing the cart, his right hand winding between the separations of the white cloth covering the Sig Sauer on the intermediate shelf.

"Room five-twenty-six," Hawkins said, also using an American accent. His wasn't as polished as his partner's, but he seldom found a need to use it.

"No," the guard said. "I told you, you got the wrong room."

He started to close the door but Hawkins stepped forward, thrusting the red and black insulated portable pizza bag into the space between the door and the jamb. His right hand was still inside the unzipped bag gripping the weapon, his left forefinger tapping the paper on top.

"Take a look at this order receipt, buddy. Right here." His left index finger tapped the paper again. "It says five-twenty-six, don't it?"

As the guard's eyes instinctively drifted downward toward the paper, Hawkins squeezed the trigger of the FNX. The detonating round made a slight plunking sound as it tore through the cardboard, the silver foil insulation, and the heavy nylon fabric. The marshal grunted and a red spot blossomed through the fabric of his light blue shirt. His hands fumbled slightly and then his right hand went inside the upper left side of his jacket.

Hawkins withdrew the FNX and let the warming glove fall to the ground. The weapon's slide had failed to cycle properly as a result of being inside the nylon encasement. A brass-colored empty shell casing rested perpendicularly in the ejection port opening. Grabbing the horizontally textured lines on the rear of the slide, he pulled it back as he tipped the weapon to the side, clearing the stove-piped shell casing. Letting the slide lurch forward, chambering another round, he again fired the weapon into the guard's chest. The sound suppressor made another sharp but muted sound, and the expended round ejected perfectly from the weapon's ejection port this time. A second crimson blossom began spreading on the man's chest, about three inches to the right of the first one. The guard crumpled to the floor and Hawkins fired a third round into the top of the downed man's head and used his foot to push the dead body away from the door.

Peregrine had shoved the cart the rest of the way into the room as he raised his Sig Sauer, achieved target acquisition, and shot two rounds into the second marshal, who was jacketless and standing off to the side with his gun still in its shoulder holster. The first two shots penetrated the man's chest, and then Peregrine added a third shot to the head, Mozambique style.

The protected soon-to-be witness, Robert Bray, was lying on the bed, legs outstretched and a stack of pillows cushioning his back. His hand dropped the remote for the television as the corners of his mouth jerked downward in a look of sheer terror. Before he could utter a sound, a round, black hole appeared in the center of his forehead and his head jerked back, a gush of blood flowing from his nostrils and mouth as his body slumped against the pillowed backdrop. Peregrine shot him two more times in the chest and side. The lack of response indicated that the man was already dead. Hawkins stepped around, surveying the rest of the room, including the bathroom, but there was no one else in the room.

"Get his badge, ID, and gun." Peregrine motioned toward the man Hawkins had killed and then kneeled beside the second fallen marshal and pulled his gun from its holster. "I'll get this one's. They'll come in handy for the other part."

Hawkins stooped down and stripped the man of those possessions, dumping them into the pizza bag. He held it open for Peregrine to drop the other one's stuff inside and then zipped it closed.

"Let's take those too," Peregrine said, pointing to three ballistic bulletproof vests in heavy black nylon carriers with *US MARSHAL SERVICE* embroidered across the fronts. With quick deliberation, he grabbed the vests and stuffed them inside the room service cart, carefully tucking the long white covering cloth back in place to conceal them.

The Hawk then took out his cell phone, placed it in

camera mode, and snapped a couple of pictures of the now-deceased Robert Bray. A little documentation never hurt.

Stopping to survey their handiwork for a moment more, Hawkins then moved to the door and peered through the peephole.

No one was visible.

He pulled the door open a crack.

Nothing either way.

He pulled the door open the rest of the way and stepped into the hallway. Peregrine followed, pushing the food cart through the door. He paused briefly to leap upward and pull the mini-cam from its position above the door of the room opposite 526, and then lightly landed on his feet to resume their trek back to the freight elevator.

All in a good day's work, Hawkins thought.

He hoped the next part would go as smoothly.

* * *

THE FIGHT ARENA
THE LUCKY STAR CASINO
LAS VEGAS, NEVADA

They were three minutes and fifty-four seconds into the third and final round when Wolf saw the opening. Dos Pastos tossed out a quick combination, but dropped his left hand as he threw his right. Wolf pivoted and delivered a straight right to the side of the other man's face. He went right down, his body crumpling like a paper lantern. The electric shock in Wolf's hand traveled right up his arm and stopped at the shoulder. It was like he'd dislocated the joint for a brief second, and then he felt normal again. But it had caused him to lose those crucial seconds to follow his opponent down to the mat and gain a superior position.

"Ground and pound, Steve," Reno was shouting. "Ground and pound!"

But just as Wolf was advancing, shaking his right hand to try and restore it, Dos Pastos was moving, doing an inverted crab-like crawl away from him and toward the cyclone fencing. Wolf tried to mount him, but Dos Pastos raised both feet off the mat and started a cycle of kicks. Not wanting to get caught with one of those, Wolf backed off and circled to the side. He still had a chance to achieve dominance, but Dos Pastos had already done a half-turn and pushed his fingers through the diagonal metallic squares, gripping the fence and pulling himself upward.

Their sweaty bodies collided and Wolf mashed him against the fence, pummeling him with left hooks and right elbows.

Wolf heard him grunt.

A good sign. That usually meant the other man was hurt.

It could be over.

"Let go of the fence," the ref called out.

Dos Pastos kept his right hand entwined in the metal but reached out and used his left arm to encircle Wolf's back, drawing him closer.

The two of them writhed together like a pair of unlikely lovers. Wolf felt himself being pulled off balance and his left arm shot out and grabbed the fence as well.

"Let go of the fence," the ref called out again, and then, "Break."

Wolf felt the referee's hand pulling the two of them apart. He repositioned them to the center of the mat.

"Go," the ref said.

Wolf could see that his opponent's eyes were clear now and focused. He'd almost recovered from the knockdown and danced artfully away, throwing a couple of effete jabs.

I can take him out if I can catch him, Wolf thought, despite the throbbing in his right hand. He lumbered forward on legs that felt as stiff as the Tin Man's in *The Wizard of Oz*.

They exchanged punches again, most of the blows bouncing off outstretched arms and sweat-covered shoulders.

"Work the body," Georgie called out. "Go for the liver."

Wolf tried, but his right slid off his opponent's slick side.

They circled each other again, and in another second, the blast from the air horn sounded, signaling the end of the round and the fight.

It was up to the judges now.

Dos Pastos, his face red and his jaw already starting to swell, stepped forward, his arms outstretched. Wolf did the same. It was time to embrace again, but this time with an air of finality and mutual respect.

* * *

WOLF'S LOCKER ROOM
THE LUCKY STAR CASINO
LAS VEGAS, NEVADA

The mood in the locker room was both volatile and somber. Wolf sat on the rub-down table and twisted the cap off a bottle of Gatorade. He then replaced his right hand back in the ice bucket that was overflowing with half-melted cubes. At least now there were no more pounds to lose. Yolanda stood close, pressing herself against him, despite her elegant outfit being next to Wolf's now rank-smelling body. He knew he'd have to hit the shower sooner rather than later, but had to take the piss test first. McNamara was off to the right and had one arm around Miss Dolly and the other around Brenda. Despite this, the expression on his face was dour looking.

Wolf knew Mac still blamed himself for causing the injury to Wolf's right hand, but he didn't know if it would have made any difference. In his mind, he felt that the weight-loss regimen trying to drop down to two-oh-six was the real culprit. He'd felt weak from the get-go. His right hand probably hadn't factored into it that much at all.

As if in reassurance, he clenched and unclenched his right a few times in the ice bucket. The numbness from the ice negated most of the pain, but he still felt a twinge or two.

"How in the hell can you beat the shit out of a guy for three fucking rounds," Reno said, "knock his ass down in the third, and come up short on two of the judge's cards?"

"It wasn't unanimous," Georgie said.

Nor could it be considered a hometown decision, Wolf thought. *Not with Dos Pastos being from Brazil.*

At least the Gatorade tasted good, and he hadn't suffered any lasting injuries other than feeling sore in all the wrong places. The main thing was that it was over.

When the decision had been announced, it had been met by assorted boos from the audience, but Wolf paid little attention to the audience. Instead, he offered his hand to Dos Pastos, who shook it and muttered something in Portuguese that Wolf assumed was "Good fight." Whether he thought he'd won or not, it hardly mattered. Every fighter always felt they'd won when it came down to a close decision. But in reality, all that counted was the way the judges had seen it.

Only one of them gave it to Wolf, so his "O" was no more.

"Well," Wolf said, managing a halfhearted grin, "at least with a performance like that, we'll have people lining up wanting to get a shot at me."

"It's all total bullshit," Reno muttered.

"I thought you won, honey," Yolanda said.

She was wearing his favorite yellow dress that complemented her luscious brown skin and showed off her great figure and enough cleavage to make Wolf wish he could just whisk her out of here and back to his assigned suite right then and there.

"You did good, Steve," Miss Dolly said.

Brenda nodded in agreement. "Real good."

Wolf wished they hadn't seen him lose, but at least it was by decision.

"I don't think I got my ass kicked too bad," he said with a wry grin.

"Well, I don't know about that," Pike said, holding a beer. "But at least we didn't have anybody shooting at us afterward like last time."

Reno frowned and rolled his eyes. "Why don't you just shut the hell up? Nobody likes a smart ass."

"I'll have you know that I minored in being a likable smart-ass in college," Pike said.

Reno clenched his fist and started toward the big fed but was restrained by Georgie.

"Been enough fightin' for one night," he said.

Pike took a swig from the bottle and remained silent.

"Yeah," Wolf said. "Let's count our blessings."

No trouble was indeed a blessing. Another shootout in a hotel after one of his fights would certainly spell the end of his MMA career. But he'd been planning on calling it quits anyway. That was until the mounting bills started to catch up to him. And the fine for being over the weight limit was going to cut into his purse even more. Reno hadn't told him how much that fine was going to be, but Wolf was sure it was going to hurt just as much as getting hit below the belt when you weren't wearing a cup.

At least the P-Patrol and his lady love were there and Wolf was sure they were probably all armed to the teeth. He knew Yolanda might be wearing her off-duty, rhinestone-covered SCCY .380, but where he had no idea. He looked forward to finding out. Mac and Pike had to be packing as well. He felt well protected, that was for sure.

"No doubt about it," Pike said. "You got robbed."

Wolf took another much-needed drink from the water bottle and smirked.

"I hope you were true to your word and bet on the other guy," he said.

"Are you kidding?" Pike said. "I did what I always do. I bet on both of you. That way, I don't lose out too much, no matter who wins. Of course, I always bet a little more on my favorite."

"I wonder which one of us that was," Wolf said.

Pike snorted and was about to answer when his cell phone rang. He shoved his beer bottle into Reno's hand and managed to fish the cell phone out of his pocket.

At least Reno did smack him with it, Wolf thought.

He took another swing of Gatorade and saw the commission official standing there with the empty plastic bottle and a somber expression on his face. Sliding off the table, Wolf handed his Gatorade to Yolanda and lumbered on sore legs into the washroom with the official trailing behind.

Once inside, he rolled down his trunks, pulled out his cup supporter, accepted the bottle, and stepped to the urinal. This was always the most difficult part. It was necessary to make sure that the fighter didn't have any banned substances in his system, or wasn't given anything illegal between rounds. After a good solid two minutes of straining and drinking copious amounts of water, he was able to fill the sample bottle about halfway.

At least it's not bloody, he thought as he held the bottle up and studied the amber contents.

After opening the door, he half-expected to hear Pike making some stupid joke about what Wolf and the official had been doing in the washroom so long, but Pike wasn't anywhere to be seen.

"Where's Pike?" Wolf asked McNamara.

Mac shrugged, his arms still around each lady.

"He took that call and then stepped out in the hall," McNamara said. "Didn't say nothing to nobody."

Wolf turned and walked to the door. After opening it, he saw the corridor was deserted except for a couple of hotel security guards.

Everybody must be over at Dos Pastos's room, he thought. Everybody loves a winner.

Wolf went back inside and was about to announce that it was time for him to go back to his room and take a nice, long, hot shower when McNamara's cell phone rang. Mac initially ignored it, and it quit ringing, only to start again a few seconds later. This time he heaved a sigh, extricated his arms from Miss Dolly and Brenda, took his cell phone out of his pocket and looked at the screen.

"Yeah," he said into the phone. "Whaddya want?"

He listened intently for the better part of thirty seconds and his face took on a somber expression, like he'd just heard some real bad news.

"Okay," he said, and handed the phone to Wolf, adding, "It's Pike."

"What's up?" Wolf said. "Where'd you go?"

"Steve," Pike said. "You and Mac need to be on high alert. They hit the safe house where they were keeping Bray. He's dead. So are the two marshals that were guarding him."

Wolf heard Pike's heavy sigh.

"One of them was Ed Quincy, a good friend of mine. The other one was named Nolan. Both good cops."

"I'm sorry to hear that," Wolf said.

Yolanda was staring at him now, trying to read him.

"Yeah, well, thanks," Pike said. "I'm renting a car now and gonna head back to Phoenix. You and Mac need to be on high alert. There's probably nothing to worry about, but we'd best err on the side of caution. Get outta that room and maybe even change hotels. Or else come back tonight."

"You think it's that bad?" Wolf asked.

He heard Pike exhale loudly. "Hard to say right now, but for all we know, you two might be numbers one and two on the hit parade. No way of knowing if they got somebody watching you."

Wolf considered the options. Changing hotels was probably out of the question. Besides, if they were under surveillance, what would stop whoever might be watching from following them to their new location. The Lucky Star had given them suites, and you needed a special key to get to that particular floor. And the hotel security was already on high alert. Driving back to Phoenix in the dark didn't seem viable either. The best course of action at the moment would be to return to their suites and stay alert.

"Mac's strapped, right?" Pike asked, shaking Wolf out of his speculations.

"Yeah," he said. "And so are the ladies."

Pike emitted a halfhearted chuckle.

"Well, there you go," Pike said. "Okay, I gotta scoot. I'll let you know more when I do. Until then, stay safe."

"Will do," Wolf said and handed the phone back to McNamara, who had a questioning look on his face.

Wolf managed to smile, but his thoughts were anything but merry.

This was getting to be like riding on a merry-go-round that was downrange at the gun club.

* * *

EXECUTIVE SUITE
LUCKY STAR HOTEL AND CASINO
LAS VEGAS, NEVADA

Wolf had spent about a good fifteen minutes in the shower soaping up and letting the hot water run off of him. Now, feeling clean and reasonably refreshed, he shut off the flow and dried himself with one of the fluffy towels. Fastening the towel around his waist, he left the bathroom and went into the bedroom section. Her bright-yellow dress was draped over the back of one of the chairs. She was sitting in the bed, the sheet artfully wrapped around her full breasts, her back against a pillow, the most alluring smile tracing over her lips. The white fabric of the sheet in contrast to her dark skin sent a thrill through him, and suddenly the exhaustion that had been plaguing him suddenly evaporated, replaced by the growing fire of desire. Wolf could tell she was naked, or at least assumed her to be, but undressing her, if she still had on any panties, would also be a treat. Her Beretta Px4 Storm with the satin-colored slide over the black frame was on the bedside table next to her.

"What happened to the fancy little SCCY three-eighty I bought you?" he asked.

She smiled. "After what happened last time, I wanted to be loaded for bear."

"Good to know," he said.

They'd already secured the safety lock and alerted hotel security. McNamara, Miss Dolly, and Brenda were all safely ensconced in an adjacent suite on the same floor, so any thoughts of the danger Pike had expressed was the farthest thing on his mind at the moment.

He went around to the other side of the bed, undid the towel, and tossed it on a chair a few feet away. Lifting the sheet, he couldn't resist and started to peer underneath it.

Yolanda's arm swept down on top of it.

"No peeking," she said. "A girl's got to maintain her modesty."

He hadn't been able to tell if she was still wearing underpants, but no matter. He sat down on the bed and stretched his legs under the sheet without touching hers.

"Okay," he said, putting both of his hands behind his head. "I'm kind of tired anyway."

"You are?"

He grinned.

She rolled closer, her hands settling on his upper chest.

"I'll bet you're hurting, aren't you, baby?" she said.

"Terribly."

Her hands began to knead his shoulders and then moved to his pectoral muscles.

"Does this feel good?" she asked.

Wolf intentionally hesitated and then said, "Kind of."

"How about this?"

Her hands moved a little bit lower.

"Keep going," he said. "I'll tell you if it doesn't."

She moved her mouth close to his, and they kissed.

Her hands moved lower still.

He brought his hand from behind his head and caressed her back. It felt smooth and sleek and muscular. His hand moved lower and felt the elastic band of an undergarment and then her bare backside.

She was wearing panties. Or rather, a thong.

"Want me to take that off?" she asked, her voice low, with the hint and promise of seduction.

"No," he said. "I want to do that myself."

CHAPTER 10

**THE HIGHWAY NEAR THE MCNAMARA RANCH
PHOENIX, ARIZONA**

The more things changed, Wolf reflected once again as he pushed his sore body through the punishing and ritualistic morning run, the more they stayed the same.

After spending a leisurely Sunday morning in bed with Yolanda yesterday, he'd justified skipping his run due to the residual soreness from the fight. Then, after lunch, they'd all headed back in the cars, caravan style—Yolanda and him in her vehicle, Mac in his Escalade, and Miss Dolly and Brenda in their ride. The P-Patrol had insisted on accompanying Wolf and Mac back to the ranch after hearing Pike's warning about the possible danger factor.

Elegant ladies all.

But Wolf was getting real tired of constantly looking over his shoulder. In a way, it reminded him of his last tour in Iraq when he was in the Green Zone and everything had pretty much been relegated to a low grade,

Alpha Blue status to Bravo Yellow when you went out on patrol. Sure, there were always concerns about snipers and IEDs, but all the major league combat clearing missions had been completed. However, he reminded himself, things had turned to shit in an instant and he'd ended up on the wrong side of a court marshal.

That was then. This was now, and here he was up at Bravo Yellow again.

It wasn't supposed to be this way on the home front, and he vowed to do something—anything to try and eliminate the threat.

But what could he do?

Not one whole hell of a lot, he decided. But at least he was wearing the Glock in the shoulder holster again.

Yolanda had on running shorts and a baggy top. He knew that underneath it, she wore a belly-band holster with the Beretta securely fitted against her abdomen. She was running beside him this morning and having no problem keeping up. Wolf couldn't decide if that was because she was in such great shape or he was just extra slow.

Of course, he told himself, she didn't have the shit kicked out of her less than forty-eight hours ago either.

"We going all the way up the mountain?" she asked.

Her face was covered with perspiration, but her respiration was good.

"That's up to you," he said. "I'm up for it if you are."

"Yeah, that's cool. You know I graduated first in my class in physical fitness at the police academy, right? And I got the award to prove it."

He remembered seeing it displayed prominently on the wall of her apartment when they'd stopped there for her to pack her overnight bag. He also remembered that she had to be back at work tomorrow for afternoon shift. That meant an early departure tomorrow morning.

She seemed to sense what he was thinking.

"Why don't you come stay with me for a while," she said. "Nobody'll think to look for you staying in Vegas."

"What about Mac?"

"He can come too, but—" She giggled. "He's gonna have to be sleeping on the couch."

"I'm sure Miss Dolly would welcome him at her place if it came to that." The ugly specter of the threat surfaced again. "But I wouldn't want to expose you to the danger."

"Danger?" She laughed and then quickened her pace. He had to take it up a notch to keep up. "I'm a cop, for Christ's sake."

They were almost to the mountain trail cut off. Wolf instinctively glanced around. No cars in the vicinity.

Back to Alpha Blue status.

"It's not fair to you," he said. "Or to Mac."

"What do you mean?"

They started the uphill trek on the dirt path up the mountain.

"I doubt he'd stay in Vegas very long," he said. "Not with Kasey and Chad here. And I'm not about to leave him to fend for himself, ex-Special Forces, or not."

Wolf was feeling a little bit of agony with each step. The incline was killing his legs.

He glanced down and caught a glimpse of Yolanda's smooth, muscular brown legs pumping and he wished they'd spent more time in bed this morning.

But there was still time after they'd showered.

That thought gave him an extra burst of energy and he felt a renewal of strength.

They both touched the mile marker and started heading back down.

Traffic was picking up, and he saw a couple of pairs of headlights moving along the road. They were too far away to tell much, but the hairs on the back of his neck began to stand up.

Back to Bravo Yellow alert status.

Was this damn thing ever going to end?

* * *

FEDERAL BUILDING
OFFICE OF US ATTORNEY BENJAMIN TURNER
PHOENIX, ARIZONA

Chester Loudermilk could feel the steady trickle of sweat dripping down from his armpits. His mouth was dry, his hands soaking wet. Suddenly, the burner phone vibrated with a text, and not just any text...it was *the* text.

They are in position. Make the call, then send the fax.

Okay, he texted back.

Damn them, he thought. They never quit. It was always something more that needed to be done.

This was definitely the last damn time, though. After this, he'd unofficially retire.

He glanced back to check on Turner's status.

The office door was closed, but the button for the outgoing phone line was still lit up. The asshole was gabbing with someone, waiting for the cup of coffee that he'd sent Loudermilk for a few minutes earlier. He pushed the cup of vending machine coffee away from the phone and made sure the little plastic lid was securely fastened. It wouldn't do to spill any, and the lid would more or less preserve the liquid's heat until it was time.

He picked up the phone, punched a button for an outside line, and dialed the number for intake and outtake section at the Federal Correctional Institute, Satellite Facility Beta. The woman who answered the phone did so crisply and professionally. Loudermilk hoped he wouldn't be dealing with her. The last thing he needed was some officious bitch that would give him a bunch of red tape regulations bullshit.

"Yes," he said, lowering his voice in the hope that it would imbue the sound of authority. "This is Chester Loudermilk from the office of US Attorney Benjamin Turner. Let me speak to whoever's in charge. I've got two US Marshals standing by outside your place for a special prisoner pick-up to be transported here for a crucial interview."

He hoped adding the word "crucial" would pay dividends.

"A prisoner pick-up?" the woman said, her voice drifting off to vagueness. After a few seconds, she added, "I've got no record of this."

"Look," Loudermilk said. "This is a highly classified operation. Her attorney contacted us over the weekend, and we just set this up. I called over there yesterday and talked to somebody about it."

"Yesterday was Sunday, sir. I have no record of it."

Loudermilk heaved a sigh. "I was worried this might happen. What's your fax number? I'll send you a copy of the authorization, but please expedite this. We're trying to get her in front of a federal grand jury later this morning."

"All right," she said slowly. "What did you say your name was again?"

"Loudermilk. Chester A." He hated to use his real name, but he knew he had little choice. More than likely, she'd want to call him back to verify he was who he said he was.

"What's the prisoner's name?"

"Last name Swenstrom." He spelled it out. "First name Bridgette." He spelled that also. "And please don't broadcast it. She's being held in isolation due to death threats. This is a highly important case."

"Okay," the bitch said. "I'll have to run this by my supervisor."

Loudermilk sighed again, adding a bit more theatrical emphasis this time.

"Like I told you, I have a pair of US Marshals standing by outside your facility with the subject's lawyer. We've got to get her here and prepped so she can go before the grand jury this morning. I'll fax you the authorization forth with. What's your name?"

"Officer Preston," she said. "My boss's name is Sergeant Criswell."

"Fine. I'll make it attention to you. Please call me back to verify it went through with no problems."

"Copy that," she said. "But I'm still going to have to run this by my supervisor. What's your number?"

He rattled off the number for his office extension and repeated his name.

"Please give this matter your utmost and prompt attention," he said. "I'm going to send the fax now."

She said she would, and he hung up.

His palms were so wet that the phone almost slipped out of his hand. He wiped them on his pants.

One hurdle down, two to go.

He scrawled her name on a fax cover sheet and then crumpled it up, deciding it was almost illegible. Using his best penmanship, Loudermilk carefully printed *ATTEN-TION OFFICER PRESTON/SERGEANT CRISWELL*. He filled out the sender information and placed the paper into the folder that contained the authorization letter he'd typed up and copied, using the signature from one of Turner's previously signed letters. They wouldn't be able to tell it wasn't authentic on the fax. His major problem was that the fax machine was on Turner's desk and he couldn't let the asshole see him using it. Taking in a deep breath, he stuck the folder under his left arm, pausing to lower it slightly when his thumb brushed over the enormous and growing sweat stain emanating from his armpit. Picking up the coffee with his right hand, he worked his thumb under the plastic lid causing it to loosen. A few drops slid over the lip of the cup and touched his skin.

All the better. It was still moderately hot.

This should work, he thought. *If not, I'm fucked.*

It was the equivalent of a Hail Mary play.

Glancing over at his desk, he saw that the phone line was still lit up.

Still gabbing away, the fat son of a bitch.

After tapping on the door, he used his left hand to twist the doorknob. Turner was leaning back in his cushioned chair, his feet on the desk, the phone cradled by his right shoulder, and a nail file in his hands.

This figures, Loudermilk thought. *The son of a bitch is sitting around filing his nails so he'll look good in court, should he ever get there, while I do all the work.*

He was suddenly glad to be making this end run.

Loudermilk strode forward purposely. Turner was smiling as he murmured into the phone, motioning with his left hand for Loudermilk to set the coffee on the desk.

Instead of doing that, he moved around the side of the desk, still holding the coffee in front of him. Stretching, as if he were going to place it on the desktop, Loudermilk extended his arm and faked a stumble, lurching forward and popping the lid off, he watched as a torrent of coffee, cream and extra sugar, cascaded outward and landed, right on target.

Turner screamed and jerked his feet off the desk.

The fat underlip of his belly was wet and so was the front of his tan pants. It looked like he'd peed himself.

Loudermilk affected an expression of horror.

"Oh, Lord, I'm so sorry."

"You stupid idiot," Turner said, rising. "What hell's the matter with you?"

"I sorry, sir. I tripped."

"What the hell…" Turner glanced down at his front and muttered into the phone, "I'll call you back. My dumbass assistant just spilled some coffee on me. Hot coffee."

He slammed the phone down into the receiver and glared at Loudermilk.

"I'm sorry, sir," Loudermilk repeated, setting the folder on the desk and taking out his handkerchief. "Let me help you."

He reached toward Turner's crotch, and the other man jerked backward.

"Get away from me," he said.

"You need to put some cold water on that right away," Loudermilk said. "Or it'll stain."

Turner brushed at his pants, snorted in exasperation, and then strode around the opposite side of the desk.

"Clean up this mess," he said. "I'm going to the men's room. I'll deal with you when I get back."

No you won't, Loudermilk thought. *Because I won't be here, you officious, self-centered, egotistical son of a bitch.*

It felt good to tell the asshole off, even sub-vocally.

After Turner had stormed out, Loudermilk quickly set the cover sheet and letter in place on the fax tray, picked up the phone, and punched in the number Officer Preston had given him. It rang twice and then the rollers of the machine took the two sheets, one by one. It made the customary squealing sounds, stopped, and then printed out a confirming receipt. Loudermilk retrieved the two sheets and replaced them in the folder. He thought about putting them in the shredder but decided to wait until he got the confirmation back. Using his handkerchief to sop up what coffee had landed on the desktop, he then wrung the cloth out while holding it over Turner's chair.

A final gift, he thought. *Hopefully, a wet ass.*

He could hear his phone ringing and hoped it was Preston calling back with the confirmation. Getting there just after the third ring, he snatched the receiver up and answered with, "Loudermilk."

"Yes, sir," Officer Preston said. "We got the authorization. She's being brought down now. Tell your marshals I'm notifying the gate."

"Okay," Loudermilk said. "Their names are Nolan and Quincy. For security reasons, they're driving an olive-drab Lexus RX 350 SUV. It's an undercover vehicle."

"Roger that," Preston said. "I can see them on the camera now."

"Thanks for all your help," Loudermilk said.

"Always thank the little people," he told himself as he hung up. He immediately texted Boulle back with a message that it was all set.

Good, came the reply.

Loudermilk looked around the outer office.

Was there anything he needed to take with him?

Only the folder with the letter and fax sheet. There was nothing else worth taking. And he did want to leave before fat-ass Turner got back. Taking a pink message slip from the pad, he scrawled that he was going home sick and taped it to Turner's door.

With that done, he headed out of the office and knew he was never going to return.

Don't look back, he thought. *I've got a flight to catch.*

* * *

FEDERAL CORRECTIONAL INSTITUTE
SATELLITE FACILITY BETA
PHOENIX, ARIZONA

Hawkins had a growing feeling of anxiety as he received the confirming call from Boulle on the burner phone.

"It is set. Loudermilk has sent the fax. Did you get the picture of the authorization letter I emailed you."

"We did," Hawkins said.

"Good," Boulle said. "The names of the officers he spoke to in the prison are Preston and Criswell."

"Got it."

"Any questions?"

"No. Sounds right as the rain," Hawkins said, thinking of all the separate pieces that had to come into play for them to pull this one off. But if they did, it would be one for the record books. He terminated the call and drove up to the huge metallic gate sandwiched between two immense cement pillars. A forty-foot wall branched out in both directions on either side of the pillars. A gate shack was built onto one of them.

Hawkins could see two uniformed figures inside, one large and masculine, the other most likely distaff, or so it looked. Seconds later, he saw that he was right. A squat-looking Black female came ambling out of the door of the gate shack, her face with a querulous expression. She was wearing a sidearm in a nylon holster, and her male partner, a big white fellow standing inside the gate shack, had what appeared to be a semi-automatic twelve gauge shotgun.

"Can I help you?" she asked. Her uniform shirt had short sleeves and there were rings of sweat staining the underarms on both sides of her tan uniform.

"US Marshals," Hawkins said, using an American accent. "Quincy and Nolan here to pick up a prisoner." He jerked his thumb at the back seat. "Got the subject's lawyer here, too."

The guard's eye went to each of them.

"Prisoner pick-up?"

"Right," he said. "The US Attorney set it up this morning. Should have faxed over the order to Sergeant Criswell."

She went back to the gate shack and stepped inside to speak with the other guard. He picked up a phone and waited.

Hawkins could feel that nervous chill run up and down his spine. It was always like this on these subterfuges. He hated being dependent on the actions of some nervous Nellie miles away who was responsible for setting things up. There was so much that could go wrong.

The female guard and the other one spoke, and then she turned, stepped out, and ambled back toward their car.

"IDs," the guard said.

Hawkins glanced at the lawyer, Moore, in the rearview mirror. The son of a bitch looked like he was about to shit his pants. He fumbled as he got out his bar card.

Hawkins pulled back his loose blue shirt. They were both supposed to be undercover operatives and were clad in soft clothes and baseball caps. Additionally, both he and Peregrine had those idiotic black surgical masks fastened around their chins. He reached into the chest pocket of his vest covering, removing the black badge case they'd taken from the dead marshal on Saturday, and flipped it open. The doctored ID now had his picture instead of that of the deceased marshal, and the alterations were virtually unnoticeable through the clear plastic overlay.

Peregrine held up his as well.

Her dark eyes flashed from one to the other and then back to her partner inside the gate shack, who nodded.

"Drive over to Building C," the guard said, pointing to a solid brick structure with a massive overhead door. "Wait for them to raise the door, pull in, and leave your weapons in the lockboxes, and they'll buzz you through the small door."

Hawkins grunted something that sounded like a thank you and saw the prison gate retracting. He shifted out of park and drove through into the main yard of the prison, feeling a distinct bump as the SUV traversed what had to be some kind of mechanical device that could be activated to deflate a vehicle's tires.

As they pulled up at Building C, the big door began to roll upward just as they arrived in front of it. The inside of the sally-port was empty except for a series of four metal boxes along one wall. Sets of keys dangled from the locking mechanism of each one. A solid metal door was to the right of them with *INTAKE/OUTTAKE* stenciled on it with black lettering. The door, like the walls, was painted a pale green color.

"You might as well wait in the car," Peregrine said to Moore.

The obese attorney nodded.

Hawkins noticed that the sweat was pouring off the man.

This one was definitely a dandy, he thought. *I'm glad we don't have to depend on him for any of this.*

Hawkins slipped on a pair of latex gloves and pulled up the mask to cover his face. Peregrine did the same. They both got out and went to the gun lockers. A Pan-Tilt-and-Zoom camera was mounted on the wall adjacent to the door, and Hawkins was glad the ridiculous COVID emergency restrictions were still loosely in effect, and they had the masks covering most of their faces.

Mass hysteria is an undercover operative's best friend, he thought.

After they'd both secured their weapons, the solid metal door to the right of them popped open with an accompanying electrical buzz. Hawkins grabbed the steel handle and swung the door back, allowing Peregrine to enter first.

The room on the other side of the door had a long counter with three telephones on it. A radio console was built into the perpendicular section jutting up at a right angle to the counter, and several television monitors were inlaid into it. Three guards, two male and one female, clad in tan uniforms, stood by in the nice, air-conditioned coolness.

No sweat stains here, Hawkins thought, conscious of his own sour body odor. But who's to complain anyway?

He smiled, even though he knew the mask was blocking the majority of his face.

"You Criswell?" he asked the one with the sergeant chevrons.

The man gave a fractional nod. He appeared to be Hispanic, which didn't fit the name, but Hawkins wasn't in the mood to speculate on that anomaly.

"We're here to pick up Bridgette Swenstrom," Hawkins said. "The US Attorney should have faxed over the order this morning."

"Right," Criswell said. "They're bringing her down now."

None of them were wearing masks and Hawkins was hoping they wouldn't question him or Peregrine about theirs. Another set of PTZ cameras were mounted on the wall above them no doubt recording this little drama for posterity and what would soon be a future investigation.

But we'll be long gone by then, Hawkins told himself, realizing that the sweat stains were probably starting to form under his own armpits, despite the relative coolness of the internal environment.

"Preston," Sergeant Criswell said. "You got that DD-ten-sixty-niner?"

"Sure do, sarge," the female said and held up a clipboard with a paper attached to it.

Hawkins flipped up the covering on his vest pocket and pulled out the doctored ID again.

Better to act official and proffer the damn thing, he thought.

He opened it up and displayed it, the US Marshal's badge on one side, the plastic slot with the picture ID on the other.

"Quincy, US Marshal Service," he said.

Peregrine had his open as well.

"Nolan," he said.

They both were doing a passable job of affecting an Americanized accent.

"Sign here," Office Preston said, tapping a blank line on the form. "Print your names and badge numbers also."

Hawkins signed first and then handed the clipboard to Peregrine. Preston seemed to be looking askance at their gloves and masks.

Seizing the initiative, Hawkins said, "You guys don't need to wear masks and gloves in here?"

Criswell snorted a laugh and patted his pistol belt, which had several pouches attached to it, but no weapon.

"We got gloves in case we come into contact with bodily fluids," he said. "As far as them damn masks, I hope you realize they ain't worth shit."

It was Hawkins's turn to laugh, and he also gave a commiserating wink.

"Yeah, I know what you mean, but..." He gave a quick shrug. "What can I say? Our boss is so anal he probably wears one of these when he bangs his old lady."

That brought a round of laughs all around, except for Preston, who accepted the clipboard from Peregrine.

A second door buzzed open and a male guard escorted a woman wearing an orange prison jumpsuit through the doorway. She had a classically beautiful face that was attractive despite being devoid of makeup. Her blonde hair had been cropped short, and she had a placid expression on her face.

Hawkins took out a pair of handcuffs but before he could administer them, Preston strode over to the woman and told her to turn around, spread her legs, and put her hands on her head, interlocking her fingers. Preston slipped on a pair of thin leather gloves.

Bridgette complied, her neck tightening slightly as

Preston began a quick but thorough pat-down. With one hand grasping the other woman's clasped hands, Preston moved quickly over the contours of Bridgette's upper body and then went lower.

"Lean over backward," Preston said. "You know the drill."

Bridgette grunted as she did so.

Preston's fingers continued her probing and stopped when she got to Bridgette's crotch.

"What's this?" Preston said and slapped between the other woman's legs.

"I'm in my period," Bridgette said, her voice hostile.

"Yeah, right," Preston said and stood up, still holding onto Bridgette's hands while walking her to the corner of the room with two holding cells.

Aw, hell, Hawkins thought. *This whole thing could turn to shit in a hurry.*

"Face that way, palms on the wall," Preston said, keeping Bridgette's front away from the men in the room. "Now spread your legs."

Bridgette hesitated for a moment but then complied. Preston pulled back on the elastic waistband and jammed her hand down the back of the orange pants. A moment later, she came up with a cell phone.

Double shit, Hawkins thought. *That's got to be the burner.*

Why the hell hadn't she left it in her cell?

"What's this?" Preston said.

Bridgette didn't reply.

Preston extended her arm out behind her. One of the male guards reached forward to take it, but Preston made a tsking sound.

"Better put on your gloves first," she said. "She had it partially in the vault."

The male guard took out a pair of latex gloves from a small pouch on his belt, slipped them on, and accepted the cell phone. A second guard pulled open a drawer on the counter and removed a paper bag, and opened it up.

"Lemme see that phone first," Criswell said. He already had his gloves on.

Preston handed him the phone, and he studied it.

It was apparently turned off.

"Where'd you get this?" he asked Bridgette, who was now turned around and facing them. Her eyes shot to Hawkins, and she said nothing.

Knowing this could easily ruin everything, Hawkins glanced at Peregrine, who usually took the lead in any type of complexities.

"Excuse me, Sergeant," he said. "But we're on a timetable here. The US Attorney's waiting and was on our asses to get her over to the federal building ASAP. He has to prep her for the grand jury and he's already running late."

"You know how those anal assholes are," Hawkins added, following his partner's lead.

Criswell held the phone in his hand for a few more minutes and then dropped it into the evidence bag.

"Write her up," he said, motioning with his head for Preston to bring the prisoner over to them. "We can deal with it when she gets back."

Hawkins felt a flood of relief.

Almost undone by the idiot hiding something in her twat. Christ, what a stupid bitch. He glared at her.

But she was good-looking. He wondered what she'd look like without that baggy orange jumpsuit.

"Turn around, Miss," he said. "And put your hands behind your back."

She did so.

He heaved a sigh of relief as he snapped the handcuffs over her outstretched wrists and pressed down the little circular pin, double-locking them.

"Good search," he said to Preston. "Thanks."

Preston shrugged. "We always make it our policy to search on entry and exit. It could have been a shiv."

"Damn straight," Hawkins said. "Let's go, Miss."

They went to the door, and it popped open with another loud buzzing sound. Hawkins walked her to the back door of the Lexus, thinking they were almost home free. After shoving her into the vehicle and fastening her seatbelt, he turned and opened the driver's door. Before he could get in, he saw Peregrine standing next to him, dangling a key on a circular ring in front of him.

"Forget something?" he said, not bothering to use his American accent.

Hawkins then realized he'd left his gun, or rather the dead marshal's gun, in the lockbox.

As he was retrieving it, he wondered if this one had belonged to Quincy or Nolan. He slid the Glock 19 back into its holster.

The overhead garage door began to rise as he got back into the SUV, and he shifted into reverse.

"Can you take these damn things off?" Bridgette said. "They're hurting my wrists."

"Shut your damn mouth until we're out of the main gate," Hawkins said, falling back into his regular Irish brogue. "You've got nobody to blame but yourself, pulling a stunt like that with the damn phone."

The lawyer, Moore, looked alarmed.

"The phone?" he said. "That cell phone I smuggled in to you? I hope they don't find my fingerprints on it."

"I wouldn't worry about that if I were you," Hawkins said with a chuckle. "Whatever trace of them there might have been has most certainly been washed away now. She was using it for a vibrator."

Moore looked at her, and Bridgette rolled her eyes.

As they approached the main gate, he saw it starting to retract once more.

"When are you going to take these fucking things off?" Bridgette said, her voice sharp. "I told you they're killing my wrists."

"Keep your knickers on," Peregrine said. "We're almost home free."

As they pulled through the main gate, Hawkins made sure he gave a quick courtesy wave to the gate guards.

They waved back.

Ah, he thought, *the camaraderie of rank and file.*

"Call Boulle," he said. "Tell him we're on our way to meet him at the airport."

CHAPTER 11

THE MCNAMARA RANCH
PHOENIX, ARIZONA

Wolf and Yolanda had just ascended the stairs to Wolf's garage apartment to spend what they had assumed would be their last evening meal together. The dinner they'd shared with McNamara, Miss Dolly, and Brenda had been lavish, Mac having outdone himself exercising all of his considerable culinary skills. Wolf was grateful to just enjoy a good meal and not have to be worried about making weight. Yolanda had finished brushing her teeth and flossing and now it was Wolf's turn in the tiny bathroom. He'd just squeezed out a bit of toothpaste when he heard her call him.

"Looks like trouble," she said.

He left the bathroom and went to stand beside her, the electric toothbrush buzzing in his mouth.

"What?" he asked.

She slapped him gently. "Don't talk with your mouth full, especially of toothpaste. And you'd best not get any of it on my hair, neither." She delivered the last line with a mock imitation of head-waggling fury.

He was about to risk inquiring further as to what she was referring to when he gazed out of the window and saw Lucian Pike leaning against Mac's Escalade. The driveway looked like a parking lot with Wolf's Jeep, Yolanda's Lexus, Reno's fortified Hummer, Miss Dolly's Cadillac Fleetwood, and now Pike's non-descript tan government Ford sedan all lined up. Pike glanced up at them and waved.

"Why is it that dude always has a habit of showing up at the worst possible times?" Yolanda said. "I was looking forward to spending the evening alone with you."

"Same here," Wolf said, careful not to eject any bits of toothpaste.

When they exited the door to the garage McNamara, Miss Dolly, and Brenda were already standing next to Pike engaged in a conversation.

"To what do we owe the unpleasantness of this visit?" Wolf said, trying to imbue both cordiality and hostility into his tone.

Pike turned to him. The big fed's face showed a bit of a strain.

"Got more bad news earlier today," he said. After a beat of about three seconds, he added, "Bridgette's in the wind."

That set Wolf back on his heels.

"I thought you were holding her in jail," he said.

"We were." Pike blew out an exasperated breath. "Word was that she was about ready to flip, too."

"How the hell did this happen?" Wolf asked.

"The same leak that gave out the location of the safe house was involved. The same hit men, too. They even used the names and IDs of my buddy Quincy and his partner, Nolan." His mouth twisted into a severe frown. "This one asshole in the US Attorney's office faxed over a fraudulent release order. The hit men and these guys are pros, came to the prison masquerading as Quincy and Nolan and picked her up, supposedly so she could cooperate."

"You got any idea who they are?" Wolf asked.

Pike shook his head. "Working on it. The fuckers wore them damn COVID masks when they were inside, obscuring their faces." He slammed his fist into his open palm. "But they slipped up and didn't realize there was a camera at the main gate to the facility. We got a fairly good picture of the driver, a half-assed one of the passenger. We're running them through facial rec programs now. And we got another one of Bridgette's lawyer, who was with them."

"Lawyer?" McNamara said. "Well, I hope you pulled that asshole in and put his balls in the wringer."

"Too late for that," Pike said. "We found him in an airport parking lot with his brains blown out."

"Suicide?" Wolf asked.

Pike shrugged. "Maybe. Or made to look like one."

"Pretty bold move," Wolf said. "I assume, since you know so many of the details, that you've found your leak?"

Pike nodded. "For all the good it does. It was the US Attorney's administrative assistant. The son of a bitch boogied. Went straight to the airport right after faxing the shit to set up the ruse."

"What's his name?" Wolf asked.

"Chester A. Loudermilk."

"With a name like that," McNamara said, "you should've known he was no damn good."

"Yeah, right," Pike said, "Anyway, I just stopped by to warn you."

"Warn us?" McNamara said. "About what?"

"I think you two are numbers one and two on the hit parade now."

"Us? What the hell for?"

Pike shrugged his huge shoulders. "It stands to reason. They're tying up all those loose ends, just like before. They took out Bray, grabbed Bridgette, and now you two are next."

The suggestion that he and McNamara were in imminent danger again, made Wolf's gut tighten.

"Which is why," Pike continued, "I've come with a proposition for you."

Wolf and McNamara exchanged glances.

"What kind of proposition?"

"Come with me now to help me track down and get the traitor."

"What?" Wolf said. "You can't be serious."

"I'm as serious as a heart attack," Pike said.

"Why us?" McNamara asked.

"I told you," Pike said. "I gotta move on this now."

McNamara's brow wrinkled. "You're telling us that with the vast resources of the G, you're calling us two exhausted warhorses out of retirement?"

Pike nodded. "I can't think of anybody better."

"Come on," Wolf said. "Get serious."

"I told you," Pike said. "I am serious. There was a leak. There may be more. I need backup. Somebody that knows their way around a firefight, if they have to, and most of all, somebody I can trust."

No one spoke for several seconds.

"Where's this guy Loudermilk at?" McNamara asked.

"He cleaned out his bank account and flew down to Mexico City this morning."

"Mexico?" Wolf said. "No way, Pike. In case you don't know, we don't have a real good track record south of the border. The last time we went down there—"

"Now just a minute, Steve," Mac said. "Maybe this ain't such a bad idea after all. What's it pay?"

"Are you forgetting our last visit down there?" Wolf asked. "We barely made it back in one piece. Remember?"

"I'm remembering that we gave as good as we got," Mac said. "And acquitted ourselves pretty damn good for having a bunch of professional mercenaries on our trail."

Wolf reflected on that disastrous mission—Mac and Reno getting wounded and how his one-man war against the Vipers had escalated to a small war.

McNamara turned to Pike. "What are you offering in the way of dispensation?"

Pike grinned. "How about my eternal gratitude and the unofficial, unrecognized thanks of a grateful nation?"

McNamara snorted. "And how about I go get Jammin' Jenny out of her lockbox and jam her muzzle up your backside?"

Pike's grin faded. "Look, I told you. I need to move and move fast, and I need people who know what they're doing and who I know I can trust. That's you two. Interested, or not?"

"We're not," Wolf said, and looked at McNamara who shrugged and blew out a long breath. He was obviously disappointed, but Wolf didn't care. He was in no mood, much less no physical shape after the beating he'd taken, to put everything on the line in some kind of unsanctioned black ops mission.

"I kinda figured you'd say that." Pike chuckled. "How about if I sweeten the pie a little?"

Both Wolf and McNamara stared at him.

"There's an eighty-thousand dollar reward for Loudermilk's capture being offered, for which I, as duly authorized federal agent, would be ineligible to collect. But you two..." He grinned and let the amount sink in and then cleared his throat. "It's all yours for the taking. I'm authorized to deputize you two as a couple of non-governmental off-the-books contract players."

"Contract players?" Wolf said. "You mean like the PMCs they used over in Iraq?"

"One and the same," Pike said. "But off the books. Think of it as being a couple of temporary unofficial deputy federal police officers."

Wolf frowned. "That sounds about as legitimate as an official Dudley Doright's Mounted police badge that used to be in the cereal packages."

"Hey, Dudley did all right," Pike said. "For being a Canadian, that is. What was that little gal's name that was always hanging all over him?"

Wolf shook his head. "No way, Pike. Forget it. It's too risky."

Mac held up his hand.

"Now wait a minute. This might have a positive side to it." He turned to Pike. "Are we talking *armed* federal police officers?"

"Armed?" Pike said. "Of course."

"You can do that?" Wolf asked.

"I'm from the government, remember?" Pike said. "I can do anything."

"So," McNamara said. "You think you can look into getting Steve's concealed carry license expedited? He applied for it but they've been stalling with a bunch of red tape."

"Consider it done. Once we get back. Now what about it?"

"Count me in," McNamara said. "Let's do it."

He looked to Wolf, who was lost in thought.

Wolf continued to mull it over. The money was good, and he sure could use it. While he might consider doing it himself for that kind of cash, taking McNamara along was stretching things a bit too far. They'd be taking a helluva chance going down there again. The last foray had damn near cost both of them their lives, and then some. Worse yet, Mac's daughter had blamed Wolf for the better part of a year for getting her father mixed up in the whole thing, even though his friend and mentor had been then, like now, eager and more than a willing participant. Mac was no spring chicken and had been through too many wars. He had enough shrapnel in various parts of his body that he still routinely set off metal detectors in airports whenever he ventured near them, and often said he was on borrowed time now.

Kasey, Wolf thought. *Maybe she was the key to keeping his best friend and mentor out of it.*

"Mac, you don't need to do this," Wolf said. "Neither of us do. What'll Kasey say?"

"Frankly," McNamara said, "I don't give a damn."

Wolf frowned. "You put in your time. You don't need to take the risk."

He doubted McNamara would actually go down there without him and began to see the doubts arising in his friend's eyes. He was this/close to declining as well.

Pike must have sensed that too, because he blurted out, "All right, I didn't want to show you guys this right now, but…" He heaved what appeared to be a particularly heavy sigh, which Wolf thought looked almost theatrical. Pike reached into his pants pocket and pulled out a black, circular disk perhaps three-quarters of an inch thick and two and three-quarter inches in circumference. It had a blue flame-like symbol on one side and what appeared to be a square magnet on the other.

"I found this on your Escalade when I pulled up," Pike said to McNamara.

"What the hell's that?"

"It's a GPS tracker," Pike said.

Mac's eyebrows rose in unison. Miss Dolly and Brenda both stared at the disc.

Pike pulled out his cell phone. "I was just about to check your Jeep."

They watched as Pike pulled out his cell phone and begin walking around Wolf's vehicle.

"I got a special app on this to detect listening and tracking devices," Pike said.

Wolf said nothing.

As Pike circled to the other side of the vehicle out of the complete view of the group, his phone chirped.

Halting, he stopped by the Jeep's right front fender and squatted down. When he stood up moments later, he was holding another of the black discs with the blue flame symbol.

"Yep," he said. "They're tracking you, or rather somebody is."

Pike tossed the disc over the Jeep's hood to Wolf, who caught it.

"What more proof do you two guys need, both of you, that you're still on the bad guy's hit parade?"

Wolf rotated the disc in his hand. McNamara was right beside him now, followed by Yolanda, Miss Dolly, and Brenda.

"The same hitmen you mentioned?" McNamara asked, looking around.

"Don't know," Pike said. "But right now, they probably know I've been keeping a close watch on both of you. And from the looks of things, they were more interested in wiping out the witnesses—Bray and Bridgette, if she's still alive." He snorted out a sigh. "But one thing's for certain. Sooner or later, they'll be coming back for you two."

It wasn't a pretty thought, and like déjà vu for Wolf.

McNamara's lips compressed into a thin line. "Those dirty sons of bitches."

"The way I figure it, we've got to stop being so reactive," Pike said. "Sitting back while they line things up the way they want, and then start taking potshots at us. We've got to start being proactive. We bring Loudermilk back and the G can really start building a case against them. It'll be our turn to kick them right where it hurts."

Wolf noted that Pike was now using the personal pronoun "we" to make it seem like they were all in the same boat now.

"Well," Pike said, "whaddya say?"

"I'm in, dammit," McNamara said. "Can't afford not to be."

Pike grinned and made a clucking sound with his mouth.

They both looked at Wolf.

"It seems like we have no choice," he said.

"Good," Pike said. "Now go pack your bags, program your DVRs, set your alarms, kiss your sweethearts goodbye, and whatever the hell else you gotta do, and I'll be back here to pick up in say, an hour."

"We gonna need our passports?" McNamara asked.

"Nah, that's where I'm going now. I already got all

that stuff taken care of. I'll give you your new names and IDs when I get back. And, Steve, you speak some Spanish, don't ya?"

Wolf nodded, thinking it was pretty damn convenient that Pike had all that stuff already set in place.

Almost too convenient.

"Excellent," Pike said. "This is all falling into place just like I hoped."

"How we going to bring this guy back?" Wolf asked. "Last I heard, extradition with Mexico wasn't the easiest thing to accomplish."

"Just leave that to me," Pike said. "I got it all worked out."

Seems like you have a lot of things worked out, Wolf thought, staring at the big fed.

"Wait a minute," McNamara said. "What about guns?"

"What about 'em?"

"You did say *armed*, didn't you? And I ain't riskin' takin' none of mine, especially Jammin' Jenny down south of the border. Not after smuggling her halfway around the world from the Nam."

"Not a problem," Pike said. "That's where I'm going now. All I have to do is put everything we'll need into a couple of special diplomatic bag. We can pick it up at the embassy when we get down there."

"Sounds like you were pretty confident we were going to accept your offer," Wolf said.

Pike grinned again. "Never had a doubt in my military mind. And don't worry. I'm working on getting a platoon of Mexican marines to hit the place. We'll just stand back and watch and then go pick up our fugitives."

"Mexican marines?" Wolf said.

"Yeah, they do most of the heavy lifting for the Mexican government when it comes to the cartels."

"Sounds good," McNamara said. "I won't mind being rear echelon on this one."

Pike held up the other circular GPS disk. "And after all, what choice do we have?"

There was that "we" again.

Wolf stared at the disk in his own hand and then at the one Pike was holding.

The big fed did have a point. When was this going to end?

"Here, catch." Pike tossed the other disk to Wolf. "Why don't you dispose of those two for me? Put 'em in a bucket of water until we get back. Or better yet…" He turned to Yolanda and the P-Patrol. "You pretty ladies are going back to Sin City, right?"

Miss Dolly gave a curt nod. "We are, not that it's any of *your* business."

"Good," Pike said. "Take them with you and leave them in some casino somewhere. That'll throw 'em off. You can handle that, can't you?"

"Yeah, we can," Yolanda said, glancing at the other women. "But what about the evidence chain of custody? Won't you need them for when you're building your case?"

Pike shrugged and then smirked. "Spoken like a true gorgeous lady officer of the law. But us big-time *federales* never sweat the small stuff. Besides, trying to pin a little insignificant something like them two disks on them at this point is like tacking a disorderly conduct citation onto a mass murderer." He motioned for Wolf to hand the two disks to Yolanda, and he did.

Pike strode to his non-descript government sedan, opened the door, and slid inside.

"See you in about an hour. Be ready." He slammed the vehicle into gear and peeled out. They all watched the government sedan pull out of the driveway and onto the access road leading to the highway.

"Hot damn," McNamara said, his face exhibiting a wide grin. "Eighty grand, only split two ways. How much you think we'll have to pay in taxes?"

"Too much, probably," Wolf said.

McNamara laughed.

"You got that right." He put his arms around the waists of both Miss Dolly and Brenda and steered them back toward the house. "Well, I'm sorry to say it looks like you ladies will be leaving a might earlier than we planned. Not that you're not welcome to stay if you want. I'll just have to show you how to set up all the alarms and such when you leave."

"It's time we get moving anyway," Miss Dolly said, the disappointment obvious in her tone.

McNamara's hand drifted downward and slapped her gingerly on the posterior.

"Well, probably just as well," he said. "I got to put Jammin' Jenny in mothballs and get my go bag ready."

Wolf watched the three of them walk slowly toward the house. Miss Dolly and Brenda seemed about as happy as Yolanda was. He glanced over at her. She stood in silence, her head bowed slightly, seeming to stare at everything and nothing.

"Hey," he said. "You okay?"

"You really have to go?"

Wolf hesitated. "Yeah, it looks like I do."

"You sure? You feeling good enough? Your hand all healed up?"

That was a lot of questions. He flexed his right hand a few times.

The painful tingling was still with him, not to

mention the overall soreness on virtually his whole body.

"I'm good," he said.

She held up the two discs. "Did you notice how he was playing it up big when he was scanning your Jeep with his phone? I think he planted these two things just to give you guys the incentive to go along with his south-of-the-border thing."

"I know he did," Wolf said. "It was the typical sleight-of-hand maneuver. Magicians use it all the time."

Her eyebrows rose as she glanced at him. "And you still want to go?"

"Yeah." He took in a deep breath and let it out slowly. "Despite all of his bullshit, he's right. It is about time we got proactive. I'm tired of standing there in the dark and letting the other guys with the night vision throw punches at us."

Her head tilted to the side. She obviously wasn't buying it.

Wolf debated telling her the real reason he had to go.

He owed her the truth.

"Besides," he said. "Mac's already dead set on going down there once he heard that eighty grand number. And there's no way I can let him do that by himself."

"He'll have Pike with him, won't he?"

Wolf forced a grin.

"That's exactly why I need to go too."

Yolanda's pretty mouth twisted into a frown.

"I wish I could be going along," she said.

"I'd love to have you, but only if we were going on a vacation." He reached out and touched her shoulder. "It'll be all right. This isn't Mac's or my first rodeo."

Her brown eyes stared at him for a long moment, and then she leaned forward and kissed him.

"Promise me you'll be careful. Don't take no chances you don't have to."

"I won't. The money's too good to pass up," he said. "And the way Pike described things, it'll probably be a cakewalk."

"Yeah, right," she said, "I heard that before." She then looked up at him again. "I guess this is what it must have felt like before when your family watched you go off to war."

"We're not going down there to fight any wars," he said. "It's just a routine pick-up of a fugitive. Worth eighty grand."

She sighed and started toward the garage. "Guess we both better get packed then."

Wolf followed her, searching for the right words to say, but they kept evading him, especially the way he felt about her.

It was just a routine fugitive pick-up, wasn't it? No muss, no fuss. That's what Pike had said. But in the back of his mind, Wolf couldn't help but wonder how accurate that would be.

When had Pike's prognostications ever been accurate?

Yolanda stopped suddenly, turned, and embraced him.

"Please make sure you come back to me," she said, squeezing him tight. "You know I love you, right?"

Without waiting for a reply, she kissed him long and hard.

He wished now, more than anything, that he could stay with her, that he didn't have to go, but he knew at this point that wasn't an option anymore.

Regrets, he thought. *I have more than a few.*

* * *

WAITING ROOM
PRIVATE AIRPLANE HANGAR
MEXICO CITY INTERNATIONAL AIRPORT
MEXICO CITY, MEXICO

The six of them sat in the small room off of the private hangar while the technicians went over the private Learjet, refueling it and performing the safety checks. It had taken longer than Boulle had planned to rendezvous with Loudermilk at the massive airport and then finally to get their plane serviced and fueled. It had stretched to several hours, but now, he'd been advised, they were almost ready. The American sat hunched over and was constantly fidgeting. The idea of fleeing under duress had clearly taken its toll. He had a sour odor about him, and Boulle was glad the man had flown down on a commercial flight and was now seated several feet away. Regrettably, the cabin for the Learjet was relatively small, so the foul scent would no doubt be more problematic once they were airborne. But it was a relatively short flight to Cancun, and Lopez could order separate cars for their transportation to the estate.

It just seemed as though time was dragging. Adding to the incremental delays was Bridgette's insistence that she be given a chance to buy a new change of clothes and the opportunity to put on some makeup. The orange jumpsuit had been a sort of red flag so Peregrine had given her one of his shirts to wear. Once they'd departed the US and landed in Mexico, Boulle had directed Hawkins and Peregrine to accompany her to a couple of shops inside the airport and let her buy her whatever she wanted. He'd humored her because he wanted to keep her thinking that she was back in Von Tillberg's good graces. Her veiled threats at having secret records that would incriminate everyone up the food chain, issued through the lawyer, Moore, had angered and alarmed the rich man and made him see her for what she truly was: a potential liability. The missing cell phone was another matter likely to cause Von Tillberg more than just a little anxiety. Luckily, it was just a burner and preprogrammed with the burner Boulle had been using. His was now disassembled and in a trash can at the private hangar of the Phoenix Airport. Still, Boulle dreaded mentioning the matter to his volatile and unstable boss.

But of course, Boulle thought, *I can blame the entire matter on Bridgette.*

Von Tillberg had previously confided to Boulle that once she was back at the compound on St Francis Island, she was to be interrogated and disposed of in an expeditious fashion. This also worried Boulle because it made him wonder how secure his own position was. She'd been Von Tillberg's confidant for several years, and if he could throw her away that easily, what would stop him from doing the same to his next in command?

It certainly was something to contemplate now as she sat across from him using a bottle and a brush to accentuate her eyelashes. He had to admit her transformation had been startling.

Hawkins and Peregrine seemed to be appreciating this latest incarnation, too. They both sat across from her in the stuffed chairs. Lopez sat farther away, seemingly unconcerned with any of them, smoking his cigarette. A cloudy haze enveloped his upper body.

"It sure took you fucking long enough to get me out

of there," she said, holding the small mirror a few inches from her face. "What took him so long."

"Fortunes of war, *cheri*," Boulle said. "It did not help that you were accused of some serious crimes. Kidnapping and attempting to murder a federal agent."

"Fuck him," she said. "If I'd wanted to kill him, he'd be dead."

That wasn't quite the way her attorney had described it, but Boulle let it go. Soon she would be doing her explaining, stripped naked and tied to a metal chair. He wondered if Von Tillberg would want to do the interrogation himself or just watch. Boulle knew quite a few persuasive techniques, especially with women. He was looking forward to that.

After checking and most likely admiring herself in the small mirror for the better part of a minute, Bridgette closed the compact and dropped it and the mascara into her new leather purse. She'd chosen a lavender tank top, showing off her ample and enhanced bosom, a pair of white slacks, and some leather sandals. Hawkins had said the bill had come to eight hundred dollars before she was finished buying things.

It mattered little to Boulle. It wasn't his money.

"*Il mefaut un verre*," Bridgette said, telling him in his native French that she wanted a drink.

"When we get on the plane," he replied in English.

"*Por favor*," she said to Lopez. "*Digame un cigarillo, señor*."

Was she showing off that she was multilingual, or was she trying to ingratiate herself in anticipation of needing assistance later? Maybe she had an idea of what was coming after all.

The Mexican's face twitched, and he smiled at being addressed in Spanish. He stood up, strode over to her, and removed a cigarette from his fancy cigarette case. She plucked one out and his hand was ready with a gold-plated lighter which he flicked on.

She brought her hand up and rested her fingers against the back of his hand.

Always the coquette, Boulle thought. *It is a shame that you do not know you have so little time left.*

"*Muchas gracias*," she said with a smile, letting the smoke drift upward as she savored the cigarette.

Lopez muttered, "*De nada*" so quickly it almost sounded like one word.

"Maybe I'll take one too," Hawkins said, his voice loud and boisterous, the grin on his face mocking.

Lopez turned his head to glare at the Irishman but said nothing. He replaced the cigarette case and the lighter in his jacket pocket and walked back to his chair.

"How much longer we going to be cooped up in here?" Hawkins asked. "I'm getting damn tired of this shit. Reminds me too much of Afghanistan."

"Hurry up and wait," Peregrine chided. "Hurry up and wait. A British soldier's solemn creed."

"But I'm Irish," Hawkins said.

"*Siempre los irlandeses son chingados*," Lopez muttered in a low voice. He blew twin plumes of smoke from his nostrils.

The Irishman's head swiveled toward him.

"Care to translate that for me, *Pancho*?"

"*Mi nombre es Pablo*," Lopez said, the corners of his mouth twisting downward. "And as for the other—"

"He said the Irish are always ready for action," Bridgette said, winking at him and then flashing a smile at Lopez. "And, of course, I can attest to that."

Hawkins seemed to doubt her veracity but didn't push it.

The Mexican inhaled on his cigarette. The smoke then seeped from his nostrils like a leaking chimney. But he said nothing.

She manipulates them both like a couple of marionettes, Boulle thought. She is definitely one to watch. A wily cat, but for the moment, this is *approprié*. We do not need any more trouble between our two bulls. At least not at this juncture. Once we land, however, the battle might be resumed. It will be amusing but also could be problematic.

He let the rest of that thought dissipate.

One of the technicians opened the door and stuck his head in.

"*El avión está listo,*" he said.

Lopez translated.

Boulle clapped his hands together and stood up.

"Come," he said. "Let us now depart."

"About damn time," Hawkins said, getting up.

"Onward to bigger and better things," Peregrine said. "And lots of money."

Hawkins grinned and grabbed the door, holding it open for the rest of them.

And on to your fates, Boulle thought as he glanced from Hawkins to Peregrine to Loudermilk and then to Bridgette. *Whatever they might be.*

* * *

WAITING ROOM
PRIVATE AIRPLANE HANGAR
MEXICO CITY INTERNATIONAL AIRPORT
MEXICO CITY, MEXICO

Wolf watched as Pike and the agent who'd met them at the Mexico City Airport circled the waiting room with their cell phones extended. They'd barely spoken then, and no one spoke at all now. A Mexican official, whom the other agent had quickly introduced as *Capitán* Estrada, of the National Police, sat across from Wolf and McNamara smoking a wretched-smelling cigar. When Wolf glared at him, the man smiled benignly and gave a fractional nod of acknowledgment. Wolf debated telling him in Spanish that his cigar smelled like a burning stinkweed, but decided not to let on that he spoke the language just yet. He'd learned that sometimes holding something back could pay dividends down the road.

The captain was wearing a tan uniform that looked anything but appropriate for a nighttime raid. He had several lines of colored ribbons and a gold braid suspended from the left epaulet of his uniform shirt. He also wore what appeared to be a 1911 Government Model Colt .45 in a shoulder holster. Wolf and McNamara wore black BDUs and OD and black jungle boots. Pike and his partner were attired in desert camos that had obviously been dyed black giving them a dark-gray color.

Pike and the other agent seemed to be performing their tasks with exceptional diligence and dedication. It brought back memories of the big fed's "discovery" of the GPS trackers on Wolf's and McNamara's vehicles. Pike had looked diligent then, too. Maybe he did have that kind of capability with his cell phone, but Wolf still doubted the veracity of his earlier claim.

That one was pure bullshit, he thought.

After they'd each made a complete circle they looked at each other and nodded, communicating with hand signals. It looked almost like a lame pantomime. Pike came back to where Wolf and McNamara were sitting and pulled out a chair.

"This room's clean," he said as he plopped down onto the seat next to *Capitán* Estrada.

The other agent, an equally good-sized man who Pike had introduced as Quincy, also sat down, forming a haphazard circle.

"Okay," Pike said. "Here's the lowdown. Quince here says we're running about an hour behind them. They landed here earlier in the day, at around fifteen hundred. They tagged up with Loudermilk at about eighteen-forty and just took off for Cancun at twenty-thirty."

Wolf glanced at his watch now.

Twenty-one forty.

Close, but no cigar.

"So it's a good bet they'll already be ensconced in the Cortez compound when we eventually get there," Wolf said.

"True," Pike said, "but that can work to our advantage. Quince has been working with the Mexican authorities since before we got here. There should be a contingent of Mexican marines suited up and ready to hit the cartel compound when we arrive. With any luck, they'll catch the bunch of them with their drawers down."

"Mexican marines?" McNamara said. "The military's involved in this?"

"The marines do most, if not all of the heavy lifting down here when it comes to policing up the cartels," Pike said. "Right, Captain?"

Capitán Estrada exhaled another cloud of foul-smelling smoke and smiled.

"*Dey* are *de* best," he said.

"And then what?" Wolf asked. "Last I heard, extradition between the US and Mexico can drag out for months."

Pike waved his hand in a dismissive gesture.

"Not this time. I've already got the State Department working it all out. The Mexicans are bending over backward to accommodate us."

"That so?" McNamara said. "The way I heard it, a lot of the Mexican government is pretty much in the pockets of the cartels." He glanced at *Capitán* Estrada, who blew twin plumes of smoke out of his nose. "No offense intended, but I ain't about to get caught holding my dick in my hand."

Estrada removed the cigar from his mouth and leaned forward.

"What you say *es verdadero...es* true, *señor*. But, in *dis* case, I can assure you we are in full agreement."

"They've been advised that Pablo Lopez, who took over after Cortez, is now harboring two wanted foreign fugitives and two other foreigners wanted in connection with the murders of two US Marshals."

"One of whom was my twin brother, Eddie," Quincy said. His expression was grim.

Wolf nodded. He'd wondered about the name similarity when Pike had introduced them. Now it made sense why this Quincy was pursuing the case with such determination.

"You got any more information on who all were looking for besides this Loudermilk fella?" McNamara asked.

"Glad you asked," Pike said. "As a matter of fact, I do."

He pulled out his cell phone and started punching the keys, calling up a color photograph of a man's face.

"This is Chester, the molester," Pike said, holding the phone so the others could see. "This gringo should be pretty easy to spot." He resumed programming his phone and showed another picture, this one of a female. "And in case you've forgotten, this is what Bridgette looks like."

Another one who would stand out, especially with her blonde hair.

It was a typical police mug shot, but the woman's face still looked exceptionally beautiful. Wolf had seen her before, but only briefly and for just a few minutes. He did remember that she was an eye-catcher and that she'd tried to slash Pike's throat.

As dangerous as she is gorgeous, he thought.

"Now," Pike said, "here are the rest of the players. This one is Pablo Lopez, the guy who took over the cartel once Esteban Cortez and his son bought the farm." He held up the phone to show the face of a Mexican national with a drooping mustache and a sinister expression. "Word is that he doesn't like to get his hands dirty, unlike his predecessor, who would often physically dispatch his enemies with a bear hug. But that don't mean he's not dangerous."

They're all dangerous, Wolf thought. He glanced at McNamara, who was staring intently at the phone screen.

"And this guy..." Pike manipulated the phone again, coming up with another pictured visage. This one had a lean, swarthy look. "His name's Pierre Boulle." He pronounced it *boo-lay* and spelled it out. "He took over as St Francis Island second in command after Bridgette and her big male associate got hammered in Vegas a couple of months ago. Boulle knew Reign, that guy that got killed in Vegas, from his French Foreign Legion days. They both served in that outfit. This little shit might not look like much, but his record, which I obtained through

Interpol, says that he's a lot tougher than he looks. His nickname was the mongoose. You know what a mongoose is, don't ya?"

"A rodent," Wolf said.

"Yeah." Pike smiled. "But a rodent capable of taking out a king cobra."

"A rat's a rat in any language," McNamara said. "Mongoose, my ass."

Wolf had come across some French Legionnaires a few times in training. Most of them were pretty tough and well-disciplined.

"Now," Pike said, swiping the phone once again. "There are two more players we're looking for and who we've got to be aware of." Holding up the phone screen, he showed another masculine headshot. "This one is Sean Dylan Hawkins, formerly of the SAS. His partner —" He swiped the screen once more, bringing up the photo of another male. "Is Charles W. Peregrine, also formerly of the SAS. Both of them did a couple of tours in Afghanistan. Hawkins was basic infantry and Peregrine flew helicopters. They both got drummed out after being accused of killing a bunch of farmers during an interrogation."

Wolf thought about his own experience back in Iraq —unjustly accused of the same type of thing and sentenced to four years in Leavenworth. If these two had merely been kicked out of the service, they had it a lot easier.

"INTERPOL told me that our two guys formed what came to be known as an assassination bureau," Pike said. "They operate on the black web and do jobs for hire."

"They're the ones that killed Eddie," Quincy said.

Wolf thought about the bond between brothers and

wondered how bitter he'd be if something happened to Jimmy, his younger brother.

"So that's about the size of things now," Pike said. "We got maybe another few minutes or so until we take off. Once there, we'll rendezvous with the *mar-oh-nos* and grab our pigeons."

Wolf almost corrected Pike's pronunciation but again held back. It turned out Estranda did it for him.

"*Marinas*," the captain said.

Pike glanced at Estrada, who smiled and gave his head a long bobbing nod.

"You got a map of the layout of this place we're hitting?" McNamara said.

"*Los marenos lo tienen*," Estrada said, then quickly added in broken English, "*De marenos, dey haf* one."

Estrada apparently understood a good deal more English than he was letting on.

Wolf continued to study him surreptitiously.

"I'd like to take a gander at it," McNamara said.

"Lemme see what I can do," Pike said, his thumb dancing over the screen portion of his phone. "But it's like I told you the *marinos*—" He stressed the word and then paused to glance at Estrada. "Will be doing the fighting. We're just observers."

"And then what happens after the fighting's over with?" McNamara said.

"We're batting clean-up, collecting our trash, and getting the hell out of there."

"To where?" Wolf asked.

"We'll simply take our prisoners to the consulate— sort of an adjunct American Embassy Office in Cancun, and arrange quick transportation back to the US. For all of us. Guarding them will be mostly up to Quincy and me here." He grinned and winked. "With you two coming along for the ride and getting that eighty thousand dollar reward when we land Stateside."

Wolf wondered what it would be like for Quincy, transporting back the men who'd most likely killed your twin brother.

"Sounds good to me," McNamara said. "And I'm sure Steve'll be ready to rescue your sorry ass if that broad tries to slice your neck again."

Pike grunted.

Wolf had been watching *Capitán* Estrada's reaction to all this, especially the mention of the reward. It had to be more money than a Mexican police captain could make in a year, or maybe two. But if the man harbored any resentment or envy, he didn't show it.

Maybe I'm making too much out of nothing, Wolf thought.

But he still didn't want to reveal that he understood Spanish, for the time being, at least.

CHAPTER 12

PRIVATE LANDING STRIP
JUST OUTSIDE OF CANCUN, MEXICO

Wolf was seated by a window and the sky outside had the look of black velvet. Far to the north, he could see a few lights spread out in various places, which he assumed to be on the outskirts of the city. A much bigger lighted area was just beyond it which he knew must be Cancun. His and Mac's last trip had been down in this region. He remembered ruins and massive pyramids and a whole lot of bullets and death. Hopefully, this trip wouldn't be as violent. But that didn't mean it wouldn't be highly complex.

The schematic that Pike had called up on his phone was pretty small, and even with the big fed expanding portions of it, Wolf felt it was lacking. From what Pike had described, the hacienda itself was a massive three-story structure set along the oceanfront and apart from the small town that bordered it. In addition to being huge, the house was also partially surrounded by a ten-foot brick wall with barbed wire along the top.

The pilot made the announcement to fasten all seat belts first in Spanish and then in English.

Everyone complied, and as the plane descended lower, Wolf caught another glance of a smattering of bright lights which he figured was the hacienda and their target. Somebody was burning the midnight oil there. He looked at his watch and saw it was, with the time zone adjustments, close to zero-three-hundred.

More than the midnight oil.

He remembered that old refrain from his army days: nothing good ever happens at three in the morning.

Hopefully, something good would happen this time.

The bright lights in the distance became obscured by a dense tree line and about fifteen seconds later, an array of landing lights became visible out of the window and he felt the first bump of the rear tires striking the ground. The pilot hit the brakes and reversed the turbines and the jet slowed to a long and protracted stop.

They were coasting now, and he glanced over and saw *Capitán* Estrada wiping the perspiration from his forehead with a white handkerchief. The man took out a cell phone and punched in what looked like a pre-programmed number.

After several rings, someone answered, and Estrada muttered something into the phone.

It was in Spanish but Wolf couldn't make it out.

Estrada terminated the call and dropped the phone back into his pocket.

The jet was coasting slowly now and finally came to a complete stop.

Pike was up and already striding down the aisle toward the exit door. He pressed the button on the wall next to the door, and it opened, extending downward, the second part of it unfolding with a set of stairs.

"Come on," Pike said. "Let's get a move on. It's not like we made a blacked-out landing or anything. And we're behind schedule."

Wolf wondered how many night flights did drop in at zero-three-hundred. He hoped those *marinos* were set and ready to go.

"What about our weapons?" McNamara asked.

"I got 'em," Quincy said. He was lugging an elongated document bag about three feet long. It had a diplomatic seal on the top in addition to a heavy metal locking mechanism.

"Come on, come on, come on," Pike said, gesturing for everyone to exit the plane. "We gotta move."

Wolf stood and followed Pike and Quincy down the steps. The ground was hard cement and Wolf saw that it was part of a fairly good-sized airfield, replete with a tower, several hangars, and a crisscross of tarmacs. The landing lights that had guided them down on their landing suddenly went out, plunging the area into darkness. Pike was in conversation with Estrada and Quincy stood off to the side with the diplomatic pouch.

"What all you got in there?" McNamara asked him.

Quincy didn't answer.

A man of few words, Wolf thought. Maybe he's focused on tracking down the guys who killed his brother, or maybe he doesn't like the idea a couple of "non-governmental contract players" being involved in this thing.

McNamara glanced at Wolf and rolled his eyes.

"That damn eighty grand's looking more and more elusive all the time," McNamara said. "I'm thinking maybe this was a mistake."

"Ya think?" Wolf said with a smirk.

Joking about the danger was the only way to deal with it at this point.

Something flickered in Wolf's peripheral vision and he saw two vehicles, one an old-style military Jeep with no canopy and a gun mounted on a center post. On the left rear corner, it had an old-style field radio with a long, whip-like antenna standing erect. The other vehicle was a dark-colored Chevy Tahoe that looked like it had seen better days. Wolf couldn't tell the year, but it didn't look new. Both vehicles were proceeding toward them without lights. He assumed they were friends, not foes, but not having their weapons available made him feel more than a little bit vulnerable.

"Hey, Pike," he said. "We've got someone approaching."

"Yeah, yeah," Pike said. "I know."

"*Son los marinos*," *Capitán* Estrada offered.

"Okay," Pike said in an authoritarian-sounding tone. "Come on over here."

He strode purposefully away from the Learjet and toward the approaching vehicles. Both of them stopped in front of one of the hangars, and a man dressed in black BDUs and wearing an ebony balaclava mask and beret got out of the Jeep. Wolf saw that the mounted gun was an M-60. A large box of what he assumed was full of belt-fed ammo was on the floor next to the gun mount. The man lowered his mask and grinned, showing a set of white teeth under a substantial mustache. He and Pike shook hands.

"This is Roberto Salazar," Pike said. "He's a lieutenant in charge of the Mexican marines."

Salazar nodded, his grin still in place.

"My men are all in place," he said. "Waiting for your arrival."

"Outstanding," Pike said, taking out his phone. "Here are the people we're looking for."

He showed Salazar the array of photos.

He nodded. "I have seen these already."

"It's important we take them alive," Pike said.

"I understand," Salazar said. "We were briefed on that. We have done some reconnoitering and have decided it is best to do a covert entry."

Pike nodded slowly.

Salazar reached into his pocket and withdrew a piece of paper that had been folded over several times. He spread it out on the hood of the Jeep and took out a mini-mag flashlight and twisted it on. It cast a red beam over the paper.

Wolf and McNamara moved closer, as did Quincy and *Capitán* Estrada.

"This is the main hacienda here," Salazar said, brushing his forefinger over the map. "*Tres*, ah, three floors. The courtyard is here." He touched what appeared on the map to be a large vacant space the size of a football field. "The men play *futbol* there. And here is the swimming pool. This area here." He made more movements around the hacienda and courtyard. "It has a wall made of stone, with concertina wire on the top."

"Looks problematic," McNamara whispered to Wolf.

He gave a fractional nod in agreement.

"We have found a weak point here." Salazar put his finger on the wall area next to the football field. "The wall was partially destroyed here. No one knows why, but it is to our advantage. I have an advanced platoon assembled there and await orders to deploy. It is our plan to enter covertly, as I said, move along here, and then take out the guards. We have Tasers and a few weapons with sound suppressors, should we need them.

Once we have secured the perimeter, we will conduct a systematic search of *la casa*."

"Sounds like a plan," Pike said. "How far away are we?"

"No more than three kilometers. Five minutes," Salazar said. "And my rear echelon unit is assembling as we speak. It has two more platoons and a medical helicopter standing by. They are perhaps fifteen minutes away, should we need them."

"I wish they had a couple of Blackhawk as well," McNamara whispered to Wolf.

"That would be nice," Wolf whispered back.

It seemed like a fairly good plan, except for traversing the *futbol* field.

"Let's roll," Pike said. "Everybody pile in that SUV. *Capitán*, you can ride in the Jeep with the lieutenant."

"Oh, no," Estrada said, fluttering his open hands. "You take *este posición*. I insist."

"What about our weapons?" McNamara asked again.

"Once we get to the ops base," Pike said. "We're already running behind. Quince, take the bag with you."

Wolf and McNamara exchanged looks.

Pike was once again showing his tendency toward being careless and unprepared.

"I'd like mine now," McNamara said. "If you please."

"We don't please," Quincy said, carrying the bag toward the SUV. "Remember, you ain't running this. We are."

"Well, pardon me all to hell," McNamara said.

Pike didn't look at them. He was already heading toward the Jeep with Salazar.

"Looks like we're SOL," McNamara said. "At least for the time being."

"Looks like," Wolf said.

He glanced back over his shoulder and saw *Capitán* Estrada sending a text.

Who the hell could that be to? Wolf wondered.

* * *

CASA DEL ESTE DE PABLO LOPEZ
ANTIGUAMENTE DE ESTEBAN CORTEZ
YUCATAN, MEXICO

The plush room was exquisitely furnished, with a mixture of burnished wooden cases containing gold figurines and Faberge eggs. Several pieces of cushiony chairs and an elongated sofa sat off to one side. Three huge full-screen TVs were along one wall, each playing a different channel as life-sized figures scurried around in the brightly colored backdrops. Chester Loudermilk was on his side at one end of the big sofa, and Bridgette Swenstrom was at the other. Neither looked comfortable and their hands were secured behind their backs.

Boulle looked at the text that appeared on his phone.

al oeste.

He caught the meaning because it was the most logical route of ingress, but he showed it to Lopez just to make sure. He was the one who would be giving the orders here anyway. Lopez glanced down at the screen.

"*Los marinos*, they will come from the west," he said, smiling. "It is just as you had predicted."

"It was nothing more than basic infantry tactics," Boulle said. "May I remind you, I was once a French Legionnaire."

Hawkins, who was standing a few feet away with a large glass of whiskey, snorted derisively.

Boulle glared at him.

The smile on Lopez's face faded.

"Something is amusing?" Boulle asked.

"No." Hawkins took a sip of the amber liquid and then shrugged. "I was just recalling how me and my boys came across a bunch of your Legionnaires that had gotten themselves pinned down and in a real pickle. In Somalia, I think it was. They were about ready to piss on themselves. Till we bailed them out, of course."

"Of course," Boulle shot back with equal derision in his tone. "Now, put down your drink and get the prisoners down to the dock. Immediately after the ambush has been completed, we shall disembark without haste."

"Huh?" Hawkins said. "Seems like we just got there. And if you want someone who knows how to run an ambush, my friend and associate here and I are your boys." He waggled his thumb between him and Peregrine.

"This is outrageous," Bridgette screamed. She rotated her body to show her restrained hands. "Get these things off of me."

Loudermilk was next to her, similarly restrained. "Mine too," he shouted.

"Hobble their feet with those leg irons as well," Boulle said.

Once the ambush had been completed, he would see about taking a photograph of each of the bodies of the Americans. Proving that those two had been terminated would pay dividends with Von Tillberg.

"I demand to be unshackled," Bridgette said. "Once my darling Edgar finds out how you have treated me, he will castrate the lot of you."

Boulle barked something profane at her in French and then added in English. "May I suggest that you shut your mouth?"

"I'll be glad to fill it up," Hawkins said with a leering grin.

"You pig," she said.

Peregrine touched him on the shoulder and shook his head.

"You would be wise to follow the lead of your friend," Boulle said. "You have done nothing but be flippant and insulting during our entire association. May I remind you that you have yet to be paid?"

Hawkins stared back at him, noticing that Lopez was regarding the conversation with a satisfied-looking, lips-only smile.

The greasy bastard looks like a happy walrus, Hawkins thought.

"And what's that supposed to mean?" he said, not trying to hide the belligerence he was feeling. "You going to assess us fines for not bending over to kiss your arse?"

Boulle stared back at him, saying nothing.

"It means we'd better get these two down to the dock," Peregrine said, flashing a smile. "Come on, tally ho."

Always the ameliorator, Hawkins thought.

Loudermilk rolled over on his side.

"Hey. Listen, I don't deserve this," he said. "I did everything you wanted. You promised me I'd be taken care of."

"And so you shall be." Boulle jerked his head toward them while staring at Hawkins and Peregrine. "When we get to the island."

"But I have to go to the bathroom," Loudermilk muttered.

Hawkins downed a bit more of his drink and laughed.

"Come along. We'll give you two a bucket to share

once we get on that yacht, just like we used to do with the Afghanies."

"I will dispatch my men for the ambush," Lopez said. "And then assemble the crew for our departure."

"You hear that?" Hawkins said, picking Loudermilk up off the couch and roughly standing him on his feet. "We're all going for an ocean voyage."

Boulle watched as Peregrine took hold of Bridgette and used a firm but gentle grip to stand her erect also.

Perhaps, once the Mexican marines and the meddle-some Americans had been dealt with and they were underway on the yacht, he would begin his interrogation of her a bit earlier than anticipated.

It might turn out to be a most amusing voyage after all.

CHAPTER 13

OUTER PERIMETER NEAR
LA CASA DEL ESTE DE PABLO LOPEZ
ANTIGUAMENTE DE ESTEBAN CORTEZ
YUCATAN, MEXICO

Moments before, the squad of *marinos* had melted into the shadows of the stone wall. The barrier had ended abruptly and appeared to be unfinished. Or perhaps it had been knocked down in a prior conflict. Wolf knew from looking at the map Salazar had shown them that the next move he and his men had to do was traverse an expanse of open field—the *futbol* field, before they could reach the rear of the huge mansion.

This was the most deadly part.

A long kill zone, and there was a half-moon that gave an unwelcome illumination to everything. Hopefully, they had the element of surprise.

If not...

It was quiet, the way it always was before a mission and Wolf felt that growing uneasiness in his gut, even though this time he was relegated to the sidelines. Somebody else was doing the heavy lifting, but that didn't ease the tension. It wouldn't cease until the op was over. The two vehicles rested in the penumbra of shadows afforded by the heavy tree line. Everyone was out on foot now and Lieutenant Salazar spoke softly into the microphone suspended in front of his mouth. He muttered a few commands and then turned back to the others.

"They are moving now," he said.

He was the only one with camo paint on.

The rest of us are probably standing out like roman candles, Wolf thought. *Good thing we're not part of the advance team.*

Pike compressed his lips. He looked nervous as all hell.

"You want to give us our guns now?" McNamara said. "I think we've waited long enough."

"Sure," Pike said. "Quince."

Quincy started moving toward the big SUV. *Capitán* Estrada fell into step beside him, motioning for the marine driver to accompany them. Wolf watched as they got to the rear of the vehicle and the driver used his key to open the hatchback. He saw movement behind the vehicle and then heard a scuffling sound. As he moved off to the right to see what was going on, the sharp burst of a gunshot pierced the stillness of the night. Wolf wasted no time darting to the front of the vehicle and crouching there. His eyes searched the darkness and then another shot sounded.

Quincy emitted a groan and stagger-stepped away from the SUV. *Capitán* Estrada was right behind him, pointing the big .45 toward the group in front of him.

A burst of what had to be automatic weapons fire erupted from the *futbol* field.

Estrada's pistol spat again, a bright flash extending from the barrel.

As Wolf was already scaling over the top of the SUV he saw Lieutenant Salazar's body twisting and falling. The scene before Wolf seemed to unfold in slow motion.

The shell casing from Estrada's semi-auto hung in the air.

The fiery yellowish blast in front of the muzzle dissipated like slow lightning.

Wolf could feel the soles of his shoes getting semi-traction on the fender and hood of the SUV.

Estrada's body rotated toward him.

Pike and Mac were in semi-crouches, slowly advancing.

Wolf's right foot slammed onto the top of the left front fender and he pushed with everything he had, launching himself toward Estrada.

The gun's barrel burst forth with another yellow blast.

For a split second, Wolf felt the round whiz by the right side of his head.

Almost, he thought, and crashed into Estrada.

The ground rushed up and slammed into both of them. Wolf's hands sought the other man's right wrist.

Seizing Estrada's gun hand, Wolf put everything he had into a heel strike to the right side of the *Capitán's* neck. Estrada's head jerked as if he'd just been given an extreme jolt of electricity. His body stiffened, and he stopped moving, his eyes suddenly half-closed with the vacuous stare of death.

Pike delivered a kick to Estrada's forehead.

The man's head jerked back from the force, but there was no other reaction.

McNamara had Estrada's .45 now and glanced around warily.

Apparently satisfied that the immediate threat had been neutralized, he snapped on the safety and jammed it into the side of his beltline.

"I'll go check on Salazar," Mac said to Pike. "You check on Quincy."

He rose and ran in a crouch toward the supine Mexican lieutenant's body. Wolf listened to the sounds of gunfire coming from beyond the wall.

The shots had two distinctly different sounds.

M-16s against what sounded like AR-15s.

Shades of Iraq and Afghanistan.

Pike was beside him now.

"The marine driver's dead," he said. "And Quincy's in a bad way. We got to get him to a hospital." His mouth twisted into a scowl as McNamara ran back to them. "I fucked this one up bad. Didn't see this shit coming."

"Never mind that," McNamara said, crouching beside them. "Salazar's all right. The round hit him in the ballistic vest. Just knocked the wind out of him."

More gunshots echoed from the killing field.

"Get those weapons out of that bag," McNamara said. "I'll see what I can do for Quincy. Where's he hit?"

"Upper right chest quadrant," Pike said. He went to the bag and began fumbling with a key. After finally inserting it into the lock, he tore open the bag and took out four Glock 19s and an extra magazine for each.

"Shit," Wolf said. "That's all you brought?"

Pike's lips drew back in a rueful smile. "What can I say? We weren't supposed to be doing a lot of shooting."

He stuffed two of the weapons into his beltline and

handed the other two to Wolf and McNamara.

About twenty feet away, Salazar was struggling to his feet.

He started staggering toward the Jeep. His stride seemed to get stronger with each step.

"*Tengo que ir a mis compadres,*" he muttered.

"Hold on, Lieutenant," McNamara said. "You ain't gonna do no good driving in there all by yourself. Let me be your gunner."

"Like hell," Wolf said. "I'll go."

"Hold on, both of you," Pike said. "This is my fuck up. *I'll* ride shotgun. Strip off that dead marine's ballistic vest."

Wolf moved to the dead man's body and started ripping off his blouse. Estrada had shot him in the back of the head and the blood had splattered over the material.

"Looks like he's got a field bandage on his belt," McNamara said.

He ripped the dressing out of its packaging and pressed it onto Quincy's wound. He groaned.

Good, Wolf thought. *At least he's semi-conscious.*

"Put some pressure on here," McNamara said to Pike.

The big fed had tears rolling down his cheeks.

"You just keep putting the pressure on there," McNamara said as he slipped the ballistic vest on over his head and adjusted the straps.

Pike nodded.

McNamara was standing now. He shoved the Glock into his waistband and handed Wolf Estrada's .45.

"Here," he said. "You take this one. Probably only has three rounds left, and I don't know if that shitbird had the wherewithal to carry any extra magazines."

Wolf checked the dead man's body but found none.

"Nothing," he said.

"Figures," McNamara said.

Salazar had the Jeep started, and the transmission made several grinding sounds as he attempted to shove it into gear.

"Hold on," McNamara yelled. In another instant, he was up and jogging to the Jeep. He climbed on board and stood behind the M-60. After popping the top cover open, he threaded the ammo belt onto the feed tray, pulled back the charging handle, and then slammed the top cover back into place.

"Hey, Mac," Pike yelled. "I told you I'd go, dammit."

McNamara's smile was quick.

"This is gonna take somebody that knows their way around a firefight and an M-sixty to do this little dance." He reached down and slapped Salazar on the shoulder. "Let's roll, *amigo*. But first, call in for reinforcements and a medivac, would ya?"

"I have already done that," Salazar said. "They are on the way."

"Mac, wait," Wolf called out. There was no way he was going to let McNamara take the point.

McNamara grinned as his head swiveled around to glance over his shoulder at Wolf.

"Marines and medivac are on the way," Mac shouted. "Tell Pike to get his man over to a cleared-off area and pop smoke for a dust-off."

Pop smoke?

With what?

Wolf yelled for him to stop again but saw it was fruitless. McNamara's face was the picture of frenzied delight.

A real, honest-to-God firefight...a treacherous gift for an old warrior.

The Jeep took off and Wolf was on his feet now and running after it, but the vehicle was speeding toward the opening in the wall through which the *marinos* had disappeared.

Wolf couldn't keep up but didn't slow his pace.

No way was he going to let Mac face that field of fire alone.

Damn him, Wolf thought.

The Jeep bounced over the hump sending both McNamara and Salazar bouncing up in the air and then down again as it barreled into the killing field.

Seconds later, the chunking sound of the big M-60 began reverberating.

* * *

THE INTERIOR OF LA CASA DE LOPEZ

They walked down the extended hallway toward the rear of the big house. Hawkins noticed the fine ornaments and exquisite paintings and marble statues and busts that lined the expansive corridor. It was quite a ritzy place. He wondered how much of it would be left after the fighting was through. It was sounding like a mini-war outside.

Glad to be sitting this one out, he thought.

He had Loudermilk slung over his broad shoulder, and the smelly asshole was squirming like an anxious puppy. Peregrine was carrying Bridgette in a typical heroic fashion, one arm around her back and the other cradling her legs. Hawkins could see she was busy whispering in a steady stream into his partner's ear. He wondered what sweet nothings she was trying to promise.

His squirming bundle shook with a renewed burst of energy and Hawkins reached up with his left hand and delivered a ridge-hand karate blow to Loudermilk's right hamstring.

"Quit squirming, you little piece of shit," he said. "Or I'll shove your goddamn head up your damn backside."

Loudermilk stopped shaking for a moment but then continued to whine.

"Please," he said, desperation edging into his voice. "I've got a lot of money. Offshore account. I'll pay you to let me go."

"Shut up." Hawkins delivered another punch, this one harder.

A staccato burst echoed from the outside firefight.

"That sounds like a bloody machine gun," Peregrine said.

Hawkins canted his head.

"Not a fifty caliber, though," he said. "Sounds more like a seven-point-six-two millimeter. Probably an M-sixty."

"As if that's not bloody enough." Peregrine pointed upward. "I hear something else, too."

Then Hawkins heard it too. The unmistakable sound of the air being sliced by the rotating blades of a helicopter.

"If that's a gunship," Peregrine said, "we'll be in deep trouble."

"Speaking of ships," Hawkins said. "Perhaps we should beat a hasty retreat, discretion being the better part of valor and all that."

Peregrine raised one eyebrow and smiled.

"You think you could pilot a yacht?" Hawkins asked.

"You think you could be a first mate?" Peregrine shot back. "But what about Lopez and Boulle?"

"Well, we'll probably have to take the Frenchie, so we can get our arses paid, but I vote we leave Lopez a life preserver on the dock so he can swim out to us."

Just as Hawkins was about to laugh at his own joke, they rounded the corner and through an open door, saw Lopez standing by an open wall safe about twenty feet away. It was a big one—almost as big as the kind you'd see at a small bank. The man was stuffing bundles of currency into a duffel bag he had standing in front of him. A second bag, already stuffed with something, lay on its side at the Mexican cartel man's feet.

Lopez paused and glared at them. A pistol lay on a table to his right, well within reaching distance.

"Take *dem* to *de* boat," he said, his voice low and guttural. To emphasize his command, he made a curt waving gesture with his right hand. It hovered over the gun. It appeared to be a semi-auto.

Hawkins glanced to Peregrine, whose face twitched with the hint of a smile. He leaned against the wall and exaggerated his breathing.

"Righto, *seenorey*," he said. "But we do need a moment's rest first."

Lopez's dark eyes flashed, and his hand reached toward the gun. Hawkins now saw it was one of those big, shiny Smith & Wesson 645s.

There was nothing quite like getting caught with your drawers down.

Hawkins and Peregrine had unceremoniously wiped clean and dumped the two Glocks they'd gotten from the dead marshals in a trash bin at the airport. The other weapons were also residing in the hotel dumpster. Boulle had insisted. Thus, they were without their guns, but like two good professional ex-soldiers, they weren't totally without weapons. Since they hadn't had to go through the regular airport security, Hawkins had kept the little SCCY .380.

As Peregrine made a show of setting down Bridgette, keeping her body wedged in the doorway, Hawkins let Loudermilk slide off his shoulder as he lurched forward.

Loudermilk screamed as his body hit the hard floor. Hawkins was already coming up with the SCCY. The little gun spat twice, both rounds catching Lopez in the face, one in the center of his forehead and one just below his right eye.

His head jerked back for an instant, and then he tumbled forward to the floor.

Peregrine ran forward and kicked the Smith away from the prone man's hand. Lopez didn't move and Hawkins assumed he was dead. Peregrine kneeled and checked, then shook his head. He stood up and glanced in the safe, took out a few more bundles of money, all rubber-banded together in nice inch-and-a-half stacks, paused to look at them, and grinned.

"All nice hundred-dollar bills," he said. "American."

He then dropped them into the open duffel bag that somehow had remained upright.

Hawkins made a clicking sound with his tongue. "Put that Smith and Wesson in the bag as well."

"Good idea." Peregrine picked up the weapon, snapped on the safety, and dropped it in the open duffel before securing the catch.

Loudermilk was lying on the floor, moaning.

"I think you broke something," he said.

"Shut your damn trap," Hawkins said.

Peregrine picked up the upright duffel bag and slipped the carrying strap over his shoulder and dragged the other one over to Hawkins. After putting his arm through the shoulder strap and securing it on his left shoulder, he stooped down and picked up Loudermilk, hoisted him up onto the right side.

"I can get you more money," Bridgette said. "A lot more."

"Now that we've been paid and sort of terminated our contract with our present employers," Hawkins said, "we just might be open to renegotiating a new deal."

"You feel like walking?" Peregrine asked her.

"Of course." Bridgette smiled. "Just get these damn things off me."

Peregrine closed the door, concealing the body of Lopez, and kneeled next to her. Using his key to unlock the leg irons, he unfastened them and stood up.

"That better?" he asked.

"What about these handcuffs?"

Peregrine looked at Hawkins, who shook his head.

"Leave them on for now," he said. "For appearance's sake. We'll take them off later."

"At least we don't have to worry about leaving that life preserver on the dock," Peregrine said with a chuckle.

* * *

OUTSIDE *LA CASA DEL* **LOPEZ**

Wolf got to the edge of the wall and leaned against it, panting to catch his breath. He felt like he was between rounds in a fight. Concentrating on his breathing, he managed to slow it down as he did a quick peek around the edge of the wall. Three men were running toward him, each carrying a fallen comrade. Two others were also running but pausing periodically to turn and fire their M-16s.

The closet man carrying his wounded comrade came abreast of Wolf and his eyes opened in shock.

Wolf searched for the right words to say so as not to alarm the shell-shocked marine.

"*No tenga cuidado*," Wolf said. "*Estoy contigo. Mi amigo es lugrtiente Salazar.*"

At the mention of Salazar's rank, the man seemed to relax.

"*El es con nostros*," the *marino* shouted over his shoulder and resumed his trek. The other two followed suit.

Wolf could see the Jeep still circulating, the fire from the M-60's barrel like an igniting bottle rocket against the velvet sky. The return fire seemed to have dissipated and Salazar steered the vehicle back toward the opening. Mac fired off three quick bursts and then crouched down.

He must be out of ammo, Wolf thought.

He took out Estrada's .45 and snapped down on the safety, ready to engage any potential targets, but none presented itself. In fact, there was no hostile fire at all. The last two *marinos* flopped down to take firing positions on either side of the wall opening.

The Jeep barreled over the cement barrier and bounced down on the other side. It continued to drive in the direction of the Tahoe. Wolf nodded to McNamara and ran alongside.

As his hearing sharpened, Wolf heard the unmistakable sound of a helicopter approaching. He looked up and saw the aircraft circling the house now, the beam of a powerful spotlight trained downward on the grounds. Flashes of gunfire erupted from the open doors of the helicopter, but no fire was returned.

McNamara jumped out of the Jeep and slapped

Salazar on the shoulder.

"Ah," McNamara said. "Nothing like introducing an old pig to a bunch of Rag-tag sorry-ass motherfuckers. We had 'em scattering like scared rats once I got that sixty clicking."

Wolf grinned, thankful that his friend had come through unscathed. But then again, Mac had been in more firefights than any twenty of Wolf's buddies in Afghanistan or Iraq.

"Better get your wounded into these vehicles and over to the LZ for that dust-off," he said.

Salazar nodded and shouted some orders to his men.

"Once we have them loaded," he said, "I will be back with my other two platoons. We will burn this place to the ground."

McNamara smiled and slapped the lieutenant's shoulder again.

"Don't forget to take Pike's amigo," he said. "He's hit in the chest."

"It will be done."

The other *marinos* were loading the wounded into the vehicles when Pike came running up.

"Reinforcements on the way," McNamara said. "They're gonna flatten this damn place."

Pike heaved a sigh.

"I hope they can get Quince to a trauma center fast," he said. "But I got the bleeding more or less stopped. I found some QuikClot. I hope he makes it."

"You going with him?" Wolf asked.

Pike shook his head.

"Nothing I can do. Besides, we gotta be this close to grabbing Chester the molester and maybe Bridgette, too."

Wolf and McNamara exchanged glances.

"Well," Pike said. "You two coming, or do I have to go it alone?"

"We ain't about to have you do that," McNamara said. "Not if that eighty grand's still in the pot."

"It is," Pike said. "Okay, looks like they were expecting us coming from the west side. Let's work our way down that tree line around and go along the water. We can hit them from the north side. When the other two squads of marines get here, the bullets will be flying and they'll be kicking ass and not taking names. It'll be too late for us to recover that prisoner."

"Sounds like a plan," McNamara said.

Wolf could tell Mac was still energized from the firefight. There wasn't any stopping him now.

If only we get through the rest of this unscathed, he thought.

All was quiet now as they went into the tress and pushed through the rough underbrush toward the water. The vegetation, cloying at first, began to thin out and then totally vanished, giving way to an expanse of sandy beach. The tiny, undulating waves made periodic sloshing sounds as the small waves broke against the shore. Pike held up his right fist, signaling a halt. The three of them squatted in the remaining shrubs and shadows.

"All right," Pike said in a low whisper. "I saw movement on that boat."

The yacht was about fifty yards away. It looked to be about eighty feet in length, with three separate levels. Wolf imagined that it had a lot of cabin space below as well. Conducting a search and possibly getting into a firefight in those close quarters would be no picnic.

"That's got to be their way out of here," Wolf said. "Once they hit the open water, we'll never catch them."

"It looks like it's still tied up to the dock," Wolf said. "If we can swim to the dock, we can come up the side and surprise them."

Pike bit his lip. "Looks like we don't have much choice. But…"

Wolf looked at him.

"But what?"

"I can't swim," Pike said.

McNamara chuckled.

"No time like the present to learn," he said. "But I've got this damn heavy vest on too. Don't really feel like taking it off now unless it's to give it to you, Steve."

"You keep it, Mac." Wolf surveyed the scene again. He saw a man ascending a set of stairs on the port side leading up to a cockpit-like portion that most likely was the bridge.

They had to move and move now.

"You two go through the water keeping at chest level," he said. "I'll swim over there now, go under the dock, and climb up the side of the yacht."

McNamara started to say something, but Wolf shook his head.

"It's my turn." He grinned.

Mac grinned back and gave a quick nod.

Wolf checked the positions of the two pistols that were jammed into his beltline. They were relatively secure. He would have preferred something more secure but there was no time. The spare magazine for the Glock was in his lower left blouse pocket, secured shut by the two buttons.

It's now or never, he thought and made his dash to the water, flattening out and just as he got there to avoid the noise of making a splashing noise. He hoped the sound of the constant waves would cover his dive.

CHAPTER 14

THE BEACHFRONT
LA CASA DE PEDRO LOPEZ
CANCUN, MEXICO

The water was warm as it enveloped him. Wolf swam at a slight angle heading out to sea to compensate for the slight tug of the tide toward the shore. He stayed underwater for several breaststrokes and then just broke the surface with just his head to take in another breath. The briny water stung his eyes, but he knew he had to keep them open even though he could see virtually nothing in front of him. Thoughts about swimming in the Atlantic on one of the rare trips to the coast when he was a child flashed in his memory. Him, Jimmy, and Pearl all jumping under each wave, their mother and father watching from the shade of a huge umbrella—a red, yellow, and white umbrella that he remembered, though why, he couldn't fathom.

He felt the current push gently on his body and then pull in the opposite direction. Even though this was the gentle Gulf, he still had to be cognizant of the undertow. Surfacing again, he checked his bearings.

About fifty more feet to go.

The man in the cockpit had a dome light on above him and seemed to be studying the controls. They were definitely getting ready to depart.

Going under once again, Wolf swam toward the yacht, finally coming up for air just before he thought his lungs would burst. Panting, he kept his head above the water, the salty taste coating the inside of his mouth.

Twenty feet more to the pier.

He knifed underneath the water again and swam until his fingers brushed against something heavy and solid. For a moment, he was terrified it might be a shark, but it felt solid and stationary.

One of the pylons of the pier.

Surfacing, he came up in the dark pocket with the heavy and weather-worn planks about five feet above his head. The hard outer shell of the hull was perhaps fifteen feet away now. He swam toward it and discovered the fatal flaw in his plan. The undulations of the cycling surf kept bouncing the hull against the series of rubber tires —called bumpers affixed to the side of the pier to prevent damage. There was no way he could climb up the side without being crushed between the yacht and the wooden structure. Wolf treaded water for about thirty seconds, trying to figure out what to do. Footsteps, several pairs of them, clattered against the wood above.

More people were coming aboard.

He had to assume they were armed.

And dangerous, he added mentally.

Wolf turned his head to try and get a glimpse of where Mac and Pike might be.

No sign of them.

Something soft brushed against his foot, and he recoiled.

Some kind of fish?

He didn't know about what kind of marine life existed down here. He'd heard of tiger sharks being ubiquitous in the Gulf.

As he kicked with his feet, he felt it again. It was a gentle touch. Sliding over to the pylon, Wolf reached downward, exploring with his hand. His fingers brushed over flowing tendrils...tendrils attached to something solid. He grasped at it and pulled.

A human head, followed by a body, slowly surfaced.

Wolf recoiled again but quickly realized the man was dead. A jagged hole had ruptured the left temple.

Gunshot wound. The entrance wound, small, neat, and round, was in the back section of the skull.

Execution style.

Another set of arms waved languidly with the next incoming wave.

A second body.

Somebody was cleaning house.

Letting the bodies slowly drift away, he swam to another of the pylons and tried for a finger-hold. The thick wood was smooth and slick, the result of an infinitesimal series of undulating waves brushing against it. Wolf realized he wouldn't have been able to climb one anyway. He paused to check his weapons.

Both were still in place.

He hoped the old myth of a wet gun not being able to shoot was just that. With the modern ammunition, Wolf didn't think this would be a factor.

Certainly, he knew he'd have to tip his weapon as soon as he got out of the water to eliminate any liquid that might have lodged in the chamber or risk a malfunction, but he couldn't do that yet.

Voices came from up above.

"Hawkins," a male voice said in a harsh tone. "What is going on? Where is Lopez?"

"Beats the hell out of me," another male voice said.

The first one had a distinct foreign-English sound to it, the second probably Irish.

Plus the foreign one had called him by name.

Hawkins, one of the ex-SAS mercenaries.

The other one's voice had a French tone.

It must be that Boulle guy, Wolf thought.

"Where is his crew?" the one Wolf assumed to be Boulle asked.

"Maybe they're on shore leave," Hawkins said. "Or maybe they went for a night-time swim. Now why don't you come on board so we can get the hell out of here before those Mexican marines regroup and come a calling?"

Boulle swore in French, and Wolf heard the sounds of someone jumping onto the boarding platform. He quickly swam toward the stern. A horizontal platform jutted out from the back side of the yacht. Wolf checked the area above and slowly pulled himself up onto the slats. Removing the Glock first, he dropped the magazine and shook it several times. Before replacing it in the gun, he stuck the mag into his pocket and pulled back on the Glock's slide to check the chamber.

Empty.

Locking back the slide, he gave the weapon several more shakes and then reinserted the magazine. The mag capacity was eighteen, as best as he could remember. But the double sack Glock magazines were notoriously hard to load, so he couldn't count on this one, or the one in his pocket, being fully loaded. Not wanting to risk making the distinct ratcheting sound of the locked-back slide being quickly released to chamber a round, he instead hit the release while keeping his fingers on the slide and eased it forward. He hoped this wouldn't impinge the weapon going into full battery.

Could anything else go wrong?

He thought about that and then mentally replied with, *Yeah, plenty.*

It was time to figure out his next move. As a combat soldier, he would have had no compunction about engaging the enemy by shooting first, but this wasn't a combat zone and he wasn't in a shoot-first-and-ask-questions-later situation. Now he had to ask himself if and when he'd be authorized to shoot.

Above him, inside the boat, he could hear voices. They sounded like they were coming from the main deck area, but he wasn't sure. There were three levels. The engine sputtered to life, and he heard more conversation. It sounded a bit heated.

"What are doing? We cannot cast off without Lopez. His men are needed to run this boat."

That was Boulle.

Wolf began to scale the ladder leading up to the deck. He went halfway up and stopped, the Glock in one hand, and peered over the gunwale. A burly-looking fellow was undoing the mooring line. He wound the rope into a loop and dropped it on the deck. The aft end of the yacht drifted sideways for a few feet and then was abruptly slammed back against the pier.

Both men did shuffle-steps, almost losing their footing.

"Dammit," Boulle said. "You do not know what you are doing. Let Lopez's men handle *dis*. Where is he?"

Hawkins smirked.

"Let's just say he's back in the hacienda, taking a nap that he's not going to wake up from."

"What? You killed him?"

"Couldn't be helped," Hawkins said. "The greasy son of a bitch pulled a gun on me." He walked toward the bow and the last mooring line. "Now, are you ready to shove off, or what?"

"We will never make it out of these waters, you fool."

The sound of a sudden explosion from the hacienda tore through the air. Gunfire then erupted.

Automatic weapons.

Another explosion.

That one sounded like a grenade, Wolf thought.

The *marinos* were back with a vengeance.

It was time to move.

"We're getting out of here now," Hawkins said, and he cast off the second mooring line. The boat slammed against the rubber barrier of the pier again and then rebounded as the engines seemed to take hold, propelling the vessel away from the dock.

Shoot, or don't shoot?

Wolf scrambled up the ladder and plodded forward, holding the Glock at a ready position.

"Don't move, or I'll shoot," Wolf yelled out. "Either one of you."

The yacht lurked forward, rising with an incoming wave that threw Wolf off balance. In the instant that it took him to regain his footing, Boulle made a dash for the cabin door, and Hawkins vanished from sight. Running forward, Wolf crashed into Boulle. The Frenchman was quick to react, driving an elbow back into Wolf's side. The blow stunned him, but he was used to taking worse. He smashed the Glock down on Boulle's temple and a stream of blood poured down the side of his face. The yacht shifted again, gaining speed now, and both combatants were thrown back, their feet shuffling to maintain their footing.

Boulle lashed out with a quick backfist to Wolf's face. He managed to slip the blow partially as it connected with his right cheekbone.

Wolf sent a left hook smashing into Boulle's kidney area, then drawing his fist back, delivered a more powerful one to his liver.

They broke apart on the shifting unevenness of the deck, and the Frenchman reached inside his shirt and pulled out a pistol. As he was bringing it up to fire, the delayed reaction of the liver punch caught up to him, and he wavered. It gave Wolf just enough time to fire his Glock. Boulle jerked backward slightly, then pitched forward. Wolf's left hand jutted outward, smacking the pistol from the Frenchman's grasp. As he started to collapse, a red stain spreading over the light blue fabric of the front of his shirt, the yacht again shifted on the water and sent Wolf staggering to the side just as felt the air ripping next to him and heard the roaring sound of a shot a split-second later.

Hawkins stood on the deck above Wolf, pointing a big silver-colored semi-auto downward.

Wolf lunged forward and tipped the barrel of the Glock upward, pulling the trigger six times. The fine woodwork above him splintered as the piercing rounds entered. Wolf had no idea if any of them went through the wood and doubted their accuracy if they had.

This wasn't a *Die Hard* movie.

He debated whether to move left or right, knowing that staying where he was would be certain suicide. Hawkins had been holding the gun in his right hand, and assuming that was his dominant hand, Wolf figured the man would instinctively drift to the right, pointing the weapon to the left. Wolf took three rapid steps sideways, moving to his right, and then shoved himself away from the wall, aiming his gun upward toward the deck above.

Hawkins was about twelve feet away, pointing the big forty-five downward, but canted to his left. He tried to adjust his aim, but Wolf was already squeezing the trigger of the Glock as many times as he could, struggling to stay on target with on the rocking yacht.

Hawkins curled forward, his big body striking the guardrail and then rolling over the top of it. He landed on the deck next to Wolf with a resounding crash.

The slide of Wolf's Glock was locked back. As he dropped the magazine, he saw another figure on the highest deck leaning over with a pistol in his hand. Before Wolf could react, twin shots rang out.

The man on the highest deck did a spasmodic quiver and collapsed in sections.

Wolf's head turned, and he saw McNamara and Pike standing on the pier about fifty feet away, each holding a pistol.

Whichever one of them it was that had hit the target, Wolf didn't care. It had been a hell of a shot.

"You gonna come back and pick us up?" Pike yelled. "Remember, I can't swim."

The yacht seemed dead in the water at the moment.

"Yeah," Wolf said, slamming the new magazine into the Glock and pulling back on the slide, chambering a new round. "As soon as I clear the rest of this damn boat."

CHAPTER 15

ON THE GULF WATERS OFF CANCUN, MEXICO

A column of black smoke curled upward from the burning compound against the nascent orange dawn hovering over the vast expanse of water.

"Looks like those *marinos* are taking no prisoners," Pike said as he refastened the second of the two well-stuffed duffel bags. He stared down at them and smiled.

"Looks like," Wolf said. "I wondered if this was the last we'll be hearing about the Cortez slash Lopez cartel boys?"

"I hope those sons of bitches are having a miserable time in hell," McNamara said. "Now which one of us is going to try to figure out which direction we need to go to get back to the USA?"

"East is obviously that way," Wolf said, pointing to the rising sun.

"Not a problem," Pike said. "I have a GPS directional finder on my cell phone."

"Is there anything you *don't* have on that damn

thing?" McNamara asked. "And ain't it gonna have to dry out first?"

"Well, normally it would," Pike said, grinning. "But not only was I a first-rate airborne trooper, but I was also an eagle scout. Be prepared."

He reached into his pocket and withdrew his cell phone, which was encased in a plastic baggie.

"I never go into combat without my special, totally waterproof zip-lock baggie," he said. "I got it at the SHOT Show a couple of years back."

"Marvelous," Wolf said. "Add another merit badge to your sash and figure out a route to get us out of here."

"Get me to a hospital," Loudermilk yelled from inside the lower deck cabin. "I've been hurt. I need medical treatment."

"And so do I," Bridgette yelled. "They abused me."

They'd left them both in the lower cabin, still trussed up in their restraints.

"Oh, we're gonna be taking good care of you two," Pike yelled down to them. "And Bridgette, sweetie, you and me got business to talk about. Remember?"

Her reply was two words.

"Now that's my girl." Pike smirked. "But is that any way to talk to the man that just saved your life?"

She repeated the epithet.

Pike stepped over and closed the door to the lower cabin. He turned around with a wide grin.

"Why don't you go shove a rag into her mouth," McNamara said.

"Nah," Pike said. "But I got no intention of letting her get near a knife."

"How far is Texas?" Wolf asked.

He looked over his shoulder at the reddish-orange

edge of the sun peeping over the edge of the horizon line.

"Just get me up to that cockpit and I'll get this tub heading for home," Pike said. "It can't be that different than driving an Abrams tank."

"Steve did all right steering it back to pick us up, didn't he?" McNamara said.

Pike held up his hand and waggled it back and forth.

"That was the least he could do," Pike said. "Besides, I'm in a hurry to get you two that eighty thousand. I think I'll use that radio once we get into open water to call and have a US Coast Guard escort us in."

"You can manage that?" Wolf asked.

"Hey," the big fed said. "I'm from the government, remember." He stared down at the two duffel bags again. "You know, maybe I'll just take care of that now. I'll just eliminate all the red tape and give it to you out of those two duffel bags here. And I'd be glad to give you a bonus for getting Bridgette back and also those two assholes, Hawkins and Peregrine. I'm sure Interpol has a bounty on both of them. That French guy, too, maybe. Whaddya say?"

Wolf looked at McNamara. The money would solve a lot of problems. But it could also open up a whole set of new ones. This would have to be a careful decision.

"Ain't that against the rules?" McNamara said. "We don't need none of those eighty-seven thousand new IRS agents crawling up our assholes."

"Rules are made to be broken," Pike said. "And we've got salvage rights to this stuff. I mean, we'll seize the yacht, of course, but these two bags..." He held up his open palms. "Want to see me make them both disappear?"

"You can do that, can you?" McNamara said with a grin.

"Like I told you," Pike answered. "I'm from the G. I can't do anything."

Yeah, Wolf thought. *Including something like planting a couple of GPS trackers on our cars.*

Pike shrugged. "I'll admit, it might take a bit of creative report writing, but our favorite uncle will be more than satisfied with our two recaptured wanted fugitives, and this nice luxury yacht."

Wolf had to chuckle at that one.

"So," Pike continued, "when we get to Texas and turn over our cargo down there..." He extended his open palm toward the cabin with the two captives. "I'll let you guys buy me a steak dinner for setting you up for that eighty-grand reward windfall. Not to mention saving your asses."

"Saving *our* asses?" McNamara said. "How do you figure that?"

"Well," Pike said. "Ah, by letting you tag along, I gave you two the chance to go on offense, didn't I? Who knows what would've happened if I hadn't been able to open your eyes to the threat."

"By planting those GPS trackers on our cars?" Wolf said.

"Huh?" Pike's face registered a half-hearted expression of surprise. "Planted? What are you talking about?"

Wolf looked at McNamara, who shook his head.

"Pike," Wolf said. "Let's just say you'll never make it as a magician."

The big fed snorted and then shrugged and then brushed things off with one of his big grins.

"It worked, didn't it? You're here, ain't ya?"

"We are," Wolf said, standing up. He flexed his right hand a few times.

Hardly any tingling at all. It was feeling pretty good, or at least good enough.

Pike shrugged. "You should see my disappearing handkerchief routine. Anyway..." He reached into the pocket of his blouse and withdrew three packaged condoms. "When we get back on US soil, we drop our yacht and the two wayward children off at the nearest federal facility and go off with our two duffel bags to a nice secluded place. I happen to know this nice little joint in Corpus Christi where we can get some feminine companionship. I'll even pay out of my share." His mouth stretched into a broad smile. "Well, whaddya think?"

Wolf looked at Mac, who nodded.

"Do it," he said.

Pivoting, Wolf sent a quick right hand plunging into Pike's abdomen. The big fed sagged to his knees, the three condoms dropping onto the hardwood deck flooring.

It took him several minutes to regain his breath, and then glanced up at Wolf and from him to McNamara.

"What'd you do that for?" he muttered. "Is that any way to treat the guy that just saved your life?"

"Bullshit," McNamara said. "That was my shot that got him."

"You had it coming, Pike," Wolf said. "I owed it to you. Just be glad I pulled the punch."

Pike held out a hand, and Wolf helped him to his feet.

"If that was pulled," Pike said, "I sure ain't betting against you in your next fight."

"You'd best not," McNamara said. "If you know what's good for you."

Pike was finally getting his breathing under control. He grinned again and motioned to the condoms.

"Pick those up for me, will ya?" I got to account for all my issued government equipment.

Wolf plucked them from the deck and handed them over.

"Thanks." He took in another deep breath and let it out. "Boy, looks like your hand's all healed up all right."

"More or less," Wolf said.

Pike exhaled again like he was emitting a satisfied breath after a good meal.

"Well..." Pike dropped the condoms back into his pocket. "I guess I only have one more question to ask you."

"And what might that be?" Wolf said.

Pike looked at him and then to McNamara.

"Now that you guys got a little taste of what the kite squad is all about, how'd you like to take a little trip with me to the Caribbean? Once I get this case all tied up with a bow on it, that is. Well, whaddya think?"

Wolf recalled Bogart's old line from the movie *Casablanca*.

"Pike, I think this is the beginning of a beautiful friendship."

IF YOU LIKE THIS, YOU MAY ALSO ENJOY: TALON

BY BRENT TOWNS

Brace yourself for a roller coaster ride of hardcore action and military strategy in this pulse-pounding adventure straight out of a pulp fiction novel.

When the British government approaches the Global Corporation about stemming the flow of human trafficking across the globe, Hank Jones turns to Mary Thurston to form a team right for the job. The end result is a motley crew of outcasts, dismissed by the world but armed with exceptional talent and indomitable spirit.

Led by disgraced German Intelligence officer Anja Meyer and SAS reject Jacob Hawk, the team is autonomous, utilizing the full force of the Global Corporation and its resources as they trek across different continents in pursuit of their elusive foe— a worldwide phenomenon known as Medusa. Armed with the extensive resources of the Global Corporation, their operation spans across continents, defying danger at every turn.

In this thrilling blend of war, action, and adventure, read along as hardened soldiers face off against a ruthless enemy, discover unconventional methods, seek personal redemption, and experience a relentless pursuit of justice. Talon isn't just military pulp fiction—it's a gritty, high-stakes war against the dark underbelly of society.

So gear up, soldier, and join Anja, Jacob, and the team everyone fears on an audacious crusade by ordering your copy today. Let the action begin!

AVAILABLE NOW

ACKNOWLEDGMENTS

I wish to thank Dave Case and Shauna Washington, my beta readers, without their advice and assistance, this book would never have gotten off the ground.

ABOUT THE AUTHOR

Michael A. Black is the author of 36 books and over 100 short stories and articles. A decorated police officer in the south suburbs of Chicago, he worked for over thirty-two years in various capacities including patrol supervisor, SWAT team leader, investigations, and tactical operations before retiring in April of 2011.

A long time practitioner of the martial arts, Black holds a black belt in Tae Kwon Do from Ki Ka Won Academy in Seoul, Korea. He has a Bachelor of Arts degree in English from Northern Illinois University and a Master of Fine Arts in Fiction Writing from Columbia College, Chicago. In 2010 he was awarded the Cook County Medal of Merit by Cook County Sheriff Tom Dart. Black wrote his first short story in the sixth grade and credits his then teacher for instilling within him the determination to keep writing when she told him never to try writing again.

Black has since been published in several genres including mystery, thriller, sci-fi, westerns, police procedurals, mainstream, pulp fiction, horror, and historical fiction. His *Ron Shade* series, featuring the Chicago-based kickboxing private eye, has won several awards, as has his police procedural series featuring Frank Leal and Olivia Hart. He also wrote two novels with television star Richard Belzer, *I Am Not a Cop* and *I Am Not a Psychic*. Black writes under numerous pseudonyms and pens *The Executioner* series under the name Don Pendleton. His Executioner novel, *Fatal Prescription*, won the Best Original Novel Scribe Award given by the International Media Tie-In Writers Association in 2018.

His current books are *Blood Trails*, a cutting edge police procedural in the tradition of the late Michael Crichton, and *Legends of the West*, which features a fictionalized account of the legendary and real life lawman, Bass Reeves. His newest Executioner novels are *Dying Art*, *Stealth Assassins*, and *Cold Fury*, all of which were nominees and finalists for Best Novel Scribe Awards. He is very active in animal rescue and animal welfare issues and has several cats.

www.ingramcontent.com/pod-product-compliance
Lightning Source LLC
Chambersburg PA
CBHW011345010726
47493CB00011B/2966